A prolonged silence descended as they subsided into either fear or calculation.

Watching how each face was mostly given over to the latter rather than the former, Huxley concluded that, once the initial assault of terrorised uncertainty faded, these people had reverted to type, a type with an ingrained resistance to panic. Even Golding, though he cast a few disappointed glances at the useless inflatable, exhibited more concentration than stress. *Chosen*, Huxley decided. *Selected. All of us. We're not here by accident.*

As A. J. Ryan

Red River Seven

As Anthony Ryan

The Raven's Shadow

Blood Song
Tower Lord
Queen of Fire

The Draconis Memoria

The Waking Fire
The Legion of Flame
The Empire of Ashes

The Raven's Blade

The Wolf's Call
The Black Song

The Covenant of Steel

The Pariah
The Martyr
The Traitor

RED RIVER SEVEN

A. J. RYAN

orbitbooks.net

Cover design by Ellen Rockell
Cover Art by Shutterstock
Author photograph by Ellie Grace Photography

Orbit
Hachette Book Group
1290 Avenue of the Americas
New York, NY 10104
orbitbooks.net

First Edition: October 2023
Simultaneously published in Great Britain by Orbit

Orbit is an imprint of Hachette Book Group.
The Orbit name and logo are trademarks of Little, Brown Book Group Limited.

The Hachette Speakers Bureau provides a wide range of authors for speaking events. To find out more, go to hachettespeakersbureau.com or email HachetteSpeakers@hbgusa.com.

Orbit books may be purchased in bulk for business, educational, or promotional use. For information, please contact your local bookseller or the Hachette Book Group Special Markets Department at special.markets@hbgusa.com.

Library of Congress Control Number: 2023935078

ISBNs: 9780316518147 (trade paperback), 9780316518277 (ebook)

Printed in the United States of America

LSC-C

Printing 1, 2023

Dedicated to the late Nigel Kneale, creator of Quatermass and the master of high-concept apocalypse.

No man ever steps in the same river twice, for it is not the same river and he is not the same man.

Heraclitus

RED
RIVER
SEVEN

Chapter One

It was the scream rather than the gunshot that woke him. It was not a human scream.

He knew that there had been a gunshot, the dissipating but familiar echo of it thrummed his ears as he raised his head, blinking eyes stinging from a mix of salt and drizzle. The scream sounded again as he shifted to press his hands against chilly, rubberised metal, pushing against a surface that heaved and swayed. He jerked towards the source of the scream, the keening, piercing quality it possessed sending a jolt of pain through his skull. More blinking brought the screamer into focus, confirming its inhuman nature.

The gull angled its head at him, a stiff, grating breeze ruffling its feathers as it bobbed on the deck as if preparing for something. He wondered if it intended to fly at him – gulls could be vicious – but it merely widened its yellow beak to scream once more before spreading an impressively broad set of wings and launching itself into the air. Following the track of its flight, he watched it skim choppy grey waters before disappearing into a bank of mist.

"Sea . . ." The word scraped over a dry tongue before escaping his lips. "I'm all at sea." For no reason at all this struck him as remarkably funny, and so he laughed. The pitch of his hilarity surprised him, the loud, breathless peals of mirth causing him to descend once more to the deck as he convulsed. *Deck*, he realised as his laughter faded. *I'm on a boat, or a ship.*

His immediate impulse was to rise once more and survey his surroundings, but once again for reasons that failed to make themselves known, he didn't. For the space of a full minute he remained huddled and unmoving on the deck, his face only inches from the rubber matting. His heart raced as he tried to parse the cause of this paralysis. *I'm afraid. Why?* The reason dawned with such shaming obviousness that he almost laughed again. *The gunshot, fuck-head. There was a gunshot. Now get up before there's another one.*

Gritting his teeth, he pushed against the deck, forcing himself to his knees, head swivelling in search of threats, eyes tracking over more mist-shrouded waves, the white on grey wake left by the boat he was on and a small, tarpaulin-covered inflatable swaying a little in its tethers. *Little boat, big boat*, he thought, fighting down another wave of laughter. *Hysteria*, he corrected himself, drawing in a deep breath.

What he saw as he turned to his right drove out any vestige of humour.

The corpse lay slumped against a bulkhead, dark grey paint discoloured by the plume of red and black that had very recently emanated from the dead man's skull. He wore plain military style fatigues and boots, the jacket lacking any insignia or name. His head lolled to one side, the face a stranger, although the passage of a bullet fired beneath the chin to puncture the top of the skull will do much to alter a man's features. One arm was limp at his side, the other rested in his lap, hand clutching a pistol.

"M18, Sig Sauer." The words were a softly spoken reflex of recognition. He knew this weapon. It was a standard issue US service pistol. Seventeen-round capacity. Effective range, fifty metres. However, more significant in that moment was the realisation that, while he could name a pistol, he couldn't name himself.

A groan escaped him, expressing confusion so acute it was more like pain. He closed his eyes, heart pounding faster than ever. *My name. My name is . . . My fucking name is!*

Nothing came. Just a blank, silent void. Like reaching into an empty box.

Context, he told himself, as fear began to surrender to panic. *You've had a bump on the head. An accident or something. This is a dream, or a hallucination. Think of a context. A home. A job. Then the name comes.*

He grunted with the effort of summoning inner focus, eyes leaking tears as he squeezed them shut tighter and tighter.

A home. Nothing.

A job. Nothing.

Lover, wife. Nothing.

Mother, father, sister, brother. Nothing.

The darkness he saw shimmered with stars but refused to coalesce into anything he knew. No faces and certainly no names.

Places, he thought, a feverish tremble overtaking him now. *Name a place. Any place . . . Poughkeepsie. What the hell? Why Poughkeepsie?* Did he know Poughkeepsie? Was he from Poughkeepsie?

No. It was from a movie. A line spoken by Gene Hackman in a movie. That one with the great car chase under the El . . . *The French Connection. I can remember movie lines but I can't remember my own name?*

He put his hands to his head, slapping punishing encouragement then stopping as he felt the rough stubble that covered his scalp. *Shaved,* he realised, fingers probing the flesh, damp from the spatter of sea air. *Shaved close . . .* His fingers halted as they alighted on an interruption in the needling texture, something puckered that traced from above his left eye around to the crown of his head. *Scar.*

Thoughts of accidents and injury rose once more but quelled as he detected a regularity to the scar, a straightness that made its nature plain. *Surgery. Someone cut my brain box open.* He could detect no stitches, meaning a healed incision. But the raised and swollen feel of the wound, however neat, forced him to conclude that whatever had been done, it wasn't all that long ago.

Operated on then stuck on a boat with a dead man. His eyes strayed to the corpse again, lingering with automatic morbidity on the smear of red and black matter on the bulkhead before shifting to the pistol. *But he wasn't dead until just a few minutes ago.* Also, he saw, as he inched closer, fighting nausea and an instinctive aversion to dead things, this suicidal stranger with his military fatigues and service issue weapon had a shaven head. Closer inspection of the unshattered portions of the skull showed a livid scar he assumed to be identical to his own.

As he drew back, he noticed something else. After shooting himself, the dead man's wrist had fallen into his lap in such a way as to uncover the underside of his forearm, the sleeve pulled back to partially reveal a tattoo. Reaching out to take the pistol was a surprisingly swift, unhesitant action, as was the way he flicked the safety into place and slipped it into the waistband of his own fatigues.

Muscle memory, he mused, taking hold of the corpse's wrist and pushing back the sleeve to view the tattoo in full. It consisted of a single word, a name, inked into the skin in precise clear letters lacking any ornamentation: CONRAD.

He waited for the name to ring bells, stir the pot, bring forth a glimmer, but once again all he found was the empty box. "Scar," he muttered aloud. "Shaved head, clothing. What else do we have in common, bud?"

The buttons on the sleeves of his own fatigue jacket were fastened and he displayed considerably more clumsiness undoing them than he had in claiming the dead man's – Conrad's – pistol. *Don't you want to know your own name?* He bit down on more laughter, forcing precision into his movements until the studs came apart and he rolled up his sleeves. The tattoo was also on his right arm, same lettering, different name: HUXLEY.

"Huxley." He spoke it softly at first, just a whisper that barely reached his own ears, repeating it with more volume when once again the empty box was his only reward. "Huxley." Nothing.

"Huxley!" Nothing.

"HUXLEY!"

It emerged as more of an enraged growl than a shout, stirring no vestige of memory but it did provoke a reaction, only not from him. The noise came from within the open hatchway to the right of Conrad's body, a shadowy orifice his overburdened mind hadn't bothered to notice before now. The sounds were muffled and hard to identify, perhaps a brief shuffling followed by a short exhalation, but he couldn't be sure. What was certain was the fact that he and the unfortunate Conrad weren't alone on this boat.

Hide! The urge was instinctive, automatic. Something a criminal might think, maybe? Or just someone well attuned to the uncertainties of a survival situation, because he had little doubt that that was what this was. *Really?* he asked himself. *Got any examples you'd like to share, Huxley? Some relevant experience definitely wouldn't go amiss at this particular juncture.*

Huxley, however, could only offer himself another empty box.

No hiding. What he could see of this vessel made it pretty obvious it wasn't a large craft, meaning hiding places were few. Besides, whoever waited within that hatchway might know who he was. He moved a hand towards the small of his back but drew it back before it grasped the pistol. Pointing a gun at people is a bad way to make friends.

"Hey!" he called into the hatchway, a tremulous, croaking greeting that assuredly didn't make much of an impression. Coughing, he tried again, raising both hands and stepping into the cabin. "I'm coming inside, OK? Not armed or anything. Just want to say . . ."

The woman rose from behind a pair of cushioned seats, a Sig Sauer pistol gripped in both hands, the barrel a black circle, which meant it was aimed directly at his face.

". . . hello," he finished, lips twisting in a weak smile.

The woman stared at him in silence, long enough for him to acquire certain salient facts. One: she had a shaved head and a scar just like him and Conrad. Two: she wore insignia-free fatigues just like him and Conrad. Three: from the way her hand shook and her nostrils flared as she drew rapid, adrenaline-fuelled breaths she was shit scared and working up the nerve to shoot him dead.

How exactly he fixed upon the right thing to say in that moment eluded him, but the words flowed easy and calm from his mouth, absent of threat or plea or anything that might have panicked her into squeezing the trigger. "You don't know your name, do you?" he said.

A frown creased her brow. The combination of military clothing and a shaven head made it hard to properly guess her age. Thirty, maybe older? He saw mostly fear in her face but also a keen intelligence in those eyes, one that failed to stop the worrying tremble of her gun.

"What's *your* name?" she asked, her accent American, east coast. Boston, perhaps. How did he know that?

"No idea," he replied, turning his upraised arm to display the tattoo. "But I guess you can call me Huxley. What do I call you?"

Her frown deepened, increased fear putting a twitch to her features before she shuddered, forcing control into herself. "Stay there," she said, taking a slow backward step, followed by two more. As she retreated, he allowed his eyes to wander the cabin. It was all no frills, military functionality. Encased cables tracing over the walls and into the deck. Another hatchway off to the right with a ladder leading down. Behind the woman with the pistol the deck rose a few inches, a trio of unoccupied padded seats were positioned at a dashboard of sorts, festooned with an array of monitors and buttons but no steering wheel. *Tiller,* he corrected himself. *A boat's steering wheel is called a tiller. Don't you know anything?* The monitors were modern flatscreens shielded by heavy duty plastic, lifeless and black despite the obvious fact that this boat was in motion and, as far as he could tell, not out of control. Beyond the dashboard three slanted windows showed a grey sky and a tilting, befogged sea.

"I heard a gunshot," the woman said, snapping his focus back to her. She still pointed the pistol at him, arm outstretched as she undid the buttons on her sleeve.

"There's someone else back there." He jerked his head over his shoulder. "A dead someone. Looks like he shot himself. Name of Conrad, according to his tat, at least."

Rolling her sleeve up to her elbow, she glanced at the revealed name then shifted the gun to her other hand, showing it to him: RHYS.

"You know this name?" she demanded, voice coloured by a forlorn accusation that told him she was pretty certain of the answer.

"No more than I know this." He held up his own marking again. "Or Conrad. Sorry, lady. You're a stranger to me, as I'm a stranger to you and, for that matter, me. Here we are, two amnesiacs on a boat. Maybe pointing guns at each other isn't such a good idea if we're going to figure this out."

"How do I know this Conrad shot himself?" she asked, keen eyes gleaming.

"You don't. Same way I don't know if you shot him and made it look like suicide. Didn't see it happen, after all."

He watched her eyes shift to his scar, her free hand moving to explore her own.

"Surgery, right?" he said. "Looks like somebody did some poking around up there."

Her gun hand fell slowly to her side as her fingers continued to probe her scar. "Less than a month ago," she said, taking a half-step forward to squint at his wound. "Same for you. Judging by the rate of healing."

"You know this stuff? You're a doctor? A surgeon?"

Confusion marred her face as the fear returned, her reply emerging as a despairing mutter. "I don't know."

He began to formulate another question, something designed to unearth some medical knowledge, but the sound of a loud, angry shout from the direction of the ladder had him reaching for Conrad's pistol instead.

"Don't!" Rhys raised her own weapon again, two hands on the butt, finger resting on the trigger guard. A trained grip that, he noticed, mirrored his own.

"Relax, lady," he told her.

"Don't call me that!" Her finger twitched. "I fucking hate that!"

"How do you know you hate it?"

She paused at this, jaw bunching and teeth gritting. *Reaching into an empty box of her own,* he concluded, deciding it would be best not to allow her the time to ponder.

"Sounds like we got company." He nodded to the ladder. "Maybe we should go introduce ourselves."

She flinched as more voices sounded from below, louder than before, overlapping in a confused babble. "You go first," she said, lowering the pistol, but not all the way this time.

The ladder was steep and plainly designed to be navigated while facing the rungs, something he wasn't prepared to do. One hand gripping the rail, he placed his heels cautiously on each rung as he descended, noticing for the first time that he wore a pair of slightly scuffed combat boots. He felt a keen urge to draw his pistol, resisted due to the scared woman at his back. Had anyone in the cabin below felt the need to shoot him, there wouldn't have been much he could have done about it. Fortunately, he found them all otherwise preoccupied.

"Tell me!" a tall man grunted, one muscular arm wrapped around the neck of a considerably smaller man. The tall man held a Sig Sauer to the smaller man's temple, pressing the muzzle hard into the flesh. It came as no surprise to see that both had shaven heads and surgery scars. As did the two women who stood with their backs to a set of bunks, both rigid and indecisive. "Tell me who you are!" The taller man pressed the pistol's barrel deeper, provoking a startled gasp from his victim.

"He doesn't know."

All eyes snapped towards Huxley, now perched halfway down the ladder. The two women backed away while the tall man, predictably, found a new target.

"Who the fuck are you?" British accent, harsh and clipped. A pair of hard eyes glowered above the pistol sights, voice and weapon lacking Rhys's uncertain tremble.

Huxley laughed, his mirth persisting as he completed his descent of the ladder. A low table sat in the small aisle between the bunks and he tossed his own weapon onto it, resting his hands on the edges and gripping hard until he forced the laughter down.

"Ladies and gentlemen," he said, straightening and raising his hands. "Welcome to the all-new Saturday Night Extravaganza: *The Who the Fuck Are You Show?* With me, your host, Huxley." He turned his forearm to display his tattoo. "Apparently. Tonight our line-up of contestants will compete for a one million dollar grand prize if they can answer just one simple question. Can you guess what it is?"

He regarded the large man in silence, watching his features bunch and twitch with the same profound, agonised confusion they all shared. Grunting, he released the smaller man, shoving him away. "Tried to take my weapon," the large man muttered.

"It seemed a sensible precaution." The smaller man spoke with a slight accent that told of European origins, but it was too subsumed by fluent English to be identifiable. "You being the biggest among us."

He ran a tentative hand over his scalp before undoing the buttons on his right sleeve. Rolling it back, he revealed a wiry forearm inscribed with a name: GOLDING.

"Plath," one of the women said, displaying her own arm. To Huxley's eyes she appeared the youngest of the group, but not by much. Late twenties at the least.

"Dickinson," the other woman said. She was the oldest of the group but lean with it, all cross-fit muscle and angular cheekbones.

"What a literary crew we are," the large man said, extending his own arm to reveal the name: PYNCHON.

"Writers?" Golding asked, squinting at his tattoo.

"Yeah." Pynchon traced a finger over the letters inked into his flesh. "*The Crying of Lot 49* is a great book. I know that the same way I know the sky is blue and water is wet. But I can't tell you where or when I read it."

"Makes you wonder what else we know," Huxley said. He looked at the pistol on the table, recalling the ease with which he reeled off its name and specifications. He started to fumble for another example, but Rhys spoke first.

"The lung capacity of an average adult human male is six litres," she said, moving to Huxley's side. Any sense of comradeship the gesture might have conveyed was dispelled by the tightness with which she crossed her arms, muscles flexing and veins stark under the skin. Like Dickinson, she was gym-toned, but not so sculpted: the work of months rather than years. "Something I just . . . know," she added, eyes darting around the group.

"In arctic conditions a human being requires upwards of three thousand, six hundred calories a day," Dickinson stated. "The height of the Matterhorn is four thousand, four hundred and seventy-eight metres."

Golding went next, irritating Huxley with the unplaceable lilt to his voice: "Benjamin Harrison was the twenty-third president of the United States."

"Thirty-fourth?" Huxley asked.

"Dwight D. Eisenhower."

"Forty-fifth?" Plath enquired.

Golding gave a distasteful grimace. "I don't think I'm supposed to say in polite company."

Pynchon snorted and looked around the cabin, eyes lingering on various details as he spoke. "This is a Mark VI, Wright Class US Navy patrol boat. It has a water jet propulsion system powered by twin fifty-two hundred horsepower diesel engines. Top speed forty-five knots. Maximum range seven hundred and fifty nautical miles."

"Which begs the question," Plath said, looking at the ceiling, "who's driving?"

"No one," Huxley told her. "There's no . . . tiller. But she's definitely following a course to somewhere."

"So, where's here?"

"The middle of the ocean." Huxley shrugged. "An ocean, anyway. I saw a seagull."

"Not far from land then," Golding said.

"That's kind of a myth," Pynchon told him. "Gulls can range for hundreds, thousands of miles out to sea."

"We know all these things," Dickinson said, speaking with the precise deliberation of one voicing recently organised thoughts, "but not our own names. We clearly have expertise and knowledge. It is therefore reasonable to conclude that we were placed on this boat for a reason."

"Some sicko experiment," Huxley suggested. "Cut out our memories then stick us on a boat with loaded weapons to see what happens."

Dickinson shook her head. "I can't imagine the purpose in that."

"And cutting out specific memories simply isn't possible," Rhys said, raising a hand to her scar then lowering it again. "Memory doesn't reside in some nice, discrete region of the brain. Taking away the ability to recall personal history but leaving behind accrued knowledge and skills, that's beyond anything in any neuroscience journal I've ever read." She closed her eyes and sighed. "Or think I've read. Right now, I can't remember a single examination or patient consult, but I *know* I've done them."

"Conrad might've had an inkling," Huxley said. "Must've had some reason for doing it."

"And who exactly is Conrad?" Pynchon asked.

"Entry and exit where you'd expect them to be." Rhys squatted to peer closely at the ragged hole torn into the underside of Conrad's chin. "Contact burns on the dermis surrounding the wound." She shifted back from the body, head angled fractionally in Huxley's direction. "If it was staged, it's a convincing job."

"If I killed him," Huxley replied, "why leave him here instead of just tipping him over the side?"

"Suspicion is inevitable in the circumstances," Dickinson said, face stern as she viewed the body. "And you were the first to wake, as far as we know."

"No, he was the first to wake." Huxley nodded at Conrad. "But I'm pretty sure we were all placed in the bunks when this whole thing started." He held up the second pistol now in his possession, the one found in an empty bunk below. "I think this was mine. I left it there when I woke, stumbled up here, maybe following Conrad, maybe not. I have no memory of it. All I know is, when I came to, here he was."

"So why?" Golding asked. He had positioned himself near the inflatable boat, Huxley noting the care with which he examined it for any signs of damage. "Having no memory of who he was drove him to the point of suicide?"

"Maybe his reaction was more severe than the rest of us," Rhys said. "Whatever procedure we underwent was obviously pretty radical, possibly even experimental. Stands to reason there'd be some unpredictable side effects."

"Or . . ." Huxley settled his eyes on Conrad's slack, blood-drained features, wondering if there might be some expression there, a small crease to the brows or angle to the lips that told of hopelessness. Or perhaps the face of any corpse was like a Rorschach test and he saw what he expected to.

"Or what?" Rhys prompted.

"Or he remembered," Huxley finished. "The operation didn't work and he remembered why we're on this boat. If so, looks like he really wasn't looking forward to the journey."

"This is all idle speculation," Dickinson said. "We can only make decisions based on what we know. Most importantly, where we are and where we're headed." She turned to Pynchon. "So far, only one of us has displayed any detailed knowledge of this craft."

Pynchon stood in the hatchway, one meaty arm resting on the frame, expression set in careful concentration. Gesturing to the misted sky and banks of fog drifting over the waves beyond the rails, he said, "No compass, no charts. We could be anywhere." He paused, shaking his head as his frown deepened, adding in a soft mutter, "Weird it's still lingering like this."

"If I could see the sun," Dickinson said, squinting at the occluded sky, "I'm pretty sure I'd be able to gauge our heading. Based on the angle of the light I'd guess we're currently following a westward trajectory. If the fog burns off by nightfall, the stars will provide a rough estimate of our general position on the planet." She pointed beyond the front of the upper cabin. "What about the controls?"

"Come take a look." They followed Pynchon to the padded seats where he reached between them to pat a hand to a grey steel panel in the centre of the dashboard. "A Wright Class patrol boat is steered with a joystick and throttle arrangement located here. As you can see, it's gone. This boat is on autopilot." He tapped fingers to the black screens. "Also, no displays. No GPS. No compass. Not even a clock. I took a quick look topside and there's a lidar sensor which I guess enables the autopilot to avoid obstacles and keep a straight course, but there's no radar or radio antenna."

"We're not supposed to know where we are," Huxley concluded.

Pynchon's brows knitted in sombre agreement. "And there's no way to change course."

"What about the inflatable?" Golding asked.

"No outboard motor," Huxley replied. "I guess you failed to notice when you were looking for holes in the hull. I'd also bet if you look inside you won't find any oars. So, unless you want to cast off and float around the ocean until you die of dehydration, it's not much of an escape hatch. Someone is very keen to keep us on this boat."

A prolonged silence descended as they subsided into either fear or calculation. Watching how each face was mostly given over to the latter rather than the former, Huxley concluded that, once the initial assault of terrorised uncertainty faded, these people had reverted to type, a type with an ingrained resistance to panic.

Even Golding, though he cast a few disappointed glances at the useless inflatable, exhibited more concentration than stress. *Chosen*, Huxley decided. *Selected. All of us. We're not here by accident.*

"Dickinson's got a point," he said. "We need to establish what we know. Not just about this boat but about us. Specifically, what skill sets we have, because if we're looking for reasons why, I'd guess that's where we'll find them."

Chapter Two

Predictably, it was Rhys who found the other scars. It got dark not long after their inspection of what Pynchon called the wheelhouse. Lights, presumably triggered by a sensor, flickered to life on the fore and aft decks, which Huxley felt added to rather than alleviated the sense of isolation. The fog had failed to burn off, denying them even a glimpse of stars or moon, and the sea had become an ink-black roil of depthless threat. Beyond the reach of the lights there was nothing, the boat marooned on a glowing speck in an anonymous and endless void.

They all agreed to Dickinson's suggestion that they conduct a thorough inspection of the boat before delving deeper into their respective skill sets. However, this was quickly interrupted by a bout of dithering over what to do with Conrad. Suggestions of covering him up with the inflatable's tarpaulin soon gave way to the more pragmatic course of consigning him to the waves.

"Without refrigeration, he'll decompose a lot quicker than you think," Rhys said. "And we've no idea how long we'll be on this tub."

They rifled his empty pockets then Pynchon and Huxley gathered him up, pausing when Rhys noticed something as Conrad's olive drab T-shirt came free of his waistband. "Stop, set him down."

With Conrad back on the deck, Rhys rolled him onto his side, pulling the shirt up to reveal scars on his back. There were two, one on each side a few inches below his ribs.

"More surgery," Huxley said, which provoked an exchange of meaningful glances before they all began tugging at their shirts. Huxley's scars felt to be in much the same state as the one on his head, puckered but lacking stitches. "Isn't that where the kidneys are?" he asked Rhys.

She spent a moment feeling at her own set of marks before rising to examine his. "Not far off. Renal transplant patients have similar incision points. These are wider than typical and double incisions are rare for transplants."

"Someone took our kidneys?" Golding's eyes grew wide as he fumbled at his back.

Rhys spared him a faintly withering glance. "No. If they had, we'd all be dead."

"They put something in or took something out," Huxley said, receiving a sober nod in response.

"No way to tell which without an X-ray."

"What about him?" Pynchon nudged Conrad with the toe of his boot. "It's not like an autopsy is going to kill him."

Rhys threw him a disparaging look, which quickly gave way to a contemplative frown. "I'm pretty sure I'm not a pathologist. Unless the procedure was obvious in nature, chances are I wouldn't be able to tell what it was."

"Still," Pynchon said, "worth a try, don't you think?"

Rhys frowned again, arms crossed in a gesture Huxley felt to be her primary stress response. "I'll need a scalpel," she said. "Or a very sharp knife."

They found a combat knife in the military-style packs Pynchon unearthed from under duckboards in the crew cabin. There were seven packs in all, each one with identical contents: knife, LED flashlight, night-vision goggles, canteen filled to the brim with water, dry rations for three days, first aid kit, three magazines for their pistols and another five for the M4 carbines that had been placed alongside each pack.

"Didn't skimp on the weaponry, did they?" Huxley observed, hefting one of the carbines. As with the pistol, his hands moved with automatic familiarity to draw back the bolt and check for an empty chamber before ejecting then reattaching the magazine. "Makes you wonder what it's for."

"Twenty-five millimetre chain gun on the foredeck too," Pynchon said. His examination of the weapons had been considerably more thorough, laying them out on the table to be disassembled into main constituent parts then slotted back together, all in the space of a few minutes. "Inactive, but the targeting gear is intact and still drawing power. They took the radar and GPS but left us a big fucking gun. Seems unlikely they'd do that if we weren't expected to use it at some point."

"This a radio?" Plath asked, reaching into the hold to pick up one of two additional objects. It was about the size of a smartphone but made from hard steel painted black with a stubby antenna protruding from one end. It also had a small, bulbous lens on one side. Huxley noted how the deftness with which she handled the device, and the sharp scrutiny of her gaze, made her appear older than his first estimate. This was someone accustomed to technology, even if they couldn't recognise it.

"It's a targeting beacon," Pynchon said. "Sends out two different types of homing signal – infrared and radio. You use it to guide airstrikes onto a target."

"Airstrikes," Huxley repeated in a murmur, finding it far from comforting.

Pynchon consigned both beacons to his own pack. "Nice to know we might have some air support."

The inventory also included two coiled bundles of rope, each one attached to a steel grappling hook with retractable claws. "Fifty metre length," Dickinson said, handling each coil with clearly practised hands. "Basic static climbing rope. Eighteen hundred kilo weight bearing limit." She looked at the now-empty storage space and grimaced. "No belays or carabiners. We'd better hope there's no serious climbing ahead or we're screwed."

They found another two duckboards that refused to budge despite a great deal of heaving. "Has to be something in there," Pynchon concluded, palming sweat from his brow. "Why seal an empty container?"

Huxley stamped a boot to the duckboard's edge, noting the way it failed to yield even a little. "Something we're not allowed to see, yet anyway."

Rhys went about the business of cutting Conrad open with scant sign of hesitation and none of the preliminary hand-washing Huxley expected. Laying the body face down on the rear deck, she inserted the tip of the combat knife into the terminus of the right-hand scar and started slicing. Huxley thought Golding would be the first to throw up but, surprisingly, Dickinson beat him to it, moving to the rail and leaning out so the wind would carry off the vomit. Golding joined her shortly after while Plath, although notice-ably queasy, stood and watched the whole thing, as did Pynchon but with only a few grimaces to betray his nausea. Besides Rhys, Huxley was the least affected, suffering only a small pulse of revulsion when the knife parted skin to unleash a sluggish flow of part-congealed blood.

Seen this before. Another thing he knew but didn't know how. He certainly wasn't a doctor, nor did he think he had been a pathologist, but there was no doubt in his mind this was not the first body he had watched being cut open.

"No obvious signs of disease," Rhys said, grunting as she tugged a fist-sized red object from the opened incision. Taking her canteen, she washed the kidney, holding it up to the beam of Huxley's flashlight. As she turned it, Huxley saw a line crease her forehead.

"Something?" he enquired.

"This—" she tapped the knife blade to what appeared to him as a patch of pale gristle on the upper portion of the organ "—is the adrenal gland. Seems larger than normal, not by much. Certainly not enough to warrant suspicions of illness." She gave the kidney another look over then, sighing, tossed it over the side. "There really isn't much else I can do without proper equipment. Whatever was done to us, it didn't leave clear traces."

"So now what?" Golding asked.

Standing, Rhys tossed her knife onto the deck and used the rest of the canteen water to wash her hands before casting a final look at Conrad's limp and defiled corpse. "A funeral seems in order."

No one suggested saying anything of ritual significance. Huxley took the arms and Pynchon the legs and together they swung Conrad up and over the railing. He made a small splash, rolled over and bobbed briefly as the passage of water carried him into the wake, where he swiftly disappeared amid the black and white churn. The absence of sentiment caused Huxley to wonder if callous indifference was another character trait that had placed them on this boat.

"Right," Dickinson said, her bearing a little stiff. Huxley assumed she felt the act of throwing up to be an embarrassing lapse into weakness. This, he decided, was a woman with an ingrained sense of self-control, also a desire to assert authority. "Skill sets."

Pynchon was a soldier. That much was obvious. He could recite reams of weaponry-related jargon without pause or hesitation. However, any indication of where he had learned it – along with name, rank, and serial number – had been stripped from his mind. It also transpired that the name on his forearm wasn't his only tattoo. Celtic and gothic spirals decorated his upper arms and shoulders, interrupted here and there by bare patches that jarred with the overall sense of a cohesive design.

"Unit insignia, maybe," Huxley said. "Lasered off. They really didn't want us to have any clue to our own identity."

"You're saying 'they' a lot," Golding pointed out. The concentration Huxley had noticed before was back but ramped up into a patently suspicious squint. "Who's they?"

"Oh." Huxley held up his hands. "You got me. Caught out by my own arrogance. 'They' are a secret cabal of Martian, reptilian, globalists who eat Aryan children for breakfast and they stuck us on this boat as part of their endlessly opaque and unfathomable conspiracy to do something or other." He held Golding's gaze, steady and humourless. "I don't know who the fuck they are. So how's about we find out who you are?"

As before, Golding's instinct went to the historical. "In 1848, both ships of the ill-fated Franklin Expedition to find the North-west Passage became ice bound in the Victoria Strait. Attempts to walk to safety failed and the surviving crew resorted to cannibalism before perishing from hypothermia and starvation." He paused to offer a weak, rueful smile. "Can't think why that came to mind."

A succession of random questions revealed Golding as a repository for a considerable wealth of facts, from the trivial to the vaguely relevant. "One of the earliest examples of how brain injury affects personality comes from the tale of Phineas Gage, a man who underwent a radical change in character after an accident with some explosives sent a railroad spike through his skull—"

"You're a historian," Huxley cut in. "I'd guess they thought bringing a walking, talking reference library along would prove useful."

"Makes what they did to us even more impressive," Rhys commented, once again running a hand over her scar. "To leave so much behind while taking so much else."

"If they did leave anything," Plath said. Huxley had

first pegged her accent as British, like Pynchon, but a few rungs up on the privilege ladder. Now he detected an Antipodean twang to the vowels that made her long-term expat Australian. She was the most reticent of the group, listening to everything with a carefully blank expression Huxley knew to be a mask. He saw it in the way she kept her hands still on her knees, perched on the edge of her bunk, back straight, chest swelling in careful, regular intervals. Breath control was a standard technique for dealing with panic, and apparently so ingrained in her it was more instinct than memory.

Not like the rest of us, he decided. *Last minute replacement, maybe? Or they were just short of recruits.*

"How do you mean?" he asked her.

Plath swallowed before speaking on, voice modulated to strip it of the quaver he didn't doubt threatened to make itself known at any moment. "Phineas Gage, remember? Brain injury changed him, made him someone else. How do we know the same hasn't been done to us?"

A pause as exchanged glances became frowns of uncomfortable introspection, pained confusion showing on every face.

"We don't," Rhys said, offering Plath a grimace of a smile. If she intended it as reassurance, it failed. "We can't. We can only ascertain what we know in this moment. Which brings us to you."

"I'm not sure." Plath shook her head. "I don't feel like I'm especially good at anything."

"I'm pretty sure you wouldn't be here if that was the case," Huxley said. "We need to focus, get granular."

She squinted at him. "Granular?"

"Details. Small questions to reveal the bigger picture. Give me a name, any name, first one that comes into your head."

"Smith."

Golding gave a disparaging grunt. "That's useful." He blanched and fell silent at a hard glower from Pynchon.

"A song," Huxley said, shifting his attention back to Plath. "Speak, don't think."

"'Someone to Watch Over Me'."

"Nice song." *But not in any way revealing.* "A colour."

"Green."

"A number."

"Two hundred and ninety-nine million, seven hundred and ninety-two thousand, four hundred and fifty-eight." Plath blinked, head tilting as thoughts churned. "The speed of light in a vacuum in metres per second."

Rhys leaned forward in her bunk, gaze intent on Plath's face. "Name the constituent parts of an atom."

"Protons, neutrons, and electrons." Plath closed her eyes. "The atomic weight of hydrogen is one point zero zero eight. Nuclear fusion occurs at temperatures exceeding one million degrees Kelvin . . ."

"We get it," Golding said. "You're a scientist."

"A physicist," Rhys corrected. "I'd guess, if we were to compare IQ points, we've already found the winner."

"I dunno." Golding arched an eyebrow at Huxley and Dickinson. "We've still got two contenders for the prize."

"I'm a mountaineer," Dickinson said. "I can name the heights and most common approaches to all major climbable mountains on earth, and a bunch of others not commonly known to popular culture." She gave a short, patently forced laugh. "Kind of weird that someone decided to stick a mountaineer on a boat, huh?"

"That's all?" Huxley asked her. "Just mountains? No family? No people?"

"No, just facts and figures. Got a lot of knowledge about the effects of extreme climate, especially the cold, so I'd guess I wasn't content with just climbing mountains. Probably a couple of polar expeditions under my belt too . . ." A distance crept into her gaze and she lowered her head. Huxley saw creases line her forehead, a soft grunt escaping her lips. When she spoke again her voice was a softened contrast to the strident tones from moments before. "Aurora borealis, I can remember that."

"The Northern Lights," Rhys said. "Kind of thing that makes a big impression if you see it firsthand."

"No." Dickinson blinked hard a few times, a vein standing stark in her temple. "Feels like more than just a memory. Feels like a moment, something significant." More blinks, a faint shudder as she fought to retrieve whatever nugget of knowledge she had unearthed. "It's hard. The more I reach for it, the more it hurts. But I think there was someone else there when I saw the aurora, someone I knew, someone important to me."

"Husband?" Huxley pushed. "Sister? Wife?"

"I . . ." She sighed and shook her head, a faintly sardonic lilt colouring her voice as she said the phrase they had all come to dread in a very short time. "I don't know."

"Amnesia is almost always temporary," Rhys said. "Surgically induced or not. The brain is very good at repairing itself. Keep recalling the image of the aurora, it might force connections, maybe even lead to partial recovery."

"Partial?" Pynchon asked. "You mean there's a chance we might never remember who we are?"

"I mean this is all one big fucking mess and I've no more idea of how best to deal with it than you do." Rhys took a calming breath and shifted her focus to Huxley. "Looks like you're up."

"Yeah, I've been wondering about it—" he began, only for Golding to cut him off.

"You're a cop. A detective. FBI agent maybe." He shrugged in response to Huxley's aggrieved frown. "The way you phrase things, questions in particular. Something very procedural about it. Seemed pretty obvious."

"Definitely," agreed Pynchon.

"OK." Huxley quelled his annoyance with an effort, wondering why their perception bothered him so much. "Detective." He patted his chest. "Mountaineer and or polar explorer. Physicist. Doctor. Soldier. Historian. All together on the same boat. What's that add up to?"

"A set-up for a really shitty joke?" Golding suggested.

"Specialists," Pynchon said, ignoring him in the way someone ignored background television babble. "A team composed of specialists, which would imply a mission which, in turn, implies an objective."

"We're going somewhere." Huxley's eyes drifted to the ceiling, the steady thrum of the engines loud in his ears. "To do something."

"Something that involves guns." Rhys gestured to the weaponry set out on the table. "And a boat full of very clever and capable people with no memory of who they are."

This brought an interlude of silent conjecture, Huxley wincing as the painful confusion swept through him again. "Does anyone else experience pain when they try to remember?" he asked, recalling Dickinson's discomfort in dragging up her one potential real experience.

"Hell yeah," Rhys said. "Thought it might be an after-effect of the surgery. But if it's not just us two . . ." Receiving confirmatory nods from the others, she grimaced. "Then maybe it's no accident."

"Aversion therapy," Huxley said. "The more trying to remember hurts, the less you want to do it."

"But why?" Dickinson asked, their complete inability to answer heralding another, more prolonged silence.

It was Golding who spoke first, mounting anxiety raising his voice an octave higher. "I can't be the only one thinking there has to be some way to turn this thing around."

"Controls are sealed," Pynchon told him. "I took a look at the engines – same thing. And we have no tools besides guns and knives."

"The engines are diesel turbines, I assume?" Plath asked.

"Yeah, but anything that makes them go or stop has been removed or covered in hard steel, so forget about shooting our way in."

"Diesels have to have vents to work." Plath shifted, coughing and sniffing in another display of masked stress. "We could shoot into one of them."

"Leaving us adrift," Huxley said. "With engines that might be on fire. And who's to say if anyone's going to come and rescue us?"

"We must be being monitored somehow," Dickinson said. "Trackers, cameras, listening devices."

Pynchon shook his head. "If there's a camera on this boat, I haven't found it. Doesn't mean there isn't, of course, just means it's so well hidden, finding it might be impossible. Placing a transponder on board is more likely, since you could put it any number of places and we'd never see it. Could be attached to the underside of the hull for all we know."

"So we can assume they know where we are," Dickinson concluded. "Even if we don't."

"It's probably not a good idea to assume anything beyond what we've already established," Huxley said.

"Which amounts to not very much at all." Golding let out a heavy sigh and settled back onto his bunk, forearm over his eyes. "I intend to sleep," he announced. "Synapses require regular bouts of REM sleep to operate at full efficiency, do they not, Doctor Rhys?"

"It's a fair point." Rhys shrugged in resignation. "We should sleep, come at it in the morning with clearer heads."

"I don't think I can," Plath said, hands clasped together now, knuckles white.

"Try," Rhys told her, swinging her legs onto her own bunk. "You might surprise yourself."

They all slept, and quickly too, even Plath. Huxley felt the onset of fatigue as soon as his head met the thin padding of the pillow, but forced himself to stay awake for a time, hearing the slow, regular breaths and absence of movement that indicated true sleep. None of them snored, although Golding was prone to a faint but irritating wheeze.

Should've set someone to keep watch, he chided himself as the shadows crowded in and his eyes fell shut. *Surprised Pynchon didn't suggest it . . .*

Dreams were woven from the fabric of memory so should have been absent. Yet, he did dream. It was a vague, ephemeral thing of shifting colours: an overlapping haze of blue and gold, a white, spectral shape moving across his line of vision. He thought he heard the ocean, crashing waves rather than the slap of choppy waters against the hull and, closer, more vibrant, the sound of a voice, a woman's voice . . .

The confusion hit hard when he woke, the headache rousing him from his bunk to rummage in one of the first aid kits in search of painkillers. "Maybe they want us to suffer," he grunted, tossing the kit aside when his rummaging unearthed only bandages and Band-Aids.

"That felt long," Golding groaned, sitting up, mouth gaping in a yawn. "I mean, really long. Everything's stiff, like I slept for weeks."

Huxley frowned in silent agreement. Despite his pain, a general lessening of fatigue told of a deep and lengthy sleep. Also, the stubble on his chin felt rougher and his bladder was uncomfortably full. He was forced to conclude this hadn't been a natural sleep. *Something else they did to us*, he decided, fingers tracing his scars. *Explains why Pynchon didn't suggest keeping watch.*

His thoughts were interrupted by another jolt of pain in his head, potent enough to send a hiss through clenched teeth. "Don't suppose you found any Advil in there?" he asked over the roar of the flush as Rhys emerged from the toilet at the rear of the crew cabin.

"Drink water," she advised. "Dehydration will make it worse."

They ate a breakfast of cold rations – granola bars

and dried fruit washed down with water since they hadn't been provided with anything more flavourful.

"Should we ration this?" Plath wondered, pausing in the act of raising a canteen to her lips.

"There's about ten gallons stacked in the engine room," Pynchon said. "We'll be fine for a while yet."

Dickinson's brow creased in calculation as she chewed a granola bar. "Ten gallons split between six people . . . seven including Conrad, is not actually that much. With all this—" she gestured with her half-eaten bar at the packets scattered on the table "—I'd say we have calories and water enough for seven days, at most."

Plath's voice became a whisper as she screwed the cap back onto her canteen. "We're only supposed to last a week."

"Maybe there'll be a resupply when we get to where we're going . . ." Pynchon offered, trailing off and cocking his head at the ceiling, eyes widening.

"What . . . ?" Huxley began but Pynchon waved him to silence. They all heard it then, a distant but rhythmic murmur, one they all recognised.

"Plane," Plath breathed, scrambling free of her bunk, but Pynchon was first up the ladder.

They all crowded onto the aft deck, peering up into a sky still occluded by fog. Huxley found it impossible to gauge a direction from the steady throb of the approaching aircraft, but Pynchon's apparently more experienced ear caused him to point directly astern.

"It's on the same course."

"Looks like they do know where we are," Dickinson said.

"If it's them." Huxley squinted into the drifting cloud, wondering if it hadn't taken on a new, pinkish hue overnight. "Could be anyone."

The engine noise grew, building into a roar that drowned further conversation. Huxley could track the source now, head swivelling to follow as it passed directly overhead. Still he saw nothing, not even a faint silhouette in the mist.

"Four engined," Pynchon said. "Pretty sure it's a C-130."

The multiple turbo-prop growl dwindled into the befogged void beyond the bows, fading to nothing with dispiriting swiftness. They continued to stand and stare in its wake, straining for a return, hearing nothing.

"If it comes back," Golding said, "should we shoot at it?"

Pynchon spared him a disgusted glance before turning to Rhys. "What was it you said? About being clever and capable?"

"Oh, fuck you," Golding retorted.

"Even though I don't know if we met before yesterday," Pynchon said, "I'm sure of one thing: I really don't like you."

"This isn't productive," Dickinson stated. "We need to establish facts, remember? You said it was a C-130. That's a cargo plane, right?"

"Yeah." Pynchon blinked, turning away from Golding to stare into the obscured distance beyond the bows. "Commonly known as the Hercules. Range twenty-two hundred nautical miles, but that can be extended through mid-air refuelling."

"Cargo," Dickinson repeated. "So, it was either delivering something or picking something up."

"Not necessarily. There are multiple variants of the C-130 – gunships, maritime surveillance, electronic warfare . . ."

Huxley's attention drifted as Pynchon surrendered to his penchant for military jargon. *His stress response, maybe?* As Huxley's eyes slipped towards the wheelhouse interior, they caught a glow that hadn't been there moments before.

"Guys," he said, interrupting Pynchon's flow to point at the previously lifeless control panel. One of the display screens was active, and it showed a map.

Chapter Three

Pynchon's finger traced over the screen, following what appeared to be a coastline interrupted by a broad inlet. The map was stark in its simplicity, flat colours and thin lines lacking any digits or text. "Well," he said. "At least we know we're not on another planet."

"Did you seriously think we were?" Rhys asked him, receiving a shrug in response.

"I don't think anything would surprise me any more."

"So," Huxley cut in with a measure of forced patience, "what are we looking at?"

"No names as you can see." Pynchon's finger tapped the coastline. "But this is definitely the Thames Estuary. And this—" his finger shifted to a pulsing green dot in the centre of the screen "—is our position. My reckoning: we're about fifty miles off the south-east coast of Britain, approaching the Thames river which leads directly into London."

"What's that?" Rhys pointed to another pulsing dot, this one red in colour. It sat at a point where the estuary narrowed to river-like proportions.

"No idea," Pynchon replied. "But, at the current speed and heading, we'll find out in about an hour."

"Does London mean anything to anyone?" Huxley turned to face them all, seeing only the typical confused frustration. "Hometown, maybe?"

"I can tell you that Anne Boleyn had her head chopped off in the Tower of London on the nineteenth of May 1536," Golding offered. "And that Lloyds of London was first established as a corporate entity in 1686. The original Roman name was Londinium, famously sacked by Boudicca in . . ."

"Yeah, that's not remotely fucking useful," Pynchon told him, turning to Huxley. "We should arm up. Get ready. Something's waiting for us and we have no way of knowing if it's good or bad."

Huxley glanced again at the pulsing dots inching towards each other on the screen. *Good, bad, or indifferent?* One thing he felt certain of: when they reached that dot at least they would get some answers. "OK, what do we do?"

Pynchon positioned himself and Huxley on the foredeck, standing on either side of the squat, insectoid menace of the chain gun. They both held loaded carbines. Bolts cocked to chamber a round. Stock fully extended and pressed into the shoulder. One hand on the fore stock, the other the pistol grip. Fingers resting on the trigger guard. Thumb on the safety.

Handling the weapon felt easy and familiar, but donning the webbing less so. Huxley slipped it over his shoulders and fastened the various buckles with a precision that bespoke only a modicum of muscle memory. By contrast, Pynchon shrugged on the canvas belt arrangement with all the swiftness of a reflex, checking the fit of the magazines in the pouches before attaching the Velcro-sheathed combat knife to his waist.

Dickinson, Rhys and Plath were on the aft deck, also armed with carbines. Golding had been consigned to the wheelhouse with instructions to report any change in the map display. The boat continued to plough a steady but unhurried course through the water, the engines maintaining the same rhythmic thrum. It was as Huxley began to discern a long, low shadow in the fog that the drone of the engines altered pitch and the boat slowed.

"That a coastline?" Huxley asked Pynchon. They both had their carbines raised. There were no binoculars on board but each carbine had an optical sight offering 3x magnification. Viewing it through the sight made the shadow only marginally less vague, but Huxley discerned the faint white glimmer of breaking waves along its base.

"North bank of the estuary." Pynchon's carbine tracked slowly from right to left, eye unblinking on the sight.

"What do you make of this fog?" Huxley lowered

his own weapon, squinting at the pink-tinged mist. "I mean, it doesn't seem natural, right? Fog doesn't hang around for this long. And the colour . . ."

"Not a meteorologist." Pynchon frowned then raised his eye from his sight. "Maybe that was Conrad's speciality. Who knows?" He returned to his survey. "Whatever it is should be dead ahead . . ." The barrel of his weapon stopped and he removed his hand from the fore stock to point. "There, twelve o'clock. See it?"

Huxley found it quickly, the sight tracking over clouded waves before coming to rest on a flare of colour among the grey: a bright shade of orange, designed to draw the eye. The colour formed a bulbous cylindrical band around a yellow-and-black-striped cone, bobbing sluggishly in the swell.

"Airdropped beacon," Pynchon said, and Huxley saw the mess of cords cascading down the cone's side to the water, where the billowing white shape of a collapsed parachute trailed just below the waves. "Looks like the plane was delivering something after all."

Huxley kept his sight on the beacon as the boat brought them closer, making out the riveted plates that comprised the sides of the cone. He saw no markings beyond the black and yellow stripes but did discern the curved edges of a rectangular hatch.

The abrupt fade of the boat's engines and Golding's shout from the wheelhouse happened simultaneously.

"Message!" The historian's voice was muted by the

thick glass of the windscreen, but his frantic gesticulation was clear enough. "There's a message!"

The boat became less stable without forward propulsion, Huxley and Pynchon creating a distinct list as they made their way aft. The others were already clustered around the display. The map had disappeared, replaced with a set of words in plain text, white on black:

INVESTIGATE
TWO ONLY
OUTBOARD MOTOR IN THE HOLD

"Short and to the point," Golding observed.

They all started in alarm when the engines flared to a growl, raising a plume of white and causing the boat's prow to shift to starboard. A second later the engines died again.

"It's just keeping position," Pynchon said, moving to the ladder. "We have an outboard to find."

They found one of the sealed duckboards in the lower deck raised up an inch, Pynchon hauling it away to reveal the long pole, propeller and control stick of an outboard motor.

"Shouldn't it be bigger?" Rhys asked, viewing the machine with a doubtful grimace.

"All electric." Pynchon patted the Kevlar-covered box at the top of the pole. "Battery pack. I think we can assume the range has been limited to make sure we don't take the inflatable and sail away."

"This is kinda nuts, isn't it?" Golding said, face bunched in mystification and voice taking on a shrill edge as he continued. "I mean, it's clear they can communicate with us. Why drop a buoy in our path and order us to go take a look? Why not just tell us what we're doing here?"

"It's a test," Plath said. "Basic reasoning and cognition. Read the message, find the motor, fix it to the inflatable, make it to the buoy. They're checking to see if we're still alive and capable of following instructions."

"Meaning," Rhys put in, "they weren't sure if we would be alive and sane at this point when they stuck us on this boat." An utterly humourless smile flickered across her lips before she stated the obvious: "Conrad isn't."

"Test or not," Pynchon grunted, taking hold of the outboard and hauling it clear. "I don't think we're going anywhere until we check out that beacon."

There was no discussion about who would go. Pynchon hauled the inflatable's tarpaulin clear, attached the outboard, pushed a lever to activate the grapple that lowered it into the water, then inclined his head at Huxley. "Shall we?"

"What if . . . something happens?" Rhys asked.

"Define 'something'." Huxley gave a helpless shrug as he settled at the inflatable's prow, Pynchon taking command of the outboard. "Thinking it's going to blow up? Turn into a killer robot, maybe?"

He hadn't seen humour on her face before and felt that the brief, grudging half-smile made her look a good deal younger. "Don't worry." She assumed a frown of grave assurance. "We'll definitely leave you to die if the worst happens."

Huxley touched his fingers to his forehead in a mock salute. "Where we go one, we go none."

According to Pynchon's annoyed estimation, the outboard proved capable of no more than three knots at full throttle. "If that thing does blow up, there's no way we're getting clear of the debris in time."

"If they could airdrop it into our path, they could've just dropped a bomb. And why go to all this trouble just to kill us now?"

Pynchon eased the throttle when they were within a few yards of the beacon. Up close it was much larger than Huxley first thought, ten feet tall with a ledge and handholds above the inflated orange doughnut that formed its base. Taking hold of the rope affixed to the rubber ring at the inflatable's prow, Huxley braced himself then leaped for the beacon. The ledge was wet but formed of a metal grate that prevented him from slipping. He tied the rope to one of the handholds, the knot sturdy and formed with the same slow but precise movements with which he had donned the webbing. More muscle memory.

He held the rope firm while Pynchon killed the outboard and clambered across from the inflatable. They both had their carbines slung crossways on their backs but Pynchon made no move to unlimber his – there was nothing to shoot at.

"It was on this side," Huxley said, moving from handhold to handhold as he made his way right. The hatch was about twelve inches square and lacked any obvious means of opening it. After a few seconds of ineffectual staring, Huxley pushed it, feeling it give a quarter-inch. A faint, mechanical whirring then the hatch slid aside, revealing a yellow rectangular object in a cradle.

"Sat-phone," Pynchon said.

"Remember any numbers offhand?" Huxley reached for the sat-phone then stopped when it let out a loud but low-pitched trill. His hand hovered near the device's thick plastic casing, trembling. He found it notable that Pynchon also made no move to pick it up.

"Somebody wants to talk," he said, wiping a spatter of seawater from his upper lip that Huxley knew also contained a measure of sweat.

Why? he asked himself, making a fist to banish the tremble. *Why does this scare me so much?*

Grimacing, he snorted a deep breath and picked up the sat-phone, holding it to his ear, saying nothing. *You want to talk. So talk.*

The voice that came from the speaker was female and modulated to an uninflected flatness, lacking anything that might be called emotion. "State your name."

Huxley had to swallow before he could grunt back an answer. "Who is this?"

"State your name." A bland repetition, just as flat.

He exchanged a glance with Pynchon, receiving a shrug then a nod.

"The name Huxley is tattooed on my arm."

"State the names of the other members of your party."

Another nod from Pynchon, leaning close enough to hear, his sweat now obvious in his odour.

"Pynchon," Huxley said. "Rhys, Dickinson, Plath, and Golding."

A pause, a very faint click from the speaker before flat-voice returned. "Where is Conrad?"

"Dead."

"How?"

"Suicide."

"Describe the body."

"Unresponsive with big holes in his head resulting from a close-range gunshot wound."

"No other injuries or signs of illness?"

Huxley's turn to pause. Beside him, Pynchon worked his lips, breathing slow and heavy. *Illness?* Something about the word, even though it had been spoken with the same lack of inflection, carried a definite weight.

"We all have recently healed surgical incisions," Huxley said. "But that's not what you meant, was it?"

Another pause, this time long enough to provoke him.

"Answer my question." The sat-phone's casing creaked in his grip. "What other signs of illness should we have seen?"

"That is not relevant at this time." Still no emotion, which infuriated him more than if the statement had been made with a taunting laugh.

"Fuck you it's not. What signs of illness?"

"The boat will remain inactive unless a satisfactory outcome to this exchange is achieved. Following that, further guidance on your course will be provided. Do you understand?"

Huxley bit down on an explosion of anger, taking the phone from his ear, pressing it to his forehead while a tempting but treacherous urge sprang to mind: *Throw the fucking thing in the sea.*

A nudge from Pynchon dispelled the anger enough for him to return the phone to his ear, the word emerging from between gritted teeth. "Understood."

"Do any of the others display signs of confused thinking or unwarranted aggression?"

"For a bunch of people who can't remember who they are, stuck on a boat sailing towards fuck knows what, I'd say they're about as stable as could be expected."

"Has anyone remembered anything? Anything personal?"

"No . . ." He hesitated, brow furrowed as he did a mental fast-forward through his interactions with the others. *Aurora borealis.* "Wait. Dickinson said something kind've personal, but it was just a minor detail."

"There are no minor details. What did she say?"

"Something she remembered seeing, during a trip north of the Arctic Circle, she thought."

"Specify."

"The aurora borealis. She said she felt she'd been with someone when she saw it, someone important to her." A very short pause, another distant click on the line.

"Is she with you now?"

"No, Pynchon's here. Dickinson and the others are on the boat."

"To ensure your survival it is imperative you comply with the following instructions: take this phone and return to the boat. Kill Dickinson."

A meeting of widened, baffled eyes with Pynchon, the phone almost slipping from his grasp. "What!?"

"Dickinson is now a danger to you all. To ensure your survival you must kill her."

"She's a fucking mountain climber, maybe an explorer . . ."

"Any member of your crew who recalls personal memories must be considered a danger. Return to the boat and kill her."

"That's not happening." Huxley's grip tightened on the phone, pressing it close to his lips, spittle flying as his rage won out over caution. "Listen, none of us is doing shit until we get answers . . ."

The sound that echoed from the boat mingled a dry crack with a boom, starkly unmistakable in origin. *Gunshot.*

"Return to the boat," the voice told him, just as flat as before. "Kill her."

Pynchon told him to take charge of the outboard, unslinging his carbine to perch on the prow while Huxley opened the throttle to its meagre maximum. They could hear shouting from the boat as they drew up to the stern, Pynchon jumping clear and disappearing into the wheelhouse, carbine at his shoulder. Huxley scrambled in his wake, remembering to tie the inflatable to the aft railing before following. He unslung his own carbine upon entering the gloom of the wheelhouse, foot slipping on something wet. Looking down he saw a smear of red on the deck.

"Fucking hell!" The grunting shout came from Golding, on his back, blood welling between his fingers as he clutched both hands to his thigh. "She shot me! Fucking bitch shot me!"

Rhys was at his side, unfurling a bandage from one of the med-kits. "Sit still! Pretty sure it's just a graze."

"Doesn't feel like a fucking graze!" Golding let out a whimpering yell as she prised his hands away from the wound, peering at the crimson mess through the rent in his fatigues.

"What happened?" Huxley demanded, scanning the wheelhouse but seeing no one else.

"Dickinson." Rhys took a canteen and splashed water on Golding's wound, grunting in satisfaction at what she found. "Took some meat off but no through-and-through or bullet lodgement. You got lucky."

"Yeah?" Golding's face paled and throat convulsed in the signature expression of a man about to lose his breakfast. "I feel so lucky right now . . ."

"Dickinson did this?" Huxley persisted.

"Started talking just when you reached the beacon. Rambling really." Rhys grimaced as Golding turned his head to throw up, but she stoically continued to apply the dressing to his wound. "Wasn't making much sense, getting increasingly agitated. We tried to calm her but she started screaming, pointing her gun at the deck as if there was something there. Then she pulled the trigger. This—" Rhys tied off the bandage with a deft twist of her wrists "—was a ricochet."

"Where is she now?"

"Crew cabin. She dropped that." Rhys nodded to a fallen carbine on the deck nearby. "Plath's trying to talk to her. Is that a sat-phone?"

Huxley had the phone tucked into one of the ammo pouches on his webbing. "Yeah."

"So you spoke to someone, right? What did they say?"

Huxley looked at Pynchon, finding him tense, eyes downcast as if in shame, though there was no sign of a tremble in the hands that held his carbine.

Huxley moved to the ladder. "I need to talk to Dickinson."

"You heard what it said," Pynchon muttered. Huxley brushed past him, descending the ladder to the crew cabin where he found Plath crouched beside a huddled Dickinson. The woman's face was a picture of guilty misery, eyes moist and lips repeatedly drawing back to reveal teeth set in a hissing grimace.

"I saw . . ." she said, putting a palm to her forehead.

"What?" Plath prompted. "What did you see?"

"You saw it too, you must have."

"There was nothing there . . ."

Plath fell silent at the sound of Huxley's boots on the deck, she and Dickinson both looking up at him with a different kind of fear in their eyes. "She's calmed down a lot," Plath said, her tone making him wonder if she saw a decision in his gaze he didn't know he had reached.

"Is it still up there?" Dickinson asked him, her expression stark in its desperate entreaty. "It's gone, right? Please tell me it's gone."

Huxley knew he was no psychiatrist, but some ingrained instinct told him with complete certainty that he was now looking into the eyes of a woman who had, in the space of a half-hour, slipped into insanity. *Dickinson is now a danger to you all.*

"It's gone," he told her. "Pretty sure you scared it off."

"Thank you." She closed her eyes, resting her head against the side of a bunk, words coming in a whispering torrent. "Thank you, thank you, thank you."

Huxley heard Pynchon descend the ladder, boots thumping onto the deck with loud intent. Glancing over his shoulder, Huxley fixed Pynchon with a steady glare, shaking his head.

"Let me talk to her," he told Plath, touching a hand to her shoulder to ease her aside. She retreated, casting nervous glances at both him and Pynchon.

"Any idea how it got here?" Huxley asked Dickinson, crouching before her and ignoring the soft scrape of Pynchon's carbine sling as he adjusted his grip.

"No!" Dickinson shook her head, fast and fierce. "I mean, it's impossible right? Papa killed it. I watched him. He made me watch."

"But you saw it, here and now."

"Maybe . . ." Dickinson's tongue licked over her lips, throat working and a manic comprehension glinting in her eyes. "Maybe this is part of it, the . . . experiment. Whatever. Maybe this isn't actually real." Her hand slapped at the bunk and then the wall behind her. "A simulation!" Her eyes widened, breath emerging in a gasp of realisation. "Of course! We're not really here. That's it. That's the only way . . ."

"The bullet wound in Golding's leg looks pretty real," Huxley pointed out.

"Well it would, wouldn't it?" Her expression became peevishly judgemental, exasperated by his failure of insight. "That's how a simulation works."

Huxley had the distinct impression she was preventing herself adding the word 'dumbass' or 'dipshit' to her statement. Softening his tone, he tried a different tack. "You mentioned your father. So you remember him now?"

"Papa? Yes." She relaxed a little, letting out a short, shrill laugh. As it faded, her expression darkened, mouth twisting in anger, voice growing thick, words emerging in a series of grunts. "I remember Papa. I remember what he did, what he'd still like to do. That's why he did it. Bought me a puppy just so he could kill it in front of me, because I wouldn't any more, because I threatened to tell Mama . . ."

The attack came without warning. No pause or shift in her posture. Just an unhesitant lunge of pure aggression, feral and animal quick. Her muscular frame hit him with the force of a battering ram, bearing him down, impossibly strong hands digging fingers into his shoulders. "Papa!" The word was formed of a growl, flecked in drool leaking from her mouth. She reared above him, teeth bared and head angled like a cat seeking the best place to bite. Before the booming crack of Pynchon's carbine sent a bullet through her skull, Huxley saw something change in her face, a shift of muscle and bone, twisting it, transforming . . .

He blinked in the shower of blood and other matter, both hard and soft, ears ringing from the gunshot. He fought a gag reflex as Dickinson's lifeless body collapsed atop him, warm blood dripping from the ragged hole in her forehead. Pynchon dragged the corpse off to allow him to scramble back, trying to scrape the gore from his face but only smearing it.

Pynchon sniffed, flipping his carbine's safety catch, eyebrow raised as he surveyed Dickinson's corpse before nodding to the sat-phone tucked into Huxley's ammo pouch. "Looks like it wasn't lying, anyway."

Chapter Four

"Remembering personal details." Rhys didn't look up from Dickinson's body as she spoke, her attention fixed on the woman's altered features. "That's what it said?"

"Anyone who recalls something about who they are is a danger." Huxley lowered his head to douse the nape of his neck in canteen water, fingers working behind his ears to scrape away the last gritty bits of bone and flesh. "It also asked about signs of illness on Conrad's body. Wasn't too specific, though."

"Why do you keep saying 'it'?" Plath asked. "You said the voice was female."

Huxley began to shrug in dismissal, pausing as it occurred to him that her scientist's mind might have happened upon something significant. "It sounded female," he said. "But not like a person. No real emotion."

"Could be a machine voice," Pynchon suggested. "Automated voice warnings on military aircraft are all female – they command more attention."

"Can we focus on the matter at hand?" Rhys straightened from Dickinson's body. They had laid it out on the aft deck, a process that involved liberally spattering the boat's interior with blood and other, less colourful fluids. Once again, the sight of violent death repulsed Huxley but not to the point of nausea. *Seen it all before.* He resisted the impulse to nudge at the realisation in the hope of stirring true recollection, grateful now for the pang of discomfort that accompanied the thought. *Maybe they made it hurt to protect us.*

"Cause of death seems pretty obvious," Golding said, though any annoyance the remark might have aroused was obviated by his pale-faced misery and the quaver that coloured his tone. He hobbled from the wheelhouse into the open, clutching at the railing as agonised winces passed across his face. Deeper rummaging of the packs from the storage lockers had revealed no painkillers of any kind.

"There are clear physiological changes here." Rhys touched a hand to Dickinson's jaw, finger pressing the flesh to explore the bone beneath. "And here." Her hand moved to the part-destroyed forehead, playing over the brows. "Rapid and pronounced morphological change."

"Seems like signs of illness to me," Huxley said.

Rhys inclined her head in agreement. "Oh yeah. But we didn't see anything like this on Conrad's body."

"Maybe he didn't have time. Dickinson went batshit

insane − to use the technical term − first, before . . ."
He waved a hand at the dead woman's disfigured
features. "Maybe Conrad knew what was happening
and . . . took the appropriate action."

"Any notion of what form of disease could cause
this?" Pynchon asked Rhys.

"Although I still can't remember my own name, I'm
pretty confident that the real me had never seen
anything like this in her entire career."

"Someone has." Huxley's gaze lingered on the
distorted flesh beneath the blood covering Dickinson's
face, recalling the predatory aspect she had taken on
just before Pynchon shot her. He had no doubt about
the danger she posed and no recriminations for
Pynchon − left alive, she would have killed them all.
"They knew it might happen."

"So we are test subjects," Plath said. Paradoxically,
Huxley felt that her persistent fear had diminished in
the aftermath of Dickinson's death. She remained tense,
hands still clasped together but not with the same
tightness. She raised them to her lips, eyes closed in
thought, almost in a gesture of prayer. "A failure rate
of two out of seven, so far. In some drug trials that
might be considered a positive result."

Golding let out a disgusted groan and fixed Huxley
with a demanding stare. "What else did it say? What
are we doing on this boat?"

"Answers were pretty thin on the ground. It did say
the boat won't move until . . ." He trailed off when

the sat-phone emitted its low-pitched chirp, the device thrumming against his chest. *Perfectly on cue. Can't fault their timing.*

The others followed him into the wheelhouse as he tugged it from the pouch. Raising a hand for silence, he thumbed the green button, angling the speaker towards his ear as they crowded in to hear.

"Is Dickinson dead?" No greeting or preamble. Same voice as before.

"Yeah," Huxley said. "She's dead."

"Any other casualties?"

"Golding got a bullet graze to the leg. Rhys says it's not serious. She is the doctor here, right?"

"Do any members of the party display signs of confused thinking or unwarranted aggression?"

His gaze roamed over the others. Golding's features were grey with pain and drawn in the effort of containing a flurry of questions. Pynchon grim and thoughtful. Plath still with her hands pressed to her mouth. Rhys, arms crossed once again, not bothering to keep the fear from her face.

"No."

Golding started to speak but his voice was smothered by the sound of the engines flaring to life, water churning white beyond the stern.

"Dispose of Dickinson's body," the sat-phone instructed. "There are obstructions ahead. You must clear them in order to continue. You will find one of the locked containers in the hold is now open. It contains explosives. Pynchon possesses the skills and knowledge to use them correctly. As you proceed, ensure you are armed at all times. If you encounter anyone else, kill them immediately. They are a danger to you."

"Am I talking to a real person?" Huxley asked the voice. For some reason it seemed the most pertinent question in the moment. "Are you . . . an AI or something?"

A short pause, a series of clicks. "Communication will resume in twelve hours," the voice said, the hiss of an open line dying as the phone went dead.

Grunting an incoherent obscenity, Golding lunged for the device, stumbling due to his leg but managing to latch a hand to it, yelling into the receiver: "What are we doing on this fucking boat? Who are you?"

"It's gone." Huxley shoved him away, Golding colliding with a seat then slumping to the deck. He pressed both hands to his face, shuddering as sobs escaped his lips. Huxley thought it best to leave him to it.

"Map's back." Pynchon nodded to the one live display, once again showing a pulsing green dot now making its way deeper into the estuary, leaving the red dot behind. He shouldered his carbine, moving to the ladder. "Guess I better take a look at our new toys."

"Is that what I think it is?"

Pynchon raised an eyebrow at Huxley before reaching into the hold, lifting the object clear. It had a vaguely rifle-like appearance but lacked a rear stock. Instead of a magazine, a small, pressurised tank was positioned to the front of the trigger. Below the muzzle was a triangular box with a small spout.

"If you're thinking it's a flame-thrower—" Pynchon flicked a switch on the underside of the triangular box, igniting a finger-sized jet of blue fire "—you're right."

The flame-thrower was one of two, both sitting atop a base consisting of what appeared to be cardboard-covered bricks. "C-4," Pynchon said, hefting one of the bricks to read the text stencilled onto the wrapping. Some further rummaging unearthed a canvas bag filled with dozens of thin metal rods and neatly coiled wires. "Detonators, timers, fuse wire." Pynchon set the bag aside with more care than he had shown when handling the actual explosive. He pursed his lips as he surveyed the hold's contents. "This is a lot, but not enough to put a dent in what we're going to run up against before nightfall."

"And what's that?"

"The Thames Barrier. Several thousand tonnes of steel and concrete designed to save the capital of these great islands from the flooding that would have claimed it years ago."

"Unless that's where the journey ends."

"I get the feeling we're not going to be that lucky." Pynchon returned the brick of C-4 to the hold but kept the bag and one of the flame-throwers. "Golding," he said, voice low. "Confused thinking."

"He just got shot. A heightened level of stress seems justified in the circumstances. Also, I haven't noticed any unwarranted aggression. And he shows no signs of remembering personal details."

"That he's told us about. Seems to me everyone on this boat now has an incentive to keep any memories to themselves."

"The effect of this . . . thing, whatever it is, seems more immediate than that. Dickinson went from sane to homicidal in the space of minutes."

"Meaning we can't hesitate if it happens again. Regardless of who it happens to."

"Even you?"

Pynchon gave him a frown that was as offended as it was puzzled. "Of course. I start talking about the good old days at school I'll expect you to put a bullet in my dome post-haste. And don't worry." He patted a hand to Huxley's shoulder before getting to his feet, bag and flame-thrower in hand. "I'll happily do the same for you."

"I don't even want to think about what that's for," Golding said, eyeing the flame-thrower with equal parts distaste and trepidation.

They gathered in the wheelhouse after tipping Dickinson over the side, another ad hoc funeral marked by a complete lack of ritual. With nothing else to do, they spent the time watching the map display. "I'm guessing this is far from the boat's top speed," Huxley said, seeing the way the two dots on the screen inched apart in gradual increments.

"I estimate about one-fifth of what she can do." Pynchon leaned forward to peer through the windscreen. The banks of the estuary were visible as indistinct, bulky shadows in the fog, but it was clear the channel was narrowing considerably with each passing mile. "It'll be a few hours before we reach the barrier . . ."

Huxley saw the flash and felt the heat before he heard it, a powerful shudder running through the boat from stern to prow. The sound, an echoing, bone-deep boom, reached them as he turned to see the bright orange plume blossoming in the fog, the shrouding miasma dissolved by the blast. The water below the explosion transformed into a shimmering white disc at least five hundred yards in diameter.

"The buoy," Huxley said, a statement that felt both redundant and necessary.

"Thermobaric bomb." Pynchon stared at the fading orange flower with a distinct absence of surprise. "At close range the blast has a similar force to a low-yield nuclear warhead."

"So if we'd still been bobbing around it . . ." Huxley blew air through his lips, feeling twin urges towards both laughter and profanity-laden rage. "At least it wasn't a killer robot."

"Why set it off now?" Rhys wondered.

"Termination of live subjects." Plath had finally unclasped her hands and spoke with a flatness not dissimilar to the voice on the sat-phone. "Typical response in the event of a failed experiment."

"It was probably on a timer," Pynchon said. "If they hadn't turned the engines back on within a set period . . ." His brow furrowed in realisation. "AI on the phone. Timed explosions. Remote activation of key components. Looks like they're keen for as much of this mission to be automated as possible."

Huxley watched the fog close in again as the last glimmer of white faded from the water. *Really must ask about this fog next time,* he decided, touching a hand to the phone.

True to its promise, the phone stayed silent as they continued to follow the estuary until it truly became a river. Both banks were more easily viewed now, the hard vertical and slanting lines of buildings discernible among the softer silhouettes of trees. A few lights glimmered here and there, mostly around the thin spires of what he took to be industrial sites or docks. However, they revealed nothing of the world beyond the lingering mist. The shoreline also remained silent until, about two hours after the explosion of the beacon, they heard a very distant rumble.

"That's not thunder." Pynchon cocked his head, straining to hear more. They had moved to the aft deck at the first murmuring boom. The noise continued but they saw no alteration in the fog or the meagre lights on shore.

Detecting a very brief pause between the peaks of the sound, Huxley turned to Pynchon. "More explosions?"

He nodded. "Pretty sure it's artillery."

"And gunfire," Golding said, pointing to his ear in response to their questioning glances. "Clear as day to me. Maybe I was chosen for my pristine hearing."

A few seconds more of strained listening and Huxley heard it too: repeated staccato drumbeats that told of automatic weapons fire.

"A battle," Rhys concluded. "But who's fighting who?"

"Last war I can name was Afghanistan," Huxley said.

"No wars have been fought on British soil for over two centuries." Golding gave a half-tilt of his head. "If you don't count Northern Ireland."

"No traffic noise, minimal lights, now this." Pynchon grimaced. "Looks like things have really gone to shit."

"Just here or elsewhere?" Plath said.

Of course, none of them had an answer and the question heralded a long silence. Eventually, the song of battle faded, only to be replaced shortly after by something even more discordant. It was made more unnerving by its direction, seeming to come at them from above rather than the shore, a plaintive, dissonant wail.

"A gull?" Golding wondered, peering up at the occluded sky.

Huxley remembered the screeching gull that had,

along with Conrad's pistol, first roused him. This was very different, wavering and prolonged instead of a rhythmic keening. Also, he hadn't caught sight of a single gull since that initial waking.

"It's human," Rhys said. Like all of them, she stared up at the unseen sky, eyes narrowed. "But from where?"

Pynchon let out a soft grunt of realisation, gesturing with his carbine at a large grey shape resolving out of the mist beyond the prow. It was a structure of monolithic proportions, huge concrete legs joined by a massive spar ascending to fog-bound heights.

"A bridge?" Plath said.

"The Dartford Crossing." A curious, faintly baffled expression flickered over Golding's brow before he added in a softer tone, "Or the Queen Elizabeth Bridge to be exact."

Feeling a pulse of alarm, Huxley's grip tightened involuntarily on his carbine. He tried not to stare at Golding's features in search of recollection, but the historian noticed anyway. "Relax," he said, edging away. "Just seemed like a strange title for it, all of a sudden."

"Without context, some names, especially place names, will probably feel weird," Rhys said.

A fresh upsurge of wailing snapped their attention back to the obscured bulk of the bridge. The boat had now drawn level with the featureless monolith, conveying a sense of passing beneath the legs of a giant.

"Just screams and screams." Golding winced, fingers

twitching on his own carbine. Like all of them he held the weapon with a practised grip, but still it looked odd in his hands, out of place. "No words that I can hear . . ." He trailed off as the wailing suddenly grew louder, echoing down the flanks of the giant's grey legs.

Pynchon and the others raised their carbines but Huxley resisted the urge to do the same. An undefined instinct failed to signal a threat here. Consequently, he was the only one who saw the small dark shape plummet through the fog, his crewmates still intent in pointing their guns at empty mist. The formless cry continued as the shape descended, Huxley seeing it flail and twist in the air – a person, falling, screaming. Gender and age unknowable. They impacted the water almost exactly at the mid-point of the bridge support, raising a tall splash. The wailing died instantly, as, Huxley assumed, did the anonymous faller. Air hissed from between his lips as he watched the column of water fall and the ripples spread. *Like falling onto bare rock from that height.*

"No movement," Pynchon confirmed, carbine levelled at the body. It was face down in the water, clothing ballooned around it, arms splayed. As the boat continued its course, the body bobbed and turned over in the wake, but sank before Huxley could train his optical sight on its features.

"That didn't tell us much," Golding said.

"Told us one thing." Pynchon raised his gaze to the

misted heights once again. "The bridge span is gone, otherwise they couldn't have splashed down where they did. Like I said, things have really gone to shit here."

The Thames Barrier came into view in the early evening, a long procession of tall, peak-curved silhouettes in the darkening mist. The boat showed no inclination to slow and it soon became clear that this particular landmark wouldn't prove a barrier at all.

"Can't say where or when, obviously," Pynchon said, tracking his sight along the row of cathedral-sized piers that formed the barrier, halting at the broad gap in the middle. "But I know I've seen damage like this before."

The pier in the centre of the barrier was a ruined and diminished version of those to either side. The aluminium curve of its roof had vanished and much of its bulk was reduced to a stump of rubble jutting only a few feet above the waterline. The gates that gave the barrier purpose were all raised between the surviving piers, but around the flanks of their destroyed sibling the river flowed through in a rapid churn of spiralling currents.

"Air-dropped ordnance." Pynchon lowered his weapon. "Laser-guided five-hundred pounders, probably."

"Somebody wanted to flood London," Huxley said.

"Or, maybe somebody wanted to make the river navigable," Plath suggested.

"You think this was bombed just to let us through?"

He was struck by the new-found composure evident in the look she gave him, just a little shy of withering in its judgement. "I think we're a bunch of amnesiacs with guns on a boat sailing into the middle of one of the largest cities in the world which, as yet, shows no signs of life apart from suicidal lunatics screaming in the fog. We already agreed we're here for a reason. It's not too huge a leap to assume this is part of it."

"This was done a while ago," Pynchon said. "Days, weeks maybe. Before this shit closed in." He flicked a hand at the encroaching fog. Huxley felt its pinkish shade had deepened over the course of the last few hours, although that may have been the effect of a fading sun.

Plath inclined her head in acknowledgement. "Which would indicate this mission to be the culmination of extensive planning and effort. The obvious conclusion is that we are here in response to whatever has happened to this city."

"Rescue maybe?" Pynchon gave a doubtful grimace. "If there's anyone left to rescue."

"There's still an unopened container in the hold," Huxley reminded them. "Doesn't take Sherlock Holmes to connect that particular fact to our ultimate objective."

The boat slewed as it passed through the barrier, the twisting current causing the bows to lurch to port and starboard with anxiety-inducing violence. However, it righted itself quickly, the pitch of the engines rising then falling as a burst of increased power brought them clear of the churn. The first wreck came into view shortly after, the prow of a large, dark-hulled vessel breaking the surface a short distance from shore. Its anchor chain formed a straight, diagonal line into the water, bisecting the portions of the part-submerged name painted in white letters on the hull: *LLIE HOLIDAY.*

"Looks like someone was a jazz fan," Golding observed.

"I think it's a dredger," Pynchon said. "Big vessel. Take a lot to sink her."

The boat slowed soon after, more wrecks appearing, rendered into little more than abstract shapes in the gloom-laden fog. The boat's prow shifted every few minutes, an unseen hand making course adjustments to avoid these new obstacles. The banks of the river were closer now, details still concealed by the diminishing light and the mist. Using his carbine sight, Huxley made out rippling shadows around the bases of structures that told of an inundated city. Unlike the eastern stretches of the river, there were no lights at all here, just a passing wall of silent, blank buildings.

"Uh-oh," Pynchon grunted when the encroaching darkness all but banished the riverbanks. He and Huxley stood on either side of the chain gun, carbines pointed into the void beyond the prow. Pynchon had activated a laser pointer attached to the fore stock of his carbine, flicking the pinpoint of red light from one vague shadow to another until it came to a wavering halt on a particularly broad shape dead ahead.

"What is it?" Huxley peered through his sight but saw only a jumble of shadowed curves and angles.

"Looks like a load of wrecks all bunched up together." The laser dot tracked from right to left several times before he lowered it. "Can't see a passage through."

As if to underline his judgement, the engines churned louder as they went into reverse, bringing the boat to a halt before shutting down. Pynchon lowered his weapon, the light from the wheelhouse gleaming on his sweat-beaded skin. "I guess this is where the C-4 comes in."

Huxley scanned the incoherent wall of shadows. "In the dark?"

Pynchon gave a half-amused snort. "Christ no." He gripped the railing to steady himself as the engines gave one of their brief, station-keeping roars, then started to work his way aft. "We'll wait for morning. And this time we're keeping watch. I'll take the first shift, wake you in two hours."

"You think they'd have at least given us an anchor." The complaint sounded strange from Rhys's lips, uncharacteristically peevish in a way that made Huxley reflect on the absurdity of ascribing character traits to someone who didn't know who they were. Her annoyance arose from the engines' habit of growling into life at random intervals to keep the boat in position.

This, and the extremity of their situation, made sleep difficult, at least for her and Huxley. Pynchon hadn't had to wake him for his turn on watch, Huxley spending the interval in contemplation of the underside of Golding's bunk. The historian had dropped into a sound slumber almost immediately, as had Pynchon after reporting an uneventful two hours. Huxley assumed the ability to grab sleep whenever opportunity arose to be an ingrained habit of military life. Plath took longer, lying on her bunk with hands resting on her chest. Her eyes remained open for a while and when they closed her posture didn't change, making him wonder if she was in fact sleeping. Upon ascending the ladder, he found Rhys seated at the front of the wheelhouse.

"If they had we might be tempted to drop it," Huxley replied, arcing an eyebrow, "never to be raised."

Rhys consented to a shallow curve of her lips before lapsing into silence, resting her head against the seat back. They both sat at the control panel, the world beyond the windscreens rendered black by the glow of the unchanging map display. Huxley had been tempted to drape something over it, but the sight of a red dot pulsing in the centre of a blue stripe proved irresistibly fascinating.

After a lengthy pause, Rhys spoke again, voice dull with fatigue and frustration. "It's different this time. Sleeping, I mean. You remember that first time after we tipped Conrad over the side? Like falling into a coma. Now it's just . . . sleep." She shifted in the seat, drawing her legs up, grimacing as she failed to find comfort. "And, it turns out I can't. Maybe insomnia was a regular thing for me."

"Or maybe it's something to do with these." Huxley played a hand over the scar on his head. "What they did to us. Maybe that first sleep was a side effect, or a necessary part of the procedure."

"Maybe," she repeated in a mutter. "Maybe, maybe. Seems like we're living in a world of endless maybes."

He wanted to offer reassurance but had nothing. No anecdotes. No exemplars of resilience in the face of tragedy or disaster. *If I was really a cop there must be something. That time I talked down a methed-up skinhead with a shotgun? Or a victim of violence, a stabbing or shooting, who I kept alive until the paramedics came?* But these were inventions not memories. It was just as possible he had spent his life behind a desk scouring spreadsheets in pursuit of money launderers or fraudsters. Or he hadn't been a cop at all and he was playing a role his equally damaged companions cast for him. He felt the absence of a personal history more keenly than ever, the pain returning but with a new sharpness as he suffered the dislocation of being severed from something fundamental, something necessary.

"You probably shouldn't try to remember," Rhys cautioned, huddled posture unchanged but her gaze now considerably more focused.

"I wasn't." He forced a smile. "Promise."

She relaxed a little, resting her chin on her raised knees. "Been thinking about the pain. I don't think it's a side effect."

"Yeah, that's what I thought. Try to remember and it hurts. Negative reinforcement, or something. Do wonder how they did it, though."

"Implants. It has to be. There's a device called a shunt which is used to treat patients with short-term memory loss, sends electrical signals through certain parts of the brain to stimulate recall. It's not hard to imagine something that does the opposite."

"Didn't work on Dickinson or Conrad, did it?"

She raised her eyebrows in grim agreement. "No, but that's to be expected with technology that's still in its infancy. Plath might be right, you know: this could all be an experiment."

Huxley inclined his head at the blackness beyond the windscreen. "If so, they've gone to pretty extreme lengths."

"I don't mean what's out there, I mean us. We're clearly here as a response to whatever happened, but that doesn't mean we're not an experiment, a test bed for the real attempt."

"Or we are the real attempt." He settled back in his seat, staring at the blinking dot on the map display. "All this automation, there has to be a reason for it. Didn't it occur to you that we might be all that's left?"

"The last hope for humanity." She let out a long

shuddering breath that he judged a failed attempt at laughter. "That may be the most depressing thought yet."

She lapsed back into silence, tilting her head to press her cheek to her knees. When she spoke again the words were soft, tremulous. "I have stretch marks and a Caesarean scar. Not too extensive so I'm guessing just one kid. I want to think I had a daughter rather than a son. Isn't that horribly sexist of me?" The question was starkly rhetorical so he said nothing, Rhys continuing with scarcely a pause. "How old is she? Does she play with Barbies or action figures? What brand of cereal does she eat? Does she miss me? It hurts, but I can't help reaching for it."

Huxley didn't look at her, knowing he would see tears if he did. Not looking was cowardice, he knew that. If he turned and saw those tears it would invite a connection, one that scared him. *If she remembers her daughter's favourite brand of cereal, I'll have to shoot her.*

Distraction, both welcome and dreaded, came in the form of a shrill chorus of screams from the north bank of the river, muted by the confines of the wheelhouse but they still heard it.

"Seagulls are back," Huxley muttered, hefting his carbine and heading to the aft deck.

The fog made peering into the night a redundant exercise. It had settled in thick drifts over the surrounding water to catch the meagre light from the boat and create a pale, impenetrable wall. Huxley wondered if it somehow amplified the screaming, which sounded too loud to be the product of human throats. It began as a babble, what might have been laughter mixed with an overlapping prating of inchoate gibberish. Huxley could draw only two conclusions, one being the patent fact that this noise came from a group rather than a solitary person, their evident insanity being the other.

"Sounds like a helluva party," he grunted. He had the stock of his carbine pressed against his shoulder but hadn't yet raised the weapon, there being nothing to shoot at.

"Are they screaming at us?" Rhys held her own weapon with much the same combination of familiarity and discomfort shown by Golding and Plath, cheeks red from rapid wiping as she stared into the fog.

"Can't see anyone else here, can you?"

"How can they see us in this?"

"Light carries far when it doesn't have much competition."

He jerked his carbine up as the babbling chorus underwent a sudden change, the screaming nonsense merging into one great shout. Huxley heard rage in it, also a great deal of pain, but mostly he heard fear – the collective yell of a terrorised group. *Are they threatening us or warning us?*

The group scream died away quickly, but didn't herald silence. Now there came a voice, just one, male, and still screaming but this time forming words, indistinct at first, garbled as if spoken by an impaired mouth.

"I . . . know . . ." the invisible screamer told them, Huxley hearing the splash of a body leaping into the water. More splashes followed, the voice growing louder as the screamer thrashed his way towards them. "I know . . . who you are!"

Huxley put his eye to the optical sight, searching the fog, seeing nothing.

"I know who you are!" Closer now, but still no sign of anything to shoot at.

"Seems he knows something we don't." Rhys's voice had a clipped, throaty quality to it that told of forced humour. Glancing to his left, Huxley saw that she also had her carbine raised, safety off, fire selector set to semi-auto. She coughed before speaking again. "Let's ask him some questions."

"I KNOW WHO YOU ARE!"

Huxley saw it then, a scattering of white amid the reddish grey, a body struggling in the current. His finger shifted from the guard to the trigger, but he held off from squeezing it. He wanted to see the screamer's face, see if it in any way resembled Dickinson's when she tried to kill him. Rhys, however, didn't share his curiosity.

Her carbine barked twice, muzzle flash huge in the gloom, tall white spikes spouting in the fog. Huxley jerked instinctively from the hot sting of ejected cartridges striking his neck. When he returned his eye to the sight, all he saw were ripples. The far shore was silent once again, the screamers' chorus quieted by fear or indifference.

"We might have learned something . . ." he began, but Rhys was already turning away, snicking her carbine's safety catch into place.

Before she disappeared into the wheelhouse he caught a mutter, "I have to be alive to remember her."

Chapter Five

The dream came again when he snatched a fitful two hours of sleep before sunrise. It was more defined this time – the blue-gold haze resolving into sea and beach, waves pounding a sandy shore at high tide. Sparse clouds dotted an otherwise pristine azure sky and he felt the wind on his skin, delightful in the freshness of its chill. The white spectre that had ghosted across his vision before became a figure, cotton skirt flaring as it pirouetted over the sand, one hand holding a straw hat to a head of trailing curls. And the voice, still indistinct but wonderfully familiar . . .

The pain dragged him from the dream with heartless insistence, its grip resembling icy steel fingers sunk into the centre of his brain. He was unable to contain the agonised gasp as he came awake, the violence of his spasm almost tipping him from the bunk. *A dream is not a memory*, he told himself, heart pounding and relief flooding when he realised he was alone in the crew cabin. *They're not the same.*

He lay there for a time, waiting for his heart to
calm, pulse slowed then quickened by bouts of fearful
conjecture: Did he feel different? Did he want to hurt
himself? Did he want to hurt the others? He disliked
Golding and felt a growing aversion to Plath, but was
that born of acquaintance or memory? Besides, he
didn't think he wanted to kill anyone. But one question concerned him more than all the others: Who is
the woman on the beach?

The sound of Pynchon's voice brought an end to
his immobility, shouting down the ladder with gruff
authority. "Wake up, Mister Policeman. Time for
another excursion."

Dawn revealed the scale of their task in dispiriting
detail. The obstacle consisted of a jumble of intertwined
boats, all damaged to varying degrees. Most were small,
dinghies and pleasure craft forced into splintered union
with far larger vessels forming the bulk of the barrier.
A three-quarter submerged tugboat served as the
chaotic structure's right-hand bulwark. On the left, a
yacht-sized cabin cruiser Pynchon dubbed "the queen
of gin palaces" created a tilted, impassable wall. However,
the main obstruction, and the one he chose as their
objective, was the long, glass-roofed river barge in the
centre. The whole untidy edifice spread out before
them, ominous and uninviting in its many hatches and
rent hulls, shadowed portals made darker by the fog. It
hadn't faded with the morning sun, not that Huxley

had expected it to. Also, the reddish tinge was even more noticeable now, leading to an obvious conclusion.

"This isn't really fog, is it?" he said, turning to Plath.

From the guarded, slightly chagrined arch of her brows he deduced she had already reached the same conclusion but decided to keep it to herself. "I don't think so, no."

"Then what is it?"

Her answer was coloured by a grating disparagement, like a teacher addressing a slow student. "Do you happen to have a mass spectrometer handy? No? Then I can't tell you what it is."

"Hypothesise," Huxley instructed her, meeting the resentment in her gaze with a steady glare. From the annoyed twist of her mouth he suspected she might have ignored him but for the expectant stares of the others.

"A gas of some kind," she said, speaking with piqued precision. "The refraction of sunlight into this red hue indicates a density greater than the constituent gases of the atmosphere. The absence of an odour or respiratory difficulty makes it non-toxic, or at least slow-acting in its effects, otherwise I assume those who planned this mission would have provided respirators. Beyond that, I have no conclusions to offer."

"Can't be a coincidence," Rhys said. "London's a disaster zone and just happens to be covered in all this red shit."

"You're thinking a chemical attack?" Golding said.

They had spared him a shift on watch, yet, despite the length of his sleep, his face was gaunt, eyes sunken. Huxley ascribed it to the pain of his wound but, judging by the depth of appraising scrutiny Pynchon directed at the historian, not everyone agreed.

"I'll concede there is a high probability of a connection," Plath said. "But without further data there is no point in further speculation."

"She's right." Pynchon fastened the Velcro straps on a pack laden with C-4. He straightened, slipping the pack over his shoulders and nodding to the jumble of wrecks beyond the prow. "We need to get on." He handed the bag containing the detonators to Huxley and webbing with full ammunition pouches to Rhys. "Three person job. Two to set the charges, one for security."

"Thanks for giving the opportunity to volunteer." Rhys grimaced but donned the webbing without complaint.

"If anything happens . . ." Huxley began, turning to Plath and Golding, then trailed off. If anything happened they were all screwed, since the boat wouldn't go anywhere. "Maybe they'll call again," he said, plucking the sat-phone from his fatigue pocket and tossing it to Plath.

The barge was so securely jammed in the wall of wrecks it barely tilted when they climbed aboard. Pynchon steered the inflatable towards the barge's stern, a portion of which jutted out just enough to allow for an entry point. Huxley's boots crunched glass when he heaved himself over the rail, aiming the carbine one handed at the dark hatchway in the deck.

"Best check it over first." Pynchon clambered over next, extending a hand to help Rhys. She ignored it, switching her carbine to her back then gripping the rail with two hands to leap nimbly to their side. Pynchon grunted and turned to make a thorough survey of their surroundings. When he leaned over the barge's starboard rail he stiffened, then beckoned them both to his side.

Leaning forward to follow the line of Pynchon's finger, Huxley could see only another layer of wreckage beyond the barrier, more boats and barges jumbled into ruin. "What are we looking for?"

"There." Pynchon pointed again, finger stabbing at the hull of the tugboat pressed into the barge's stern. Looking closer, Huxley made out a ragged hole in the vessel's side, stretching from the thick rubber skirt covering its upper hull to the plating below the water-line. The hole's edges were twisted iron petals, blossoming out not in. "Charges on the inner hull," Pynchon said. "Metal's still scorched."

"Meaning?" Rhys asked.

Pynchon drew back, eyes shifting to the misted river beyond this accidental barricade. "Someone already blasted their way through."

"Then why is all this junk still here?"

"Current. Rivers don't stop flowing. It would've happened days or even weeks ago. More wrecks floated in to fill the gap and squish the tug up to the surface."

"We're not the first," Huxley said. "Maybe not even the second. How long has all this been going on?"

"Won't get any answers dossing about here." Pynchon sniffed and turned to the barge's upper cabin, activating the LED flashlight fixed to his webbing. "We stay together at all times. No splitting up to cover more ground crap."

"You sure?" Rhys shifted her carbine to her shoulder, adopting the usual trained grip and stance. "Kinda fancied myself as a final girl."

Huxley huffed a laugh, more through obligation than humour. Pynchon didn't. "And no more talk until we have to." He nodded at Huxley, pointing his weapon at the hatchway. "Mister Policeman, if you wouldn't mind leading the way."

"Because I'm the most expendable, right?"

"Because a law enforcement officer will have experience navigating an unfamiliar interior containing potential threats." A rare smile flickered over Pynchon's face. "And yes, I'd rather lose you than the good doctor."

"Not even sure I am a cop," Huxley grunted, switching on his own flashlight and crouching as he entered the cabin. The barge's glass roof was shattered in numerous places, the cabin a weirdly intact arrangement of seats and tables. Fragmented glass was everywhere, glittering as his LED played over it.

Moving deeper, he found nothing of particular interest beyond scattered cutlery and smashed crockery until he came to a chrome balustrade. It arched down to the deck, disappearing into a sturdy wooden hatch which seemed at odds with the rest of the decor.

"Seems solid," Huxley said, crouching to test the hatch with a hard shove. "No lock though."

"Secured from the other side." Pynchon was more forceful, stamping his boot into the centre of the hatch. It shuddered but failed to give. "This is scavenged wood," he said. "Probably taken from the other wrecks."

"Somebody's keen to keep things out," Rhys observed.

"Then I'm guessing they won't be welcoming of visitors," Huxley added.

"Welcome or not—" Pynchon gave the hatch a final look over then flipped the fire selector on his carbine to fully automatic "—here we come. Stand back. Cover your eyes."

He aimed for the centre of the hatch where its two parts joined. Huxley raised his forearm to his face and turned away as the carbine roared, two short bursts, a pause, then a third. Lowering his arm, he saw Pynchon once again stamping on the hatch, this time with more success as his boot crunched through timber transformed into splinters by high-velocity rounds. A few more kicks and he had created a hole large enough to grab with both hands, wrenching the hatch apart then standing back, carbine trained on the revealed stairwell.

Huxley moved to his side, motes of dust and fragmented wood drifting in the beams of their flashlights. The shards of more than one twisted and broken bolt lock littered the steps and, below that, he saw the gleam of lapping water.

"Flooded. At least she won't take a lot to sink." Pynchon stood aside, inclining his head at Huxley.

He descended the steps in a crouch, keeping the carbine at his shoulder, tracking the barrel in tandem with the flashlight. It played over ankle-deep water and another sprawl of disturbed hospitality, tables and chairs in disarray, a wine glass bobbing in the slosh as he reached the base of the stairs. Water seeped into his boots as he waded on, coming to a halt after a few steps when his flashlight caught an unusual piece of floating debris, something dark and red. *Rat.* He stooped for a closer look at the rodent's corpse, finding its mouth agape, small sharp teeth bared in the rictus of death. More concerning was the state of its body, black fur and flesh torn away down to the bone, the ribcage and spine exposed while its tail was a flaccid pale worm, coiling gently in the ripples.

"Didn't die of disease, anyway," Rhys said, coming to his side to take hold of the rat's tail. Plucking it from the water, she held it close to her flashlight for inspection. "This little guy was eaten. And they didn't bother to cook him first."

"Also the first sign of animal life we've seen," Huxley pointed out.

"We don't need any distractions, people." Pynchon moved past, carbine still at his shoulder and affording the rat only a brief glance. "Job to do, remember."

Rhys tossed the rat away while Huxley raised his carbine and returned to scanning the cabin. His flashlight came to a halt as it illuminated a bar on the far side of the deck, lingering on the remarkable sight of an intact bottle on the marble counter. It glowed in the LED beam with a gilded seductiveness that drew him straight to it, regardless of instincts that warned him to check his environment. The bottle was all chunky, rectangular familiarity, sending a pang through his head as it rebounded from his shielded memory. It had a black label, ruined by damp but still legible in places, the words "Tennessee" and "Daniel's" being the most noteworthy. He took hold of the bottle, the amber liquid displaying a pleasing sluggishness as it moved within its glass prison. Huxley found that his lips were pressed together and he had to stiffen his arm to prevent his hands shaking. He could taste the whiskey, even though not one memory of ever drinking it came to mind. The feel of it on his tongue, the wonderful burn, and the accompanying invitation to oblivion . . .

"If I wanted to lay a trap for unwelcome visitors," Rhys's voice, a harsh whisper in his ear, "a bottle full of inviting liquor laced with something nasty would seem like a very good idea." She tapped a finger to the broken seal of the bottle's cap. "Sure you want to risk it?"

More pain, this time not all in his head. It came from his gut too, a roiling, desperate need far beyond thirst or hunger. He tried to keep the shake from his hand as he set the bottle down, but Pynchon saw it. Also, as he stepped closer, face bunching both scrutiny and disdain, he saw something else.

"Looks like we've uncovered another aspect of your character, Mister Policeman," he said, eyebrows raised, mouth curling in an almost apologetic grin. "You're a fucking drunk, mate."

It was foolish, a display of churlish anger and defiance, once again painful in its familiarity, but also not one Huxley could contain. Taking up the bottle again, he gripped it by the neck and brought it down on the edge of the marble counter, amber droplets and crystal shards exploding. "Fuck you," he rasped at Pynchon.

The soldier angled his head, lips quirking in amusement now, although his gaze was steady and unblinking.

"Get the measuring tape out later, boys," Rhys said in weary disparagement, wading towards the far end of the deck where another balustrade gleamed in her flashlight beam. "Job to do, remember."

Pynchon held Huxley's gaze a second longer, then turned away to follow Rhys. Huxley found himself preoccupied by Pynchon's unguarded back, the neck of the shattered bottle still clutched in his fist. A spasm of self-reproach and disgust jerked his hand open, letting it fall. *Something a drunk would do*, he decided, bemused by feeling both shame and embarrassment for a past he couldn't remember. *A cowardly drunk at that.*

There was no hatch guarding the stairwell to the barge's lowest deck. The flashlights revealed an identical set of steps submerged by debris-flecked water, the space below lost to absolute blackness. "Looks like I'm swimming," Pynchon said, shrugging off his pack.

"Is that really necessary?" Rhys eyed the flooded stairwell with keen trepidation. "Can't you set the charges here?"

"Needs to be below the waterline where her hull meets the tugboat, or they won't sink." He beckoned to them as he sloshed his way back to the bar, setting the pack on the counter and opening it to extract two blocks of C-4. "Detonators," he said, extending a hand to Huxley.

"Won't you need magnets or tape or something?" he asked, handing over the bag. "To attach them, I mean."

"Just need to rest them against the hull. Water pressure will do the rest." Pynchon placed the C-4 blocks side by side and slowly pressed a pen-sized detonator into each of the bricks. He attached the fuse wires next, thumbing the plastic timer switches on each with careful precision. "Fifteen minutes. Should be plenty of time to get clear."

He removed his boots and fatigue jacket before returning the C-4 to the pack and carrying it to the flooded stairwell, flashlight in his other hand. "Two minutes max," he said. "More than that and I've drowned. I'll leave it up to you if you want to come down after me."

He took a few short, shallow breaths before a final, wide-mouthed gulp then plunged into the stairwell. They saw him descend into the gloom, flip end over end then disappear from view, the glow of his flashlight dimming quickly.

"One-one-thousand, two-one-thousand," Rhys began to count with a concentrated precision Huxley felt to be pointless. Pynchon was coming back or he wasn't. He soon found her rhythmic muttering unaccountably annoying, although it may have been due to lingering pique over the whiskey bottle. Either way, he opened his mouth to utter a waspish suggestion to lay off, then stopped as something disturbed the water behind them.

Their flashlights danced as they whirled, carbines at the shoulder, safeties flicking off, the beams tracking over rippling water and bobbing detritus. "Another rat?" Rhys wondered.

"I really hope so." He knew with a dispiriting certainty that the sound hadn't come from a rat. Whatever was left in this city, it didn't consist only of vermin.

Another slosh, off to the right, their flashlight beams converging on the corner of the cabin. The figure crouched there was so still, Huxley's light tracked over it without pause at first, then snapped back when his eye caught the outline of a human shape. He saw a pair of eyes glittering in a face liberally smeared in something dark and viscous. Steady, unblinking eyes.

"Don't move!" Huxley shouted in what he assumed to be cop-reflex. The figure jerked at the sound, emitting a short gasp that was unnervingly close to a snarl. *If you encounter anyone else, kill them immediately.* The sat-phone voice, loud and unemotional in his head. *They are a danger to you.*

"Huxley," Rhys began, finger shifting to her trigger.

He removed his hand from his carbine's fore stock, waving her to silence. "Wait." He took a long, slow step forward, keeping his hand raised, fingers spread wide. "We're not here to hurt you," he called to the figure. The words drew another gasp, eyes blinking for the first time, the blackened shape crouching smaller. "I'm Huxley. This is Rhys. Can you tell me your name?"

The figure shuddered, Huxley making out the droplets of a congealed substance dripping from its chin. It was so distorted, so inhuman that when it spoke, the words were shocking in their clarity: "I'm not going home." A female voice, young, scared but defiant.

Huxley halted, replying with a nod. "OK. If that's what you want . . ."

"I'm not going home," the young woman repeated, another cascade of slime subsiding from her face, more words tumbling forth in a rapid torrent. "You can't make me. I don't care what your fucking book says."

"That's fine." He tried a smile but the woman became increasingly agitated, shifting from side to side, his flashlight catching the stains her hands left on the wall. "Whatever you want . . ."

"It's *your* book." The snarl he had heard in that first gasp returned, the woman's eyes blazing now, head jutting forward on a neck that appeared at least an inch too long. Her teeth became visible as her lips peeled back, impossibly white amid the oozing mask. She spoke with a kind of triumphant rejection now, a certain pride colouring the words she cast at him as if delivering a long-nurtured denunciation. "Your scripture. I don't give a shit about it. You know what? I never did . . ."

A splash behind him; Rhys adjusting her position for a better shot. "Get out of the goddamn way!" she snapped, when Huxley moved into her line of fire.

"We need answers," he hissed back.

Turning to the ordure-covered woman, he found her bobbing up and down, tensing for a rush, head trailing the movement on her overlong neck. "You don't need to be afraid of us," he told her, a bald and naked lie. "We just want to help . . ."

If, at that moment, Pynchon hadn't erupted from the stairwell in a flurry of flailing arms and churned water, the scenario might have played out differently. Huxley might have extracted something of use from this deformed, maddened woman, but he doubted it.

Pynchon's appearance was the starting gun for her

attack, the too white teeth and bright eyes blazing in the centre of a mass of twisting, clawing shadow. She leaped with such swiftness he knew she would have caught him had he stood only a few inches closer. As it was, he managed to train his carbine on her gaping, white-toothed mouth and fire four rapid shots before she got close enough to land a blow with her flailing limbs. He saw red blossom in the glistening shadow before it collapsed, convulsing in the water. Huxley back-pedalled, carbine still pointed at the twitching mass. Rhys, apparently unwilling to tolerate more risk, emptied a full magazine into the body, three long bursts, muzzle flash blazing and cartridges arcing in a glittering cascade.

When she stopped to reload it took a few seconds for the buzzing ring in Huxley's ears to subside, finding that Pynchon was shouting something at him. He had retrieved his carbine from the bar and swung it from one darkened corner of the cabin to the other, droplets scattering from sodden skin and clothing. "Are there more? Wake up, Policeman!" He paused to deliver a hard shove to Huxley's shoulder. "Are there any more?"

Huxley shook his head. "Didn't see any."

"Good." Pynchon hurried to retrieve the rest of his gear. "Charges are set. Reckon it's time we pissed right off out of here, don't you?"

Rhys lost no time splashing towards the stairwell, Pynchon close behind. Huxley began to follow but found his gaze drawn to the limp black shape floating in the centre of the cabin. His LED played over crimson water laced in black before glistening on the surface of the deformed corpse. As his eyes lingered, the beam caught a straight-lined highlight among the otherwise soft mass.

"For fuck's sake!" Pynchon said, midway up the steps.

Huxley ignored him and moved to the body, reaching out a tentative hand to the highlighted object. It jutted from slime-covered fabric, which revealed itself as the flap of a backpack as he leaned closer. The backpack was almost entirely subsumed into the gelatinous bulk but not this hard, patently artificial item, one he recognised in a rush of excitement as the edge of an intact laptop.

"Huxley!" Rhys shouted, the anger in her voice joined with a surprising note of concern.

"One minute!" he shouted back, flexing his fingers before taking hold of the laptop. As he drew it clear of the backpack his skin brushed the surrounding slime, birthing an instant gag of revulsion. He fought it down and pulled the device free, an Apple MacBook Air, the logo surprisingly clean and bright. Straightening with prize in hand, he noticed something else, the dead woman's eye, still open, staring up at him from the mask of black goo. *No, not a mask.* Disgusted realisation dawned as he stared back at that eye, noting how the lids were entirely formed of the stuff. *Skin. It's her skin . . .*

A muffled burst of gunfire from beyond the confines of the barge banished any further urge to loiter, Huxley turning to see Pynchon and Rhys crouched just below the hatch. "Looks like we stirred something up," Pynchon said, another burst of fire echoing down the stairwell. He braced his carbine against his shoulder and nodded for Rhys to continue, casting out a harsh final warning at Huxley: "Stay or go. We won't wait for you."

Huxley splashed his way to the steps as Rhys and Pynchon disappeared through the hatch, gunfire erupting almost immediately. He paused to shove the laptop into the detonator bag and tied it to his belt before following. Another blast of carbine fire, accompanied by the shattering of glass, caused him to duck the moment he reached the upper deck. Crouching between two tables, he caught sight of a dark shape sliding from the glass roof, leaving a red smear as it tumbled into the river.

"We're moving!" Pynchon barked, making for the barge's stern, carbine pointed straight ahead. "Rhys, watch the flanks. Huxley, guard the rear."

Scrambling upright, Huxley fell into place behind Rhys. She swept her carbine right and left while he moved backwards, weapon trained on the roof. He understood the automatic precision of their formation to be more muscle memory, something trained into them over the course of weeks or even months, something they were permitted to remember.

More gunfire greeted them as they emerged onto the stern, Huxley's focus immediately shifting to the boat where both Plath and Golding were blazing away with their carbines. Plath fired to starboard and Golding to port, aimed shots, two rounds at a time. A splash drew his gaze to the wrecks beyond Pynchon's crouched form, seeing a body, details lost to the fog, flail in the current before being swept from view. Another two shots from Plath and a second figure, equally hard to make out, detached from the barricade, letting out a plaintive screech as it fell.

"Get to the inflatable," Pynchon instructed, rising to aim at the southern stretch of the barrier. He fired three lengthy bursts before crouching to change magazines, hands moving with reflexive dexterity. Rhys was already hauling the rope to bring the inflatable closer, dragging it up to the barge's hull then waving urgently at Huxley to get aboard. He leaped over the rail, one foot landing in the inflatable, the other in the river. He pivoted, collapsing onto his back beside the outboard, quickly taking hold of the tiller and activating the battery. Rhys held the rope while Pynchon climbed in, the soldier resuming his barrage as soon as he settled himself, single aimed shots now, switching from right to left. The inflatable heaved when Rhys jumped onto the prow, water lapping over the rubber sides but not enough to swamp them.

"Go, go!" Pynchon shouted, ejecting then loading another magazine, Huxley already opening the throttle and pushing the tiller hard to port to bring them about. He ignored the ongoing gunfire, fighting the impulse to look anywhere but at the stern of the boat. He saw Plath continue to fire from the rail as they circled the starboard hull, muzzle flash lighting her face to reveal teeth bared in a feral expression that almost seemed like a smile. Golding left off his own barrage to hurry to the aft deck, catching the rope Rhys tossed to him.

"Did you do it?" he asked as they jumped from the inflatable to the lowered ledge at the rear of the aft deck. "We heard firing then this lot started crawling out of the woodwork."

"Got about eight minutes left," Pynchon replied, turning to help Huxley haul the inflatable aboard. "Maybe less."

"Not sure we'll last that long if they keep coming."

Freed of his obligation to steer the inflatable, Huxley shifted his full attention to the barrier, seeing figures crowding its undulating mass from end to end. The fog continued to frustrate attempts to perceive details, save for an overall impression of disarrayed humanity. Plath fired again and he saw another body detach from the anonymous silhouette of the crowd, plunging into the water with a tall splash. Some had reached the barge now, affording a clearer view, Huxley making out a distinct non-uniformity in appearance. One appeared to be covered in some kind of blanket and crawled on all fours, its movements more crab-like than human. Others shuffled forward in a crouch, darting from cover to cover in full awareness of the danger. Others stood tall, unconcerned, serene sentinels in the drifting mist. He caught the hues of unclothed flesh among them, also the varied but muted shades of ragged clothing. The noise they emitted was similarly lacking in concordance, shouts and screams mingled with a low murmur that might have been taken for calm conversation. The only conclusion he could form after a brief survey was that they all displayed no inclination to get in the water.

"Hold off," he told Plath as she let rip with another salvo. "They've stopped."

She fired one more time, a figure, tall and pale, jerking and disappearing from view as the bullet took it in the head. From the satisfied cast to Plath's face as she lowered her carbine, Huxley judged this as an act of basic spite. He put his subsequent conclusion down to more cop instinct: *No way this one hasn't killed before. She might not remember doing it but she remembers how to enjoy it. What kind of scientist is also a killer?*

"Now what?" Golding asked, wide eyes tracking across the array of twitching, shouting or silent figures covering the barrier from end to end.

"Load up and wait. Nothing else we can do." Pynchon's features bunched in worried annoyance as he squinted towards the wheelhouse and the inert form of the chain gun visible through the windscreen. "Really could've done with that right about now."

"They might be saving it for something worse," Huxley suggested.

"Oh great." Golding wiped sweat from his brow, although Huxley noted that his hands no longer shook. "Thanks for that."

"You . . ." the call echoed from the barrier with loud but plaintive insistence, Huxley's gaze quickly fixing on the source. It was one of the standing figures. The fog obscured much of it, but he got the impression of a bearded face and an arm extended to point back downriver. "You . . ." the figure called again, Huxley hearing an effort in the sound, as if the words were being formed and spoken with ponderous concentration. "You should . . . go back . . ." The call faded then resumed after a short pause, more strident, less faltering, the speaker confident now that their words made sense. "You should go . . ."

The barge exploded, instantly swallowing the pointing man in a gout of yellow flame and black debris. The blast sent a cloud of fragmented wood and metal in all directions, Huxley diving for the deck along with the others, the boat's engines roaring to life once again to keep station in the suddenly violent water.

"Eight minutes?" he asked Pynchon, teeth gritted, hands over his head and flinching while bits of boat and flesh rained down.

Pynchon responded with a wince of marginal apology. "Mental arithmetic might not be my strong suit."

The boom of the explosion faded into the grind and rush of the barge sinking and taking the tug with it, white water frothing as the river claimed them. Bodies bobbed and turned in the displaced current, some struggling, a few screaming. Before it sank from sight, Huxley caught an unobscured glimpse of one within a few feet of the boat's stern. It slipped below the surface quickly, body apparently so torn it had lost any vestige of buoyancy. As the water lapped over its face Huxley made out a protruding snout and upraised ears, lacking fur, but plainly the face of a dog, and an ugly one at that.

A mask, he told himself, knowing it was wrong. That face had been formed of distorted and stretched skin, human skin. *One made of slime and another turned into a dog? No disease does that.*

The pitch of the engines took on a deeper note and the boat lurched into motion, taking them into the newly created gap in the barrier. As they passed through, those figures not destroyed by the explosion continued to watch, standing, crouching or fidgeting, but this time completely silent. Soon the fog closed in again and they were gone, mute witnesses lost for ever to the red haze.

Chapter Six

Beyond the barrier the boat slowed to a yet more glacial pace in order to navigate a river rich in wrecks. The occasional manic or forlorn shout echoed from the banks, but nothing appeared to bar their steady if incremental progress. Pynchon had expressed some concern that wrecks and river-borne detritus might have gathered under Tower Bridge to create another obstacle but they passed beneath its bisected and raised span without incident.

"Most people think it dates back to Tudor times, you know," Golding said, speaking in the distracted way that told of an inner monologue given voice. He stared at the twin castles rising above, windows dark, panes broken in places, stone flanks besmirched by soot. "Or even before. But it wasn't built until the late 1890s . . ."

"I'm sure I speak for us all when I say I don't give the most aerodynamic of fucks," Pynchon told him before turning to Huxley, nodding expectantly at the laptop he held. "Don't keep us in suspense, Mister Policeman."

They congregated in the wheelhouse to inspect Huxley's prize. He knelt and placed it on one of the seats while they crowded in to peer over his head. Upon raising the screen the first thing he noticed was the battery indicator: 4 per cent. Pynchon assured him there was no means of charging it on this boat. He watched in relief as the device continued to power up without complaint, the screen showing a standard desktop complete with numerous app icons littering a mountain-scape wallpaper. The slightly blurred quality of the image indicated a personal photograph rather than something from the standard library, as did the two young women posing in the foreground. They both wore quilted jackets and hiking boots, broad smiles and fingers raised in the V sign of victory or peace.

"That the Rockies?" Golding wondered, peering closer at the screen.

"Andes," Rhys said. "Probably the Inca Trail. A widely travelled girl."

"No password screen," Plath observed. "Maybe the owner wanted people to find what's on it."

"Video uses a lot of memory," Huxley mused, tapping a finger to a folder on the desktop labelled 'WATCH ME'. Clicking on it revealed a list of MP4 video files, all tagged in numerical order that matched the sequential date of creation. "Video diary," he concluded. "Last one created over a month ago, first one . . ." He trailed off, blinking in surprise. "Fourteen months."

"Wasting time," Pynchon said. "Battery."

"Yeah." Huxley tapped the finger pad to open the first file. The video started without preamble or title card, a young woman with hair dyed a bright shade of pink staring fixedly into the camera. Her eyes had a sunken look that mingled fatigue with a level of fear that went beyond mere worry. The background was entirely taken up with a bookcase laden with fantasy and science fiction novels, as well as a few academic volumes that he thought might relate to biology. Her library was adorned here and there with various figurines and genre-related bric-a-brac.

"My name . . ." the young woman began, only to immediately fall silent, head tilting as a sigh of frustration escaped her lips. "Fuck." A jump-cut, then she was once again staring into the camera, speaking with a forced level of calm and precision. "My name is Abigail Toulouse. This is my real name, as in the name I have chosen for myself. It is the name I consider most valid to my identity and therefore the name I wish to be known by should anyone find this . . . record. I hope, whoever you are, you will honour this request."

She paused again, lips pursed and chest swelling as she took a deep breath. She wore a waterproof, olive drab smock, zip opened to reveal a shiny black lining he thought might be Mylar. "I wondered if I should start at the very beginning," the young woman said. "But if you're watching this, whenever or wherever you're watching this, I guess it's all history now, recent or otherwise."

"It really isn't," Golding said in a sour mutter, falling silent at a glare from Pynchon.

"Suffice to say," Abigail continued, "everything began properly going to hell about six months ago. I've been thinking about the exact date but can't really pin it down." She frowned, shaking her head in a gesture eerily reminiscent of Dickinson when she talked about the aurora. "Late June, early July, I think. At least that's when we began to notice. Mrs Hale down the hall was the first to go, the first person we knew to become . . . dangerous. But we'd been seeing things on the news. Random attacks, random murders, usually within families. People sitting down to watch Netflix then hacking away at each other with carving knives by the end credits. Then the riots started happening, but they weren't really riots. No protests, no placards, just mobs of people doing bad things for no reason anyone could work out. Some doctor or psychiatrist on *Newsnight* put it down to mass hysteria brought on by climate uncertainty. Julie said at the time he was talking bollocks and she wasn't wrong."

Abigail stopped speaking, closing her eyes and sighing in self-reproach. "They know all this," she muttered. "Tell them what they don't know." She took another breath, opening her eyes to stare into the camera. "Mrs Hale may be a typical case, or not, who knows? A sweet old lady two doors down who used to share the cupcakes she baked, mainly so she'd have an excuse to talk, but we didn't mind. Then one day she knocks on the door and when Julie answers this nice old gran calls her a filthy dyke whore and tries to brain her with a rolling pin. And her face . . ." A distance appeared in Abigail's eyes then, mouth forming a hard line. "That wasn't her face, that was someone else. I don't mean her expression. I don't mean she was just mean and nasty all of a sudden. Parts of it were still recognisable but it had changed, physically changed. If it had still been her I don't think I could've done it. I'm pretty sure I didn't kill her, I mean it was an ornamental katana I got on eBay, not even sharp. Cheap metal, the blade bent when I hit her. When we cracked the door open an inch the next morning there was no body in the hall. Bit of blood, but no body. So, yeah, I definitely didn't kill her."

She coughed and blinked before speaking on. "We holed up in here after it happened. We heard other things in the block, pounding on the walls and the flat above, screams . . . crying. We'd stocked up a bit when the news started getting bad, lot of canned goods, stuff you don't need to cook. Julie's idea. She's always been the practical one. So at least we could eat. The power stayed on for most of it, which was a surprise. Then about six weeks ago the army showed up and we thought that would be it, all over." She fingered the olive drab jacket she wore. "They handed out clothing, rations, medical supplies. Their officer made a speech about security and order and how more help was on the way and all we had to do was stay calm and follow instructions, or 'sensible guidelines' he called them." She gave a short, bitter laugh. "There's a bullet hole in our balcony window. Came from a soldier's gun. Apparently he killed the officer and three others before the rest of his squad shot him to pieces. Weird thing, him and the others wore gas masks most of the time. Didn't stop it, whatever it is. A few days later, we heard a load of guns firing in the park, explosions too. In the morning, all the soldiers were gone, or lying there dead. Left a tank behind, if you can believe it. It's still sitting there now."

"Three per cent," said Pynchon, pointing to the battery indicator.

Huxley hit the pause button, not without regret. Closing the file felt like a betrayal. This young woman had fought through her trauma to record her experiences only for it to be treated like a clip library. But this particular video still had ten minutes to run and he doubted the battery would last that long. "We'll skip ahead. How far?"

"Midway," Plath said. "Then the last, if the battery holds out. At least that'll give us some kind of narrative."

The backdrop was different in the next video, the bookcase replaced by a bare concrete wall, streaked with damp. Abigail was different too. The pink in her hair had diminished to a light brown, her eyes more sunken and a nasty-looking scab on her forehead. The army-issue smock remained, but it was stained and torn in places. Despite her appearance, Abigail spoke with an unhesitant briskness, though her voice had lost much of its inflection, the monotone of someone now accustomed to danger and privation.

"Don't have long," she stated, eyes repeatedly darting off screen. "Eight days since we left the block. Rations holding out since we keep finding more. The Diseased don't seem that bothered about eating, and Kevin's got a real talent for ferreting out the good stuff." She glanced to her left, a forced smile twisting her lips. "Yesterday I even ate a Mars bar, can't remember the last time I did that." The flash of humour vanished, a shadow passing over Abigail's face. "Julie always called them her kryptonite. 'How am I supposed to get abs when there's Mars bars in the world?'" Eyes closed and a slow intake of breath, the ritual of someone fighting raw and recent grief.

After a second she swallowed and blinked. "Anyway. The vote among the group is to make for the river, apart from Oliver, but who gives a shit what he thinks? We know the major roads are all blocked off. Met another group two days ago who said the army are machine-gunning anyone who gets within a hundred yards of the M25. Even if we can't just sail out of here, a boat offers some kind of security. Putting water between us and the Diseased seems like a really good idea . . ."

"One per cent," Pynchon said.

Huxley closed the file and moved the cursor to the final clip in the folder. Looking at the details he was surprised to find it the longest, over three hours of video but they would be lucky to view more than a few minutes. "Try and skip forward whenever she stops talking," Golding advised but Huxley knew he wouldn't. He had killed this woman, an act that had aroused only fear in him at the time but now churned a ball of nausea in his gut. *She lived. She was real. Human. Not a monster. And I killed her.* He knew then that he had never killed anyone before today. It wasn't memory, it was knowledge, something coded deep in his psyche. Something not shared by Pynchon, Plath, or Rhys.

The video opened on a blank-faced Abigail, hair a scraggly mess tied up with frayed string. He recognised the backdrop as the pleasure barge's lower deck. The scab on her forehead had grown and another disfigured her neck. From the way they glistened in the light Huxley knew they weren't the result of an injury. Soon these marks would merge and Abigail as she was now would effectively cease to exist. Her previous forced concentration was gone, replaced by a near-listless, monotone resignation.

"Oliver killed himself this morning. He surprised me, actually. Pretty much the only unselfish thing I ever saw him do. He knew it had got him. 'The dreams,' that's what he said, standing there with the razor blade at his wrist. 'It starts with the dreams.'" She made a faint movement, features bunching in an expression of microscopic amusement. "Weird that it should've been just him and me at the end. Not the ending I'd've written, that's for sure. But still, I guess you could say he went out a hero, of sorts. Can't say the same for me." Her brow creased in shame, face growing more animated in self-directed anger. "I'm just too scared. Even though I know it won't be long. He was right, y'see? About the dreams."

She stayed silent for several seconds, Huxley ignoring the agitated consternation of the others as he let it play out and the battery indicator ticked over to zero. Still the clip continued, however, Abigail resuming her demeanour of bland acceptance. "For me it's always that last phone call I got from Mum. The one where she just spouted endless Bible verses, on and on, not listening to anything I said. Of course, it being a dream it doesn't happen the way it did. I don't just hang up and block her number, then curl up in Julie's lap and have a good cry. I keep listening, and those words, all that babbling scripture seems to seep into me, like poison. Feels like I'm rotting from the insi—"

The laptop screen went dead, flickering into a dark reflection of the five people staring into it. Huxley wondered if their silence came from the same place as his. Were they all sharing the same secret? He had the woman on the beach. What did they have? *It starts with the dreams . . .*

The sat-phone chirped, no louder than before but the sound still provoking a startled interruption of their silent vigil of the laptop screen.

"Wait," Golding said as Plath took the device from her fatigue pocket. "Don't we have some discussing to do first?"

"About what?" Pynchon asked.

"About what we just saw. We've been sent into the middle of a plague zone."

"Your point being?"

"Oh, I don't know? How about, we're all going to fucking die?"

Seeing an ominously hard focus appear in Pynchon's gaze, Huxley rose to place himself between them. "He's right," he said. "We need to talk about all of this. But we need to hear what it has to say first. Decisions can wait until we know what it wants us to do next." He turned to Plath. "Don't say a word about the laptop. As far as it knows we're still living in not-very-blissful ignorance."

She nodded and thumbed the green button. The flat female voice spoke immediately, leaving no interval. "Huxley?"

"This is Plath."

A very short pause. "Is Huxley dead or incapacitated?"

"No, he's here."

"Give him the sat-phone. I will only communicate with him."

A mingling of puzzlement and annoyance showed on Plath's face as she handed the phone to Huxley, causing him to wonder if self-importance was imprinted on her in much the same way as taking human life.

"It's Huxley," he said into the speaker, holding the device out so the rest of them could hear.

"Do you have casualties?" the voice asked.

"No."

"Do any of the others display signs of confused thinking or unwarranted aggression?"

Plath's probably a homicidal sociopath but I think you already know that. "No."

Another very slight pause. "A container has opened in the crew cabin. It contains hypodermic applicators. Each is labelled with your names. All of you are to inject yourselves with a full dose."

A flurry of shared glances. "Dose of what?"

"A compound crucial to your continued survival. By now you will have come into contact with some inhabitants of this city. It will be apparent to you that they are infected by a pathogen that causes violent delusions and severe physical deformity. You have already been injected with a variant of the hypodermics' contents. They contain a booster that will continue to protect you from this pathogen. Failure to comply with this order will result in the deactivation of the boat. Infection and death will follow shortly after. Communications will resume in three hours."

A familiar series of clicks and the sat-phone fell silent.

They found seven applicators in the newly opened compartment, narrow, eight-inch long aluminium cylinders sitting in a cut-to-size foam cushion. Each one bore a name stencilled in black lettering.

"How will they know if we don't do it?" Golding said, echoing the thought at the forefront of Huxley's mind.

"They're probably fitted with a micro-transmitter of some kind," Pynchon said. "Sends a signal when activated."

"We could just squirt it over the side."

"Something tells me they'll have thought of that."

"Also a bad idea if they're telling the truth," Plath put in. "Since we supposedly need to inject the contents to stay alive."

"*If* they're telling the truth," Rhys added.

Huxley reached into the box to extract his own applicator. "Any way to find out what's in these?" he asked her, pointing to the cylinders marked "CONRAD" and "DICKINSON". "We've got two spares, after all."

"Not without a microscope. Even then, I'm a doctor not a biochemist."

"As far as you know."

"Why are they individually labelled?" Golding asked. "Vaccine doses are universal, right?"

"Not these, apparently. I'd guess each dose is tailored to the recipient." Rhys ran a hand over her stubbled head, fingers lingering on her scar before she forced them closed. "Could be due to different biometrics; height, weight, blood group and so on."

Sensing an unspoken line of thought, Huxley prompted her. "Or?"

"Or there may be a genetic component to this, the disease and the inoculant. A genetic disease would require gene therapy of some kind."

"This is all irrelevant." Pynchon crouched beside Huxley to retrieve his own applicator. "Best if we just get on with it."

"Call me overly sensitive," Golding said, "but I'm not too keen on injecting myself with a load of chemical gunk if I don't know for certain what it's for."

"You've seen what this disease does. If this stuff stops us turning into one of them, I'm all for it." Pynchon slipped the applicator into his fatigue pocket and began rolling up his sleeve.

"Not doing every damn thing they tell us to do is worth considering," Huxley said. "We can make it to the bank without too much difficulty now. We have weapons and rations. We could load up and make our own way."

Pynchon snorted in dismissal. "You saw those vids. We know what's out there."

"I know that whoever put us on this boat didn't do it because they love us. We're heading into something, something they need us to do. Something that requires us to inject ourselves with this shit, whatever it might be."

"The voice hasn't lied to us yet," Rhys pointed out.

"Maybe because it hardly says anything. We're given instructions but almost nothing in the way of actual information. And does anyone really think that when we've done whatever we're supposed to do we'll just sail on our merry way?"

"No." Rhys stooped to pick up her own applicator. "But it's clear we've been sent to stop all this, or at least prevent it spreading. That strikes me as a task worth doing. Might even be something we volunteered for."

Golding frowned and shook his head. "Not sure about that. I don't strike me as the volunteering type."

"And leaving the boat is suicide." Pynchon took the applicator from his pocket and pressed the flat end to the exposed skin of his arm, thumb poised over the button. "I'll accept that staying on it might be too, but at least now I know what my mission is, some of it anyway. I'm not turning back, not running off to hide in a ruin and wait to turn into one of those things. We all have a choice to make. This is mine. The rest of you can go if you want, I won't try to stop you."

He clenched his teeth as he pressed the button, grunting softlty as the hypo let out a snick then a hiss. Huxley watched the veins of Pynchon's forearm bulge then relax. "But if you choose to stay, you inject yourself," Pynchon added, tossing his applicator back into the box. "I'll shoot anyone who doesn't."

Chapter Seven

They all took it in the end, even Golding. Huxley felt the historian would have demanded to be put ashore if a fresh bout of screams hadn't echoed from the south bank as he limped about the aft deck, hypo in hand. "Sixty seconds," Pynchon warned him. He leaned in the wheelhouse hatchway, carbine at his side. "I'm counting. Make your mind up time, History Man."

"Fuck off," Golding shot back, continuing his back-and-forth course.

Pynchon replied with a surprisingly affable smile. "Forty-five seconds now. I'd be happy to take you ashore if you want to walk it from here." He gestured at the bank, a part-flooded array of concrete ugliness rendered into abstract sculpture by the fog, thicker than ever now. Golding stopped, staring at the passing array of hard-edged shadows. His posture told of rigid stubbornness that shifted into slumped resignation when the screams began. They were the most discordant and indecipherable yet. The product of at least a dozen throats emitting elongated words that weren't words interspersed with screams resonant with every heightened emotion, running the gamut from confusion, to pain, to a concordance of bewildered ecstasy. Despite the dissonance, Huxley felt there to be a strange kind of unity in that sound. Although tonally incoherent, the volume of each voice rose and fell in concert, like a choir following the same conductor even though they all sang a different song.

Whatever its origin or purpose, it was enough to convince Golding that a solo expedition through this city would be ill advised. "Fuck you," he spat, pressing the hypo to his arm. "Fuck you. Fuck this fucking boat. This fucking river. This fucking city. These fucking diseased bastards." He grimaced at the momentary pain of the needle piercing his skin then tossed the applicator over the side. "Fuck it all."

"Spoken like a truly educated man," Pynchon said, disappearing into the wheelhouse.

The boat continued its steady, walking-pace course for another ten minutes before the engines faded once again into station-keeping quiescence. The reason rose before them in stark, ruinous clarity.

"Bet that put a dent in the tourist trade," Golding said. Although calmer since his outburst, his attempt at humour was forced, spoken in a strained rapid tumble of words.

"Waterloo Bridge?" Huxley asked him.

He shook his head. "Westminster."

"Looks like someone decided to blow it up at some

point." Pynchon put his eye to his carbine sight and swept it over the concrete and iron wreckage barring their path from bank to bank. "We'd need ten times the amount of C-4 we have to make any kind of hole in this."

Huxley's eyes inevitably wandered to the tall, gothic silhouette rising beyond the remains of the bridge. It was so innately familiar he worried it might stir a memory, but the absence of pain led him to conclude this could be the first time he was seeing the actual tower of Big Ben with his own eyes. They had just passed another postcard icon in the form of the gargantuan Ferris wheel Golding named the London Eye. Its upper arc was lost to the fog, the visible structure featuring some damage; jagged holes marred the glass walls of its bus-sized capsules and scorch marks defaced its otherwise pristine white majesty. The survival of these monuments, and the intact Tower Bridge, made Huxley ponder if their immunity to destruction arose from the indifference of madness or a residual reverence among the Diseased. It also struck him how quickly he and the others had adopted Abigail's term for the infected, something Plath ascribed to an innate human tendency towards appellation.

"It's a hard-wired survival trait," she explained. "To warn the rest of the tribe to avoid the hunting grounds of a smilodon, you have to know what it's called. It also serves to collectivise the enemy into a faceless mass, something inhuman. They aren't people any more, they're the Diseased."

"Well," Golding said, extending a hand to the ruined bridge, "I'd name that the end of this road."

This time Huxley was unsurprised when the sat-phone began its low-pitched chirping. "The obstacle ahead requires airdropped ordnance to clear," the phone-voice stated with the usual absence of preamble. "Accuracy is essential and on-board systems lack the resolution for precise targeting. Take one of the beacons from the hold and place it in the centre of the obstacle. Infected survivors are particularly active in this area so all crew members will take part in this mission to provide security and ensure success. Once the beacon is activated return to the boat. It will retire to a safe distance." Once again its sign off consisted of only clicks then silence.

"Looks like we're going for a jaunt after all," Pynchon said, shouldering his weapon and heading for the ladder. "Seems a good time to break out the flame-throwers."

The stretch of river separating the boat from the bulk of the ruined bridge resembled an arctic seascape in miniature, jagged bergs of cracked concrete rising from the busy current. The channels in between were thick with steel cables and mangled girders that made navigating it all an unwelcome if unavoidable prospect. Huxley assumed the inflatable would require two trips to convey them all to the artificial ridge created by the wrecked bridge, but the small craft accommodated their collective weight with surprising ease. Pynchon took charge of one of the flame-throwers and gave the other to Plath, apparently having judged her the least likely to hesitate in using it. Both north and south banks of the river were flooded by water comparatively free of obstacles, but Pynchon opted against an indirect approach.

"We don't know what's out there," he said. "Get in. Get it done. Get out. Simplicity is always the best tactic."

Huxley took up position at the prow, scanning the concrete and steel jungle as Pynchon steered them carefully through worryingly narrow channels. It seemed to take an absurdly long time to cover just half the distance to their objective, Huxley finding he had to flex his fingers to work out the ache of gripping his carbine. As he began to raise the weapon again, he caught a flash of something below the surface, a shimmering orange blur beneath the swirl. It pulsed then glided swiftly deeper, vanishing in an instant.

"You see that?" He raised himself up, carbine trained on the water. "Maybe they've mutated, gone aquatic or something."

"It was an octopus," Golding told him, not bothering to keep the mirth from his voice. He inclined his head at the mostly destroyed Edwardian-era building south of the ruined bridge. "County Hall, once the seat of local government, later home to the London Aquarium. I guess the inmates took the chance to liberate themselves when the river broke its banks. If we're lucky we might see a shark next."

Huxley's pique at the historian's tone died at the sight of his face. Golding stared into each passing shadow with wide, barely blinking eyes, face rigid with the kind of immobility that arose from terror rather than fear. Moving on, they saw no more octopuses, or sharks, but Huxley did glimpse a few shoals of colourful, darting fish. The contagion that had laid waste to this city may have scoured it of animal life above the surface, but he took a minute crumb of comfort from the knowledge that aquatic life continued below.

He saw the body by chance, something in the periphery of his vision he would have missed but for the red shirt cladding its torso. Putting his eye to the carbine's optical sight, he saw it was a man, slumped on his side on a grid of intersecting steel bars. *Killed when the bridge got blown up*, he judged. *Or swam here later, for whatever reason.* Another weird death in a city full of corpses. Thousands, probably millions of stories had ended here in a vast and forever unknowable cavalcade of horrors. He began to track the carbine away then paused as he noticed something about the body.

"Hold up," he called over his shoulder to Pynchon. "Something we need to check out."

Pynchon shook his head, hand keeping the same angle on the tiller. "Get in, get out."

"It's important." Huxley glared at him in insistence, receiving an indifferent glance in return.

"The more we find out the better our chances," Plath said. "At least slow down enough for a decent look."

Pynchon's jaw tensed but he consented to close the throttle a little. When the object of Huxley's interest came fully into view Pynchon needed no encouragement to shut down the engine, allowing them to drift closer to the body.

"That's new," Rhys said, playing the laser dot on her carbine over the vine-like growth emerging from the body. The corpse lay with its face pressed into the metal lattice, the growth sprouting from the base of the neck. Its red hue was too dark to be the result of staining by the body's fluids. It formed a half-twisted coil that abruptly bisected where it met the steel grid, expanding into sub-branches to create a matrix of root-like tendrils entwined about the rusted metalwork.

"Some symptom of the disease, obviously," Plath said. "We know it alters morphology."

"In the living," Rhys said, squinting as she leaned forward for a closer look. "This looks post-mortem. Can't see any signs of healing or scars around the point where it exits the body."

"You know of any disease that does this?" Huxley asked her.

"Some pathogens will live on in a host body after death, but this is . . ." She trailed off, shaking her head. "Assuming it's caused by the same infection, it has to be a multi-stage organism. Probably part of its reproductive process. More like a parasite than a disease."

"Then maybe we shouldn't hang around so close to it," Golding said.

"We've been exposed since we entered this city. Maybe even before. The fog isn't really fog, remember."

"And we're inoculated," Pynchon reminded them. "Sorry, Doc. This is all fascinating and everything but we need to get on."

He reactivated the outboard, resuming their wayward course through the part-submerged remnants of the bridge. "This'll have to do," he said, bringing the boat to a halt at the base of a huge concrete slab which offered a steep but climbable slope to the approximate centre of the thickest stretch of rubble. "Mister Policeman. History Man. You're up."

"Still the most expendable, am I?" Huxley enquired.

"Second most." Pynchon's gaze shifted to Golding, offering a patently false smile of apology. "Chances of success are doubled if two go. We're the base of reinforcements if anything goes wrong."

To Huxley's surprise, Golding made no objection, merely sighing in resigned annoyance before hefting his carbine and preparing to jump from the inflatable. Despite his leg injury, he performed the feat of leaping onto the concrete slope with surefooted alacrity, albeit accompanied by a painful wince. Huxley's attempt was less impressive. His boots skidded on the surface and he came close to sliding into the water before Golding reached out a steadying hand.

"Where do we put it?" Huxley asked Pynchon when the soldier tossed him the targeting beacon.

"In the centre, like the phone said." Pynchon held

up the other beacon. "Back-up in case you two . . . well, y'know. Activate it by pressing the big button on the side twice. You'll hear a beep when it powers up. Make sure you place it on top of the rubble, not below anything, so it can be seen from the air." Another blandly insincere smile. "Haven't got all day."

"He's really enjoying himself," Golding said in a low mutter as they started climbing. "I'm still pretty sure I didn't volunteer for this, but I'd lay odds he did."

They got to the top quickly, finding a narrow summit of jagged rubble spiked with twisted steel rebars. After a quick survey, they headed for a flatter expanse of wreckage a few dozen yards to the right. "I mean," Golding continued, grunting with the effort of hauling himself across, "you'd think that absence of memory would strip away personality, or at least transform it. But soldier boy is still very much a soldier. I'm still a historian. Rhys is still a doctor. You're still a cop."

"And Plath?"

Golding inclined his head a little, letting out a snort. "Not entirely sure we had it right about the scientist thing, are you? The fun she had shooting those poor bastards back there was quite something."

"You noticed."

"I think it's what I do, notice things. Useful trait for a historian. Bit like you with your detective brain, I guess."

They came to a stretch formed of two or more slabs smashed together to create a constricted, uneven pathway of sorts. Golding led the way, coming to a halt after a few short steps, transfixed by the sight of something underfoot. Following his gaze, Huxley saw a clawed hand frozen in the act of reaching up from a fissure in the concrete. Moving closer, he peered into the dark recess of the crack. The gloom was such he couldn't make out the hand's owner, but the state of the limb and digits made it clear they had been a Diseased. The bones were too large and the fingers too long, each one ending in a wicked, hooked barb.

"Like a demon clawing its way out of the under-world." Golding angled his head to study the claw, brow set in a reflective furrow. "All places shall be hell."

"What?"

Golding shrugged. "A line from Marlowe that bubbled up from somewhere. 'When all the world dissolves, and every creature shall be purified, all places shall be hell that are not heaven.'"

"You think that's what this is? Hell made real?"

"I don't know. I do know we're in pain, all of us, and I don't mean whatever they put in our heads. Having no idea about who you are isn't just confusing, it hurts. Without memory what are we? No one. Nothing. We don't come from anywhere. We don't belong anywhere. It's like being dead except for some reason you keep breathing. We're being made to suffer. And isn't that what hell's for? Not knowing why makes it all worse. It could be that I deserve this. It could be that I'm a very bad man and so are you. It could be this whole fucking nightmare is a fitting punishment.

Because, if it's not, then we're all just victims of a very sick game."

Huxley moved past him, climbing onto the upraised ironwork that formed the next portion of the barrier. "Based on what we know, I can't help thinking Rhys is right: we've been sent to end this." He crouched, extending a hand to Golding. "One other thing I'm sure of: there's no going back. No escaping it. If we're in hell, they made very sure we're not getting out until this is done."

"Redemption." Golding took his hand and hauled himself up. "Classically the only escape from damnation. You really imagine that's what'll be waiting for us at the end of this river?"

"I'm starting to think if any of us could be redeemed we wouldn't have been chosen."

They placed the beacon atop a plinth that had somehow survived the bridge's fall, remaining both intact and upright amid the chaos. "How do we know they won't drop their bombs the moment we activate this?" Golding asked as Huxley's finger hovered over the button.

"I don't think we're that expendable." Huxley pressed the button twice, standing back to look at the sky as the beep sounded. "Besides, no airplane noise. I think we've got a while yet."

They lost no time making their way back to the inflatable, scrambling aboard and reclaiming their carbines.

"Any idea how long?" Huxley asked the soldier as

he reversed the outboard then angled the tiller to put the craft into a 180-degree turn. To Huxley's surprise he saw a spasm of uncertainty pass across Pynchon's face, a tension in his jaw and neck that told of pain. "Did that stir something up?" Huxley adjusted the grip on his carbine, a subtle movement intended to bring the trigger a little closer to his hand. It didn't fool Pynchon, however.

"Seriously?" He raised an eyebrow and huffed a marginal laugh. "Just a feeling I've done this before but nothing specific. To answer your question: the battery life on the beacon is pretty long, so it could be an hour or more."

"Look," Golding said to Huxley as the craft began to accelerate. Turning, Huxley saw a smile play over the historian's lips as he angled his head to peer into the water. "Another octopus . . ."

The appendage that shot out from the inflatable's wake was no tentacle. It was hard rather than soft, jagged and bulging at intervals along its narrow, jointed length and ending in a slightly curved point that found no difficulty in skewering Golding through the neck. Huxley had time to take in the sight of the historian's bloody, desperate features before the thing that had surely killed him plucked him from the boat. A splash, a flailing of rapidly disappearing legs, and he was gone.

Chapter Eight

Huxley and Rhys fired in unison, the volley raising tall fountains around the inflatable, their guns falling silent at Pynchon's shout: "Save your ammo! He's gone!"

"Not a fucking octopus!" Huxley gasped in breathless impotence. He itched to fire again, possessed by a perverse need for revenge. But whatever deeply ingrained training he had received halted his finger on the trigger guard and shifted it to the safety catch.

"Eyes on the water," Pynchon said, continuing to steer the inflatable through the maze of wreckage. "If there was one there might be more."

"One what?" Rhys asked, voice shrill with shock.

"Extreme mutation," Plath said, her voice lacking the panic of Huxley and Rhys. She ignited the gas nozzle of her flame-thrower and settled a steady, searching gaze on the water. "Looked similar to the deformity on that body, don't you think?"

"That was post-mortem," Rhys said.

"Then it's reasonable to assume the disease isn't a hundred per cent fatal." Huxley saw Plath's mouth twitch and knew she was containing a laugh. "What doesn't kill you makes you stronger."

He wanted to tell her to shut up. He wanted to shoot something. He wanted Golding not to be dead and he especially wanted to wipe away the glistening patch of the historian's blood on the inflatable's hull. Instead, he pulled the stock of his carbine tighter against his shoulder and kept scanning the water. Discipline. Training. Resistance to trauma. Learned skills coupled with something he suspected was more innate.

They were halfway through the wreckage when the next attack came. As before, there was no warning, a thrashing, multi-limbed thing erupting from the water directly in the inflatable's path. Pynchon's reflexes saved them, hand jerking the tiller to a right angle, turning the craft in time to avoid the descending limbs with their wickedly sharp points.

Huxley was unable to discern many details among the dark, swift-moving shape of their assailant. However, he did hear its voice, harsh and grating but also entirely human, born of a mouth somewhere in the deformed mass of its being. "Bitch! Lying fucking bitch!" It lurched after the inflatable as Pynchon steered it into a wide arc, Huxley catching a glimpse of a face in the spiky shadow, a hating, teeth-bared rictus. "Lying whore!" it screamed, water churning as it continued its pursuit. "You took everything from me . . ."

Huxley aimed for where he thought he had seen the hate-filled face and fired twice. The thing jerked at the impact but kept coming, following the inflatable's wake with anxiety-inducing swiftness. Huxley and Rhys shifted position and fired again, their pursuer shuddering as the bullets lashed it but showing no signs of slowing.

"Steer left," Plath told Pynchon, voice flat and curt, her narrowed gaze fixed on the Diseased. "Then kill the engine."

Pynchon frowned at her but, apparently perceiving her intent, did as she said. Plath rose to one knee as the inflatable slewed and slowed, the Diseased closing the distance in a fury of white water, still screaming its grievance.

"Bitch! Whore! Cunt!"

The whooshing blast of the flame-thrower drowned the words, Huxley shielding his face from the heat but finding the sight of what came next too irresistible to close his eyes. The yellow and orange tongue spewed from Plath's weapon to engulf the Diseased in an instant blossom of steam and burning matter. Spindly limbs spasmed and clawed, its clear howl of utter anguish audible even above the roar of the fiery torrent consuming it. The thing slipped briefly below the surface in an attempt to extinguish the flames, but, driven by panic or madness, it re-emerged a second later. Plath maintained the blazing stream, tracking the Diseased as it scrambled to a mound of rubble. It screamed in incoherent pain as it latched its spindly limbs onto the piled debris, vainly attempting to crawl away from the inferno. Finally, its screams ended as the fire ate its throat. Huxley found he still couldn't fully discern the shape of the thing as it slumped into the water, a floating, charred island of ruin. His guts roiled under the weight of a stench that mingled spent fuel with overdone meat.

"Wasn't very polite, was he?" Plath observed, casting a judgemental glare at the Diseased's smoking remains. Resuming her seat, she waved a languid hand at Pynchon. "Home, and don't spare the horses."

Pynchon opened the throttle to full power as soon as they emerged into the open but Huxley found the inflatable's lack of speed jarringly aggravating. The journey back to the boat probably required no more than fifteen minutes but felt like hours. As the inflatable ploughed its steady, unimpressive course, all eyes were fixed on the water in expectation of another attack, apart from Plath. She had relaxed into a placid repose, cradling her flame-thrower with almost motherly affection.

Once back aboard the boat, the engines flared to life as soon as they had reattached the inflatable to its tethers. Huxley skidded across the aft deck as the boat swung around in a 180-degree turn, pointing its prow away from the ruined bridge. For the first time the engines roared to full power, twin arcs of water fountained in their wake as they sped downriver. It maintained the same speed until the remains of Westminster Bridge faded into the fog.

"This should do it," Pynchon said as the engines altered pitch and the boat slewed around once more. Silence settled upon them as they waited, eyes scanning a sky they couldn't see and ears straining for the sound of approaching aircraft.

"It's possible we might not even hear them," Pynchon added. "If it's a high-altitude drop . . ."

The groaning whoosh of a jet drowned his words, the sound sweeping from east to west. They saw nothing, not even a shadow in the red mist. Seeing Pynchon clamp both hands to his ears, Huxley did the same just as the bomb hit. To call what came next a boom was pitifully inadequate. It was a sound that was felt rather than heard, so vast as to swamp the senses, Huxley shuddering as what felt like the invisible arm of a vicious ghost swept through him.

The boat shifted as the blast raised up in a sizeable swell, the surrounding fog thinning to reveal more of their surroundings. Huxley's eyes immediately went to the sky in an instinctive desire to catch a glimpse of blue, but all he saw was a lighter shade of pink before the red haze closed in once again. Removing his hands from his ears, he heard what sounded like rain, another elemental feature that had been absent from their journey. However, multiple splashes drew his gaze to the sight of debris falling into the floodwater.

When the last chunk of rubble splashed into the river a few yards ahead of the prow, the boat's engines resumed the steady, unimpressive chug that had marked most of the journey. As they closed on the site of the explosion it became apparent that the ruins of Westminster Bridge had formed a partial dam given the strength of the current rushing into the newly created gap. The bomb had torn a 40-foot-wide hole in the barrier, creating a frothing channel through which the boat made jolting but undamaged passage. Once they settled into comparatively calmer waters, Huxley took in the sight of the newly inundated precincts of the Houses of Parliament. On the south bank, half-submerged trees swayed in the fresh torrent.

"Was this our mission, do you think?" Rhys wondered. "Flood the rest of the city?"

"To what purpose?" Plath said. "It's plainly already dead so why drown it?"

They passed beneath two more bridges over the course of the next half-hour, their middle spans destroyed by what Pynchon judged to be airstrikes. "Looks like they were trying to stop people crossing," Rhys said. "But in which direction?"

"I doubt it mattered after a while," Pynchon said. "From what the girl on the laptop said, it looks like they gave up on the city and established a perimeter on the M25. Must've been quite an operation. We'd be talking tens of thousands of troops to make it work."

"What if it didn't?" Huxley asked. "As far as we

know it could have been overrun months ago. What then?"

"Then we're living in a whole world that's gone to shit instead of just a city."

The next bridge was noteworthy for three reasons. The first being that it was fully intact, spared bombing for reasons Huxley doubted he would ever know. The second was its design: it was the first suspension bridge they had seen, three spans and two sets of tall white pillars providing anchors for the steel cables arcing between them, while also serving as the supports for its third notable feature. The bodies hung from the cables at varying heights, fifty or more swaying in the meagre breeze. Tracking his carbine sight over the dangling corpses, Huxley found many lacking obvious signs of infection, others riven by telltale distortions to face and limbs. Some were naked, others fully clothed. Some old, some young, some children. In a few cases, their executioners had felt the need to adorn their victim with signs, the daubed lettering proclaiming one elderly woman a "CLASS TRAITOR" while the child a few yards to her left was dubbed "MIGRANT SCUM". Death appeared to be the only unifying factor.

"Turned on each other," Rhys stated, voice thick.

"It's what people do," Plath said. "When things get bad and fear is the overriding emotion. They probably started with the Diseased, then anyone they thought might be infected. After that—" she shrugged "—every living soul they could get their hands on. Didn't realise they were most likely all infected themselves by then. Probably thought they were doing a good thing even as they were stringing up that little girl over there."

Despite the lightness of her tone, Huxley saw something new in her face: disgust. It was a knowing expression, one he knew to be habitual. For the first time he felt the urge to question his judgement about the true aim of this mission. *If this is what she thinks of humanity, why send her to save it?*

He began to formulate some carefully worded questions for Plath, probing enquiries aimed at revealing more of her already troubling character. It was a difficult prospect; how to elicit information from someone with a life history amounting to only two days. *Assuming she's as forgetful as she claims.* The thought surely came from his cop-brain, the product of professional suspicion moulded into second nature. Of them all, even Pynchon, Plath now appeared the most composed, the most assured of herself. It wasn't too paranoid to entertain the notion that such surety arose from a depth of self-awareness denied him and the others.

His growing list of questions quickly slipped away when, with a whirr of gears and electronics, the chain gun activated.

"What the fuck!" Rhys reached for her carbine as they all stared at the bulky contraption through the wheelhouse windscreen. It didn't fire, instead merely tracking its long barrel right, left, then up and down, putting Huxley in mind of a boxer flexing his arms before the bell. They all started again when the screen on the right side of the dashboard came to life. It flickered briefly before settling into a monochrome image of the river ahead, shifting in concert with the movements of the chain gun. Below the screen a panel slid aside to reveal a small joystick and keypad.

"Controls are active." Pynchon's voice held a mingling of both relief and anticipation as he settled into the seat in front of the display. His fingers played over the buttons and the joystick before taking a firmer hold. As he worked it, the chain gun altered its angle to match, Huxley finding its movements disconcertingly fluid, lacking the robotic jerkiness he expected.

"Got a full load of ammo too." Pynchon tapped a numerical readout on the display. "High velocity twenty-five millimetre cannon shells. Won't just take down an elephant, this'll make mincemeat of the whole herd."

"Why activate it now?" Rhys asked.

"Because," Plath said, a wry smile on her lips, "what's ahead will be worse than what's behind."

The boat began to slow when the next bridge came into view. Like the suspension bridge it was intact, but fortunately free of hanging bodies. Its supports were less encouraging in appearance, featuring another sprawl of wrecked river craft, which raised the prospect of once again having to blast their way through. As they drew closer, Huxley sighed in relief at the sight of a navigable gap in the mess. His lightened spirits soon evaporated when his gaze tracked to the largest and least damaged boat among the jumbled craft.

"Is that . . . ?" Rhys squinted at the wreck through the windscreen.

"A Mark VI Wright Class patrol boat," Pynchon finished. "Yeah."

The engines died and it was with a sense of grim inevitability that Huxley reached for the sat-phone when it began to chirp. He placed it on the dashboard and hit the green button, his greeting a terse grunt. "Huxley."

"Do you have casualties?"

"One. Golding's dead."

No pause. "Do any of the others display signs of confused thinking or unwarranted aggression?"

"Oh, get fucked. Golding's dead! Do you get that? A fucking monster came out of the water and killed him! He's dead!"

"Acknowledged. Answer my question: do any of the others display signs of confused thinking or unwarranted aggression?"

Huxley rested clenched fists on either side of the phone, bafflement and anger competing to spill more rage-inflected words at this faux-female machine. *Pointless. It's a thing, not a person, designed not to care what you think, or feel. Probably with good reason.*

"No," he said, after a few calming breaths.

"Sensors on your boat have detected a transponder signal. What is the origin?"

Huxley raised his eyes to the windscreen and the

tilted, pale-grey craft pushed up against the bridge's northern stanchion. "There's another boat just like this one ahead."

"Describe its condition."

"Immobile. Seems intact."

"Signs of life?"

"None."

A pause, then a faint series of clicks. "Investigate. Gather additional weapons and ordnance. They may be necessary for the next phase of this mission. Destroy the other boat with explosives when the task is complete."

Huxley surveyed the others, finding doubtful suspicion on the faces of Pynchon and Rhys while Plath appeared only marginally interested. "What if we find survivors?" he enquired.

"Kill them."

"Whose boat is that?"

"That is not relevant to your mission. Your boat will reactivate when the transponder on the other craft is disabled."

The signature clicks of its customary sign-off followed, then the sat-phone fell silent.

"My advice," Plath said. "Prime some C-4, toss it on that thing. When it goes boom we get to move on."

"They want us to investigate," Rhys pointed out.

Plath raised her eyebrows, smiling blandly. "And I don't give a shit." She turned away, heading for the ladder to the crew cabin. "Go if you want, but don't ask me to join you. I've done my heroics for the day, and you're welcome by the way. I think I'll have a nap."

They decided Pynchon should stay behind, since he was the only one who knew how to operate the chain gun. The north and south banks had been silent when they first halted at the bridge but the more they lingered the greater the number of distressed and delusional shouts came at them from the mist. The fog was so thick they were denied the sight of these vocal Diseased, but the growing number of ripples to either side indicated an increasing throng. Also, Huxley's eyes scanned the water in constant expectation of another spiny, spear-pointed limb lashing out from the depths.

"Might need some serious firepower before long," he told Pynchon, inclining his head at the chain gun.

The soldier nodded in reluctant agreement, his focus on the other patrol boat. "It's not a bad idea, y'know. What she said. Just blowing it up and getting out of here."

"We need to know," Rhys said. "Or I do, anyway. Who they were. What they were doing here."

"How did they get this far is what puzzles me," Huxley said. "With Westminster Bridge blocking the river, I mean."

"Bit obvious isn't it, Mister Policeman?" Pynchon gave him a grin of muted disparagement. "It wasn't down when they came through. Means they must have been here a while." His grin faded as another notion dawned. "Or they took the bridge down to stop them turning back."

He prepped four blocks of C-4, each with its own detonator and timer switch. "One in the engine room," he instructed, placing the last block in a pack and handing it to Huxley. "One in the prow. One in the crew quarters and the other on the dashboard. If that doesn't destroy the transponder, wherever it might be, nothing will."

Huxley took charge of the inflatable's outboard while Rhys perched on the prow, carbine trained on the other boat. "I know you're thinking it," she commented when they had covered half the distance.

"Thinking what?"

"Plath. She's not who she used to be."

"That's probably true of all of us."

"You know that's not what I mean." She glanced back at him, face hard with intent. "We should kill her."

"You suspect she's infected?"

"Possibly. Or she was always like this and her very particular psychology is reasserting itself. If she scored less than ninety per cent on the psychopath test I'd be very surprised. In short: she's fucking nuts and a danger to the rest of us."

"Seems a pretty significant diagnosis to make based on little evidence. She's not going to win any prizes for charm or likeability, sure. And she's certainly got a vicious streak. Doesn't make her a psychopath."

Another glance, this one more of a glare. "In a survival

situation we're forced to make life or death judgements based on available data, thin though it might be. I told you I intend to survive this. And I told you why."

Her daughter. The daughter that might just as easily be a son. A child she knew she had brought into the world but couldn't even remember their name or face. He knew then with complete certainty that Rhys had volunteered for this, driven by a fierce and implacable need to secure that child's future. It was the same need that fuelled her resolve now, the same need that made her want to kill Plath.

"A psychopath can still be useful," he pointed out, closing the outboard's throttle as the inflatable nudged the aft deck of the other patrol boat. "She proved that today."

"Because she had to. She's fundamentally incapable of giving a shit about anyone else. If she thinks it necessary to ensure her own survival, she'll turn on us in an instant."

"We're getting short on crew. You may have noticed." He hefted his carbine, shifting it so the stock rested against his shoulder. Rhys didn't move, keeping her eyes on his. "If it comes to it," he said as the moment grew uncomfortably long, "I won't hesitate. But I'm not ready to do outright murder."

Rhys's face bunched in reluctant agreement before she straightened, turning to aim her carbine at the patrol boat's wheelhouse. The craft lay half concealed in the gloom beneath the bridge's span, Huxley making out the dull sheen of the displays on its control panel, but no sign of power. Rhys kept her carbine aimed with one hand as she climbed from the inflatable to the aft deck, kneeling then activating her flashlight.

"Knock, knock!" she called out. "It's Rhys and Huxley from next door. We brought you a cherry pie. Love what you've done with the place."

No answer as Huxley hauled himself to her side. Their twin flashlight beams played over the wheelhouse interior, catching a glint of shattered glass when they touched the windscreens. "Bullet impacts," Huxley judged.

"Lot of them too." Rhys rose and moved into the wheelhouse, shifting her LED beam left and right. "All over the place. Looks like they had a full-on firefight in here."

"Bodies?"

She shook her head, lowering her flashlight to illuminate numerous expended cartridge casings littering an extensive abstract pattern of dark stains decorating the rubberised floor plates. "It's dried but this was definitely a bleed-out. Somebody died here."

Huxley went to the dashboard, finding it a stark contrast to their own. The sealed unit that was such a feature of their boat was absent. The board was rich in buttons and control panels, featuring a large joystick and levers on the right that he assumed controlled the boat's rudder and engines.

"They had full control," he said. "Can't see a

sat-phone either. No waiting around for the engines to start up for them."

"Then they knew what they were doing. They knew who they were."

"Possibly. Either way I'd bet they knew a shitload more than we do." He nodded towards the ladder. "Crew cabin. I'll lead."

"Sexist." She spoke the word in a tone devoid of objection, standing aside while he swung the carbine to his back and drew his pistol. Unhooking the flashlight from his webbing, he held it in a reverse grip alongside his gun hand. The light revealed more staining to the crew-cabin ladder but the deck below was clear. Huxley crouched low as he descended, pausing with every step, forcing himself not to flick the light around too quickly. The bodies were easy to find, two of them, slumped on either side of the narrow aisle between the bunks.

He paused at the foot of the ladder to scour the cabin with the flashlight, finding blood spatter and a scattering of detritus. Empty ration packs littered the deck along with a number of smartphones. "Clear," he told Rhys, shifting the light to the bodies. "You've got some examining to do."

Both corpses, a man and a woman, were dressed in the same non-camo fatigues Huxley wore. They were dark with the onset of necrosis, tendrils of corruption creeping through mottled flesh. The man had a dark stain in the centre of his chest and the woman a coin-sized hole in her forehead with a larger one in the rear of her skull, the wall behind dark with exploded matter. A pistol lay in the stiffened, ash dark hand resting in her lap.

"Murder–suicide," Huxley deduced, drawing a withering look from Rhys. He was grateful she didn't bother with the 'no shit, Sherlock' jibe before carrying out a cursory inspection of the bodies.

"Both in their thirties," she mused, angling the woman's head from side to side, Huxley fighting a spasm of revulsion at the creak and grind of dried muscle tissue. "Rigor's come and gone so they've been dead a while," Rhys went on, casting a critical eye over both corpses. "I'd expect more decomposition, but the disease might slow the process somehow. They were both infected, see?" She traced a finger along the woman's jawline to point out the deformities. Near the woman's chin a small spur of bone resembling a miniature rhino horn jutted from the flesh. "He's got growths at the top of his spine," she added, nodding to the dead man.

"Their scars are different." Huxley moved his light closer to the woman's shaven skull, illuminating the inch-long healed incision above her ear.

"Smaller," Rhys agreed. "I'd guess a less invasive procedure." She had to use a knife to cut away the woman's vest, matted and stuck to the flesh in places. "No scars above the kidneys. Guess they saved that just for us."

"What about names?"

Rhys moved her flashlight to the woman's forearm. The tattoo was hard to make out among the discoloured flesh but she deciphered it after some squinting. "Kahlo." The man's tattoo was easier to discern, Rhys putting it down to the fact that the blood had congealed in his hands rather than his arms. "Turner."

"Frida Kahlo and J. M. W. Turner," Huxley said. "Painters. Looks like this was the artists' boat. But only two of them?'

"Unlikely." Rhys jerked her head at the ceiling. "The firefight was inside. My guess is they killed the others when infection took hold. Tipped them over the side when the shooting ended, then . . ." She gestured to either side. "Decided on this when they realised they weren't going to make it."

Huxley turned his attention to the smartphones littering the deck. "Must've gathered them from the wrecks downriver." Picking up the nearest phone, he pushed the power button, finding it dead. He tossed the device aside and tried several more with the same result. "No good. If they learned anything, it died with them."

"Gotta be something here." Rhys rose and moved to the storage lockers in the floor. "They don't seem to have had as much gear as we do, or they used it all up getting this far." She knelt to rummage in the space while Huxley moved to the engine room. He spent a few minutes in fruitless searching, shining his light on various machinery and finding every dial inert and readout dead. A wordless exclamation from

Rhys caused an involuntary jerk of his gun hand, finger twitching, but once again his ingrained training stopped it moving to the trigger.

"What?" he shouted back.

"They left us something." Her voice held a surprisingly cheery note, like a kid finding a toy in the cereal box.

As he re-entered the crew cabin, Huxley paused when his LED alighted on a mark disfiguring the wall behind Turner's body. At first it looked like an elongated smear of his blood, dried into dark filth, but as his eye lingered, he saw that it formed a word. *Kahlo shot Turner then wrote something in his blood before blowing her brains out.* Crouching, he played the flashlight beam over it, mouthing the daubed letters, each one rendered in irregular, barely legible capitals: "A N T I B O D Y". Another short, meaningless smear he took as some form of punctuation, then a digit followed by another incomplete word: "5 F A I L U".

Five failures? he wondered. *There were five of them, but seven of us set sail on this river. Did they want an improved chance of success or just a bigger sample size?*

"Huxley," Rhys said in irritation. He began to tell her about the gruesome graffiti, then stopped. He didn't know why, but some instinct told him with unambiguous insistence to say nothing. *More cop-brain stuff*, he decided, suppressing a pang of guilt. *Keep back information that might be useful later.*

"What've you got?" he asked, moving to her side.

"Something useful for once." She reached into the locker to grasp the neck of an object about the size of a heavy duty desktop printer, but judging by the difficulty Rhys had in lifting it, considerably heavier. "Oh please," she grunted. "Don't help. I'm fine."

"What is this thing?" He took hold of the object's broad base and together they managed to heave it onto the deck. Huxley used his light to illuminate a device that seemed to be an elaborate marriage of binoculars and flatbed scanner.

"If I'm not mistaken." Rhys ran a hand over the thing's bulky head. "This is a microscope spectrophotometer." Seeing his blank look, she elaborated. "A microscope and a spectrometer in one unit. Not only will it let you image samples at micro-levels, it'll also tell you what they're made of, and—" she flicked a switch on the base, letting out a satisfied laugh when it lit up in green "—it seems to have its own fully functioning power source."

"You know how to use it?"

"Pretty sure I do."

"All right." He glanced over his shoulder at the bodies. The word daubed onto the wall was lost to the shadows. *Antibody.* "Let's get it on the inflatable. Then we'll see if there's anything else to find . . ."

The sound that erupted outside was so loud he thought at first another jet had come screaming in on a bombing mission. When it paused for a short interval before blaring into life once more he realised it was no jet. The cacophony brought to mind some kind of heavy-duty drill but much more rapid and accompanied by a high-pitched yowl that told of violently displaced air.

"The chain gun," he said, getting to his feet. "Time to go."

Rhys grunted as she attempted to lift the microscope, barely managing to get it clear of the deck. "We can't leave this."

Huxley bit down on a profane exclamation, hearing the chain gun pause then scream again, a thud sounding from above as something impacted the roof of the boat. After shrugging off his pack, he extracted one of the C-4 blocks and set the timer for five minutes, thought about it, then reduced it to four.

"This'll have to do," he said, returning the block to the pack and hurrying to place it at the hatch to the engine room. He checked the ladder was clear, seeing nothing but taking comfort from the fact that the chain gun had fallen silent. Together, he and Rhys manhandled her prize up the rungs to the wheelhouse, the chain gun letting out another scream when they reached the top. More thuds sounded above their heads, the boat heaving with the impacts. Huxley caught a glimpse of something wet and heavy sliding down the windscreen but didn't linger for a better look.

They emerged onto the aft deck to be greeted by

what at first appeared to be a bolt of horizontal lightning. The screaming report of the chain gun thrummed their ears as they ducked, Huxley looking up to see a near solid line of monstrous fireflies buzzing overhead. *Tracer*, he realised, tracking the glowing stream to the bridge. At first it seemed to be blossoming into red fireworks as it met a dark, shifting obstacle, tracking back and forth to leave a trail of crimson novas. When one of those fireworks deposited a chunk of smoking, deformed forearm on the deck, he understood the nature of the unfolding danger.

The chain gun fell silent once more and he looked towards the boat, seeing a thin stream of grey vapour rising from its barrel. He thought he saw Pynchon waving urgently behind the wheelhouse glass but couldn't be sure. From the rear of the boat he heard a steady, repeating crack, catching the muzzle flash of Plath's carbine as she fired aimed shots at something on the north bank.

A collective growl from above drew his gaze back to the bridge. Its balustrade was streaked with blood and decorated by the partly destroyed corpses of the Diseased. He couldn't see the source of the growling but assumed it came from those who had survived the chain gun's attentions and possessed enough residual reason to take shelter. The scale of the noise they produced told of a large number. While he had been able to make some sense of the utterances from the other Diseased they had encountered, this was a truly hellish and incomprehensible babble. Rhythmic yelping overlapped with plaintive wails and infuriated roars to create a chorus he would have described as bestial if he hadn't been sure no collection of animals would ever produce something so ugly.

One of the disarranged bodies tumbled from the bridge, the boat bobbing as it collided with the wheelhouse roof. More followed, Huxley seeing how they were being pushed over the balustrade directly above the boat, some whole, most not, dismembered limbs and decapitated heads forming part of the growing cascade.

"They're trying to sink us," Rhys said.

A rapid series of cracks from Plath's carbine snapped Huxley's attention back to the boat. *Four minutes*, he reminded himself, stooping to heft the microscope contraption and dragging it to the inflatable. *Closer to two now.*

The inflatable contrived not to sink under the concentrated weight of the microscope, but did bob alarmingly as Rhys cast away the rope and Huxley deposited the device in her arms before reaching for the outboard. Unwilling to risk a wayward shot from Plath's carbine, he steered to the boat's port side, the chain gun roaring back to life the instant they cleared the prow. It fired in short bursts now, Huxley looking back to see the pulses of tracer impacting the upper side of the bridge in what he assumed to be an effort to keep the Diseased's heads down. It didn't appear to have much effect, the cascade of body parts continuing without pause. The other boat listed at an increasingly acute angle under the additional weight, drifting away from the bridge stanchion, water lapping over its stern.

"New toy?" Plath enquired, sparing them a glance as they tied up the inflatable and heaved the microscope onto the aft deck. She turned and fired without waiting for an answer, Huxley raising himself up to see what she was shooting at. The ripples disturbing the flood-water off the starboard side had intensified considerably and he saw numerous silhouettes in the fog. Like the Diseased on the bridge, this group gave voice to a grotesque song, just as discordant but shot through with a burgeoning note of enraged aggression.

"One or two rush forward now and again," Plath said. Beyond her a splash appeared in the haze and she fired two quick shots. "See? Seem to be getting bolder by the second. We can't change the angle of the boat so Pynchon can get them with the chain gun."

"How long?" Pynchon called from the wheelhouse.

Huxley left Rhys to add her carbine to Plath's efforts and moved to the front of the wheelhouse, peering through the windscreen at the other boat. The stern was part submerged now as it drifted further towards the centre of the bridge, burdened by ever more grisly projectiles from above.

"I set a four-minute fuse," he told Pynchon. "Can't be much longer."

Pynchon's face bunched in consternation, hand

tensing on the joystick to rake the top of the bridge with another burst of chain gun fire. Huxley focused on the other boat, counting off sixty seconds then letting out a sigh of self-reproach when nothing happened. "Maybe I didn't set the timer right."

"Terrific." Pynchon's jaw worked in a manner that indicated he was, with difficulty, containing a stream of highly critical and profane invective. "We'll just have to hope the transponder signal is muffled when it sinks. Water's a pretty good inhibitor for radio waves. Not sure the river's deep enough though."

Huxley watched another fleshy deluge pummel the boat, the Diseased ducking down as Pynchon unleashed another short burst of tracer. "Gonna run out of ammo fast at this rate."

"Can't work out why they're so intent on sinking it," Huxley said. "I mean, they're all insane, right? The disease makes them that way. This is collective effort . . ."

His conjecture ended when the boat disappeared in an instantaneous upsurge of water. The explosion was so close the sound swamped them, spiderweb cracks appearing in the windscreens as Huxley and Pynchon ducked, hands clamped to their ears. The boat swayed and heaved in the wake before righting itself and resuming forward motion. Huxley only realised the engines had reactivated when the ringing in his ears faded.

As the shadow of the bridge swept over them, he made for the aft deck, finding Plath casting a few farewell bullets at the Diseased. The fog closed in before he could make out any details, but he gained an impression of a large mass of deformed bodies crowding the span, their collective, infernal chorus fading into the engines' roar.

Looking down, he saw Rhys engaged in a close examination of their treasure, hands playing over the various knobs and switches with tentative appreciation. "Shit," she said, glancing up at him with brows arched. "All that blood and guts and we didn't think to take any tissue samples."

Chapter Nine

The sat-phone began chirping when they were a short distance from the bridge. For the first time, Huxley felt an urge to ignore it; let it burble away for however long it took for their unseen tormentors to deactivate the engines. Pynchon read his mood, giving a half-apologetic grimace as he reached out to depress the green button. "Got no choice. You know that."

"Do you have casualties?" the phone-voice asked with its customary lack of inflection.

Huxley ran a hand over his head, memory pain pulsing once again. Perhaps he'd had a bad experience on hold once upon a time. "No."

"Do any of the others display signs of confused thinking or unwarranted aggression?"

"No."

"Describe the condition of the other boat."

"Extensive internal damage due to small arms fire. No survivors. Two bodies. Kahlo and Turner. Murder–suicide. Both were infected."

"Did you retrieve anything of interest or value to your mission?"

His eyes flicked towards the microscope, strapped into one of the chairs. "No. We didn't have time." He hadn't discussed this lie with the others beforehand but none of them piped up with an objection. "Bunch of Diseased turned up. Looked like they took exception to our presence. Acted in concert to stop us, in fact. Any idea what that's about?"

He didn't expect an answer, so the length and detail of what followed came as a surprise. "While most Diseased succumb to delusion and death within four weeks of infection, others do not. Some continue to act independently, while others form groups that display hierarchical and predatory characteristics. All remain violently aggressive in response to what may be perceived as territorial intrusion."

"If they're doing that, they can't be completely crazy. Some part of them is still capable of thinking, communicating."

A short pause, a single click. "Your empathy is misplaced and irrelevant to the success of this mission."

"Your mission."

"Also yours. Your participation was fully voluntary."

"So you say. We have no way of knowing if that's true."

Another click. "Further discussion on this point is irrelevant. The boat is approaching a stretch of deeper water where it will deactivate during the hours of darkness. You are instructed to rest but maintain a watch to ensure security. The boat will reactivate at dawn when further instructions will be provided."

"Yeah," Huxley muttered when the familiar clicks and silence followed. "Fuck you too, I guess."

"It's a complex organic compound." Rhys pursed her lips, moving back from the microscope's eyepieces. Lacking alternative samples, they had opted to test the contents of one of the two spare hypodermic applicators. She rested the device on an upturned storage box, positioned close to the wheelhouse hatch where Pynchon kept watch on the surrounding waters. It transpired that the microscope's base contained a sliding compartment filled with slides, syringes and various other useful instruments.

The boat had come to its promised halt an hour after the sat-phone fell silent, the engines resuming their intermittent, station-keeping growl. They could see nothing of the landscape beyond the fog now, nightfall creating an impression that they floated in the midst of a vast and endless ocean rather than a ruined and flooded city. Distant cries came to them through the mist but there was no sign of the conjoined and discordant chorus of the pack that had assailed them at the bridge.

"Long list of various elements, as you can see." Rhys gestured to the small fold-out screen affixed to the microscope, displaying the contents of the slide she had slotted into the base unit. To Huxley's eyes it appeared only a pink and grey smear overlaid with chemical symbols and numbers. Rhys, despite her protestations to a lack of biochemical knowledge, exhibited little difficulty in reading it.

"But that's hardly a surprise," she continued. "It's what they add up to that matters."

"And what's that?" Huxley enquired.

"Deoxyribonucleic acid and proteins in various quantities. Stem cells for short. Spectrographic analysis also identified the presence of aluminum salts."

"Why is that significant?" Plath asked.

"Aluminum salts are an adjuvant common to many vaccines."

"Adjuvant?" Huxley asked.

"It's a medical term for any substance that increases the effect of the principal component of a compound. In vaccines, aluminum salts are used to increase the body's inflammatory response, which in turn stimulates the immune response causing increased production of antibodies."

Antibodies . . . The notion of telling them about the scrawl on the other boat rose then faded from Huxley's mind, quelled once again by cop instinct.

"So it is an inoculant," Plath said.

Rhys looked at the microscope's display screen, shaking her head. "Not necessarily. Adjuvants are common to other drug therapies. Though it does make it more likely. However, what's left of my memory contains no information about use of stem cells in vaccines."

"But whatever it is might still have made us immune to this thing," Pynchon said. "I mean, none of us seem to be showing signs yet."

"Dickinson did," Huxley pointed out.

"Because she hadn't taken the shot yet," Plath said.

"Which raises another question: if it is some kind of vaccine, why didn't we get dosed with it until we were so deep into this journey?"

"It's possible we were," Rhys said. "The phone told us the shots we took were boosters. Some vaccines don't become fully effective until after a second dose. And let's not forget the scars above our kidneys. Maybe this thing needed some kind of surgical intervention to make it work, probably some alterations to the endocrine system. As for Dickinson, no two human beings are exactly alike. People respond differently to disease. Some get mild symptoms, some have no symptoms at all. Others can have natural immunity even without a vaccine. Maybe Dickinson was just more susceptible to infection. If so, the booster shot possibly wouldn't have helped her."

Pynchon nodded to the microscope. "You can check our blood with that, right? See if we're infected."

Rhys nodded. "But I'd need samples to compare. Infected samples, and we don't have any."

"There's still some of Dickinson's blood in the crew cabin," Plath suggested.

"It's dried out and contaminated." Rhys turned to the fog drifting in crimson whirls beyond the stern. "If we want a viable sample, we'll need to go get it."

Pynchon insisted that Rhys stay behind this time. "We need her expertise. No point bringing back a body if she's not alive to analyse it."

Plath gave him a wide smile. "How wonderfully encouraging."

Pynchon ignored her in much the same way he had ignored Golding, instead spending a few minutes talking Rhys through the basics of operating the chain gun. "It's pretty simple." He had her work the joystick, causing the gun to track and tilt on the other side of the cracked windscreens, the monochrome display shifting in concert. "The camera sees what the gun sees. It's set to lowlight mode so you should have a clear shot at anything that comes close. A target in the centre of the screen will be obliterated when you press the trigger. If you have to fire, do so with a light touch. Short bursts only. We've got maybe fifteen seconds of firepower left so don't piss it all away at once."

The night-vision goggles felt uncomfortable on Huxley's head, the strap too tight and the weight too cumbersome. "Get the feeling we didn't train much with these," he said, fiddling with the controls. The green melange blazed in his eyes, settling into something comprehensible when Pynchon adjusted the dial for him. Huxley blinked in surprise at the clarity of what he saw, the fog banished to reveal a swathe of placid water stretching away on either side. The southern bank was rich in the hard angles and straight lines of buildings while the northern bank was all half-submerged trees and parkland.

"Like the Everglades," Plath said, a faint electronic whirr sounding as she activated her own goggles. "Wonder if there's any gators."

"Battery life on these things is not great," Pynchon said, taking his place at the inflatable's outboard. "Two hours at most, so we can't hang around. We find a Diseased, kill it and bring it back. We hear the chain gun start up, we abandon the mission. No arguments."

He opted for the south bank, reasoning that a residential area offered a higher probability of finding a Diseased. They were a few hundred yards from the boat, the dark monolith of a lightless apartment block looming ahead, when the inflatable's hull began to scrape over unseen obstacles beneath the surface.

"Gardens," Pynchon concluded, killing the outboard to peer into the green shimmer. He raised himself up and dipped a leg into the water. It stopped at his knee. He unslung his carbine, speaking in a murmur, "We'll wade from here. I'm on point. Huxley take the rear. Plath, remember why we're doing this: no barbecuing the samples without my say-so."

Plath replied with a mock salute before hefting the flame-thrower and sliding over the side of the inflatable. Huxley took hold of the inflatable's bow rope and slipped into the water, movements slow to prevent a splash. Some underwater rummaging discovered a heavy, unyielding piece of metal he assumed must be garden furniture. He tied the rope to it and fell in behind Plath as Pynchon started off.

He made for the double doors of the apartment block directly to their front, laser sight a thin, glittering line flicking right and left as he scanned for targets. The doors were open, water invading the hallway beyond. Pynchon entered at an unhurried pace, carbine aiming up the stairwell. The place smelled of rot and sewage shot through with something far more acrid.

"Decomposition has a unique flavour, don't you find?" Plath asked in a rhetorical whisper. Huxley felt the transformed world of the night-vision goggles rendered her into something even more unsettling: a grinning, glass- and plastic-eyed goblin rather than a conventionally attractive, if patently psychopathic woman of scientific leanings. *Is she really a scientist?* The question hadn't occurred before but felt increasingly pertinent. *Or has she just read a lot of books? The kind of thing you do when you have plenty of time on your hands. Like a prisoner, or someone who had been institutionalised.*

There were three apartments on the block's ground floor. Pynchon led them in a methodical search of each one, finding two empty and one occupied by a corpse. It lay abed in one of the bedrooms, household bric-a-brac bobbing in the floodwaters lapping at the mattress. The body was weeks old and featured no obvious signs of infection. Age and identity were obscured by death and the monochrome filter of the goggles.

"Paracetamol and promethazine," Plath whispered, picking up two empty pill bottles from the nightstand. "That'll do it."

"Can't really blame them, can you?" Pynchon inclined his head at the ceiling. "People have a tendency to seek higher ground in times of crisis."

The stairwell to the first floor featured another corpse, this one in an even more advanced state of decay and showing evident signs of infection. It had the same growths along its spine as the body near Westminster Bridge but far more extensive. The distorted cadaver lay face down on the steps, protrusions rising from its back to entwine the railings in a tangle of root-like knots. These had also sprouted tendrils that extended to the walls and the stairs above.

"It's like everyone it infects becomes a plant pot when they die." Plath peered at the bulges enfolding the railings. Taking a knife from her belt she cut off a portion, the blade making a difficult course through the fibrous substance. "Won't be enough, will it?" She grimaced, consigning the sample to one of the empty ration bags they had brought along for the purpose.

"Rhys said she needs blood." Pynchon prodded the body with the muzzle of his carbine. "This guy's way too dry."

They moved on, finding another four apartments, all disarrayed but lacking in occupants, living or dead. They were heading back to the stairwell when they heard it, a muted but definite impact on the floor above. Pynchon held up a closed fist, signalling for them to hold in place. They listened for more, at first hearing nothing then, instead of another soft thud, they heard something fainter but even more compelling. It grew louder as Pynchon led them back to the stairs, Huxley feeling an instinctive urgency rise at the sound: plaintive and irresistible. *A child.* A crying child.

The night-vision goggles painted the next hallway in typically stark tones save for the blaze of light leaking from the partially opened apartment door at the far end of the hall. The weeping grew louder still, shot through with a sudden high-pitched sob that had Huxley rushing towards the door.

"Easy!" Pynchon hissed at him, forearm braced against his chest. "Slow down, Mister Policeman." He held Huxley's gaze a moment longer then nodded at Plath. She raised an eyebrow and shouldered the flame-thrower before drawing her pistol. Approaching the door, she reached up to remove her goggles, Huxley following suit when the blaze of light from within threatened to swamp his vision.

Plath crouched as she shouldered the door gently aside, pistol aimed two-handed at the interior. The glow from the apartment was surprisingly dim without the goggle's amplification, a blue-white flicker that seemed to hide more than it revealed. Plath maintained her crouch as she moved inside, Pynchon close behind, his own pistol drawn. Following them, Huxley took in the sight of a short hallway leading to a living room that he initially assumed must have been invaded by a fallen tree. The meagre light cast its inconstant glow over an interwoven web of growths. They appeared to have sprouted from two bodies lying in the centre of the room, expanding to fill this space and force their way into the ceiling and surrounding walls.

The light came from a door to the right, as did the unceasing weeping. Huxley heard pain in that sound, of body and mind, a siren call of loss and utter despair that once again urged him forward. *Find her! Help her!* He shuddered with the effort of resisting the impulse to shoulder Pynchon and Plath aside, kick the door open and give succour to the unseen infant. As seductive as the weeping was, it also chimed a warning in his head: *it's not right.* It may have been another example of cop instinct, or something more primal, but he felt no desire to see what lay on the other side of that door, even quelling the urge to shout a warning to Plath as she reached out to ease it open.

The weeping diminished to a frightened gasp as Plath shone a flashlight on the room's occupant. The figure was huddled in the centre of what Huxley assumed to have been a bedroom, although the state of its transformation had obscured much of the detail. Root-like tendrils covered the floor, walls, and ceiling.

He glimpsed the corner of a poster beneath the twisting organic melange of it all, some rock group he couldn't name, probably due to basic ignorance since the sight of it failed to stir any memory pain.

The flickering illumination came from an electric lantern sitting amid a carpet of twisting growths, its battery evidently failing, hence the aggravating flicker. The blanketed figure whimpered and shifted as Plath's flashlight played over it, the beam then tracking across the room, lingering here and there but not long enough for Huxley to discern any further details.

"Are you . . . ?" Plath's flashlight snapped back to the figure as it spoke, the voice small and tremulous, no louder than a sigh. "Are you . . . the fire brigade?"

"Come again?" Plath said.

"Mum said they would come. When things started going bad. 'Don't cry,' she said. 'The fire brigade will come and take us away.'" A part-stifled sob then a sniffle, the figure shivering as it turned its head, just enough to reveal a bright, moist eye beneath the blanket's edge.

"Uh-huh," Plath replied. "When was that, sweetie?"

"Days . . . weeks. I don't know." The sob returned, coloured by a defensive wail. The figure shuddered as it cried, slowly mastering its grief before turning back to Plath. More of the face was revealed now, pale, female, flecked with damp grit, a desperate hope in her eyes. Huxley put her age at eight or nine. "Are you . . ." She leaned towards Plath, blanket bunching as she raised a concealed hand, ready to reach out. "Are you going to take me away?"

"Oh please," Plath said with a palpable note of disgust. Then she shot the little girl in the head.

Huxley's instinct, cop or simply human, brought his carbine stock to his shoulder, centring the sights on the back of Plath's skull, finger closing on the trigger. Before he could fire, Pynchon grabbed the fore stock of Huxley's weapon, forcing the muzzle aside, jerking it hard enough to make him hesitate.

"Stop!" He fixed Huxley with a commanding glare then jerked his head at the corpse in the centre of the room. "Look."

Plath stepped forward, stooping to pull away the blanket. The revealed body was complete down to the knees where it morphed into a sprawling mass of tendrils, the matrix all connected to the chaotic lattice on the walls and ceiling. Also significant was the fact that the body was male, the sagging gut of a rarely exercised, middle-aged man partially obscuring an unprepossessing set of genitals. The face, however, remained that of an eight- or nine-year-old girl, riven by the bullet hole in its forehead.

"You were right," Plath told Huxley, her head tilted to a studious angle as she scanned the Diseased.

The blandness of her tone enraged him, the sheer incongruity and indifference of it fuelling another urge to shoot her. Huxley swallowed and forced his hand from the carbine's pistol grip. "What?"

"They can still think," Plath elaborated. "This was some real Venus flytrap shit." She shifted her scrutiny to the surrounding room, shining her flashlight on something in the corner, something round and pale. "Looks like it worked, too. Once anyway."

Moving closer to the illuminated object, Huxley recognised it as a skull sunken into the mass of roots. It seemed cleaner than it should, lacking any lingering shred of skin or hair. "Did this thing eat it?" he wondered.

"What else would it do with it?"

"I thought it was random," Pynchon mused, Huxley turning to see him peering closer at the obscene amalgam of child and man.

"What?" Huxley asked.

"The disease, what it does. What did Rhys call it?" He poked the barrel of his carbine into the point where the smooth flesh of the little girl's neck met the folds of the body it was attached to. "Rapid morphological change. I assumed whatever it turned you into was just bad luck. This would indicate otherwise."

"You think he turned himself into this?"

"Maybe, maybe not. Seems an awfully useful form to adopt if you want to keep living in a world that's changed this much."

"You're wasting time on useless conjecture," Plath said, crouching to deliver an experimental shove to the slain Diseased. "Too big to carry even if we can cut him free of all this stuff."

Hearing a metallic scrape, Huxley turned to see Pynchon drawing his combat knife. "We don't need all of it."

Huxley saw them first, a shifting green blur flashing into view the moment he reactivated his night-vision goggles. He had taken point as they exited the building, Pynchon second in line with his newly bulging pack, Plath guarding the rear. The descent to the ground floor had been uneventful, stirring optimism that Plath's shot hadn't attracted notice. It was misplaced.

"Enemy left!" He wasn't sure where this phrase came from, another deeply instilled part of his training compelling the warning from his lips as he brought his carbine to bear and started firing. The Diseased's hostility was evident in the way they moved, a dozen or more vaguely human shapes thrashing towards them through the floodwater. As they charged, Huxley recognised their screams as a lesser but still recognisable version of the collective chorus of aggression from the Diseased pack at the bridge.

The first fell instantly, two shots to the central mass sending it into an untidy splash. Huxley adjusted his aim to the right and fired again, felling another. Adjusted left and cut down two more with a rapid salvo.

"We're moving!" Pynchon shouted, rushing forward several yards before halting and firing. Plath splashed past them both then halted to loose off several shots with her pistol. They maintained this overlapping formation all the way back to the inflatable. The Diseased pack were undaunted by the gunfire, stopping only when a bullet found its mark. Huxley was dismayed to see Plath reach the inflatable first, half expecting her to take it and leave before he and Pynchon had a chance to get aboard. But she didn't. Depositing her flame-thrower in the craft, she crouched to undo the bow rope, holding the inflatable in place.

"Here," Pynchon said, piling in then scooping up the flame-thrower. "All animals are scared of fire." He tossed the weapon to Plath and reached for the outboard. Huxley paused to shoot down another two Diseased as Pynchon started the electric motor and Plath readied her flame-thrower. She unleashed its fire stream without hesitation, sweeping the twenty-yard-long plume of flame from side to side. Blinded by the glare, Huxley tore the night-vision goggles from his head and heaved himself in. He lay across the middle, carbine pointing to Plath's left, seeing a figure, wreathed head to knees in flame, caper about in spasmodic agony before disappearing under the water.

He opened up again when the fiery torrent of Plath's flame-thrower slowed then guttered to a trickle. Without the goggles he had no clear targets so fired at the screams. "All good things must end," Plath quipped in a regretful sigh, tossing the empty flame-thrower away before climbing onto the inflatable's prow.

She drew her pistol and joined in Huxley's probably fruitless barrage while Pynchon opened the throttle and brought the craft around in a rapid arc. Huxley twisted about to aim his carbine at the flames now licking over the trees and non-submerged bushes that had formed the communal gardens for this place. He stopped only when the magazine clicked empty.

Chapter Ten

"So, that's what it looks like."
The image on the microscope screen remained largely meaningless to Huxley, but, aesthetically at least, he found it far uglier than the contents on the hypodermics. The molecule was dark with a jagged yellow outline, its mass dotted with red flecks that writhed in constant motion.

"Yeah." Rhys's expression was all heavy-browed grimness, leading him to conclude that she had no good news to impart. She began her analysis an hour before first light, hoping to complete it in advance of the engines starting up again. She had exhibited a spasm of revulsion at the contents of Pynchon's pack; a little girl's head perched atop the severed neck of an adult male was certainly off-putting. Any squeamishness quickly disappeared when she set about her work. She opened the skull with one of the combat knives and used a syringe to extract the required amount of fluid.

Placing a small bead of the stuff on a slide, she slotted it into the microscope's base.

"The sample's loaded with it," she went on. "Looks like it's a fast-breeding little bastard."

"Any idea what it's called?" Huxley asked.

She grunted an utterly humourless laugh. "I'd be amazed if any medical professional had ever seen this before the outbreak. I can tell it's not a virus, its morphology and chemical make-up being more akin to a bacterium. The good news is, given its signature appearance and rapid growth, identifying its presence in another sample shouldn't be difficult." She reached for a fresh syringe. "Who wants to go first?"

Huxley's anxiety was stoked to such a high degree that he barely felt it when she pressed the tip of the needle into his arm. He had managed perhaps an hour of fitful sleep upon their return to the boat, the dream plaguing him once more, terrible in its beautiful clarity. He could feel the sand-laced wind on his skin this time, ears thrumming with the hard gusts sweeping in from the blue ocean beneath the even more blue sky. But it wasn't all beauty. The woman in the wide-brimmed hat hid her face from him as he reached for her. The movement he had thought a joyful whirl now appeared more an attempt at avoiding his touch. The shadow cast by the hat receded when she consented to turn her head towards him, revealing eyes that were both hard and tearful. She began to speak but the dream evaporated when Pynchon shook him awake.

"Well, there it is," Rhys reported after performing her mysterious communion with the microscope. At first, Huxley saw nothing but globules of red on the screen, until she adjusted the magnification, whereupon the same ugly dark cells resolved into focus. "Smaller though." Rhys punched buttons and altered some more settings. "Less frequency too, but that may be due to location. We know this thing affects the brain first so it may breed more in cranial vessels. And—" she took a closer look at the readout "—less motile. Not quite dormant, but not as fully active either."

She took samples from each of them, running her own blood last. Each one returned the same result. Curiously, Huxley's tension diminished as he absorbed the news. He felt there to be an inevitability to it, a confirmation that any hope of surviving this journey had been a fantasy. *Five*, he thought, recalling the visceral graffiti on the artists' boat. *Failure. They didn't make it, why would we?*

"So we've all got it," Pynchon said. "But it's not doing much."

Rhys inclined her head. "More or less. The question is why?"

"The injections," Plath said. "Whatever we took is slowing the spread."

"Possibly." Rhys frowned as she continued to stare at the screen. "Would explain the absence of symptoms."

"You don't sound convinced," Huxley said. "You think they lied to us about the boosters?"

"Maybe. But I think it's more connected to memory." She pointed to the scars on her head. "Dickinson recovered some memories then . . ."

"Went nuts and Pynchon shot her," Plath finished. "So?"

"So it seems likely this pathogen is connected to brain function somehow. Memory is part of our cognitive apparatus. Every Diseased we've encountered has displayed delusional behaviour. The disfigurement suffered by the girl on the laptop began to worsen when she started to obsess over that phone call with her shitty mother."

"You think they took our memories to protect us," Huxley said. "Memory is its trigger, like the open wound it needs to infect us."

"We're already infected. But it's possible the act of remembering acts as a stimulus."

Plath squinted at her. "A psychic disease? Come on."

"Memory is a physiological process of the brain. An electrochemical signal exchanged via a network of synapses. There's nothing supernatural about it. What if this pathogen needs that very process to activate?"

"Meaning," Pynchon said, "as long as we stay amnesiacs we'll be fine?"

Huxley's anxiety rose again when Rhys folded her arms. "Maybe, but the fact is we won't."

"Why not?" Plath asked. "I mean, they operated on us to get at our memories, cut them fully out for all we know."

"True, but they didn't take away our ability to form new ones. Our collective memories may only add up to a couple of days but it's still experience stored in our brains. We are still remembering, we just have less to remember."

"The longer we survive the more memories we build up," Huxley said. "The greater the chance of activating this thing."

"Not only that . . ." Rhys paused to offer a tight grimace. "Clearly the surgery we were subjected to has prevented us from remembering personal details, life history and so on, but I don't think we'd be able to form new memories if they'd taken them completely. The organic machinery that enables us to remember is part and parcel of everything else that allows us to function as human beings. You can't just rip it all out. And, like I said at the start of all this, the brain repairs itself." She paused again, arms bracing tighter across her chest. "Which brings us to the dreams. And don't tell me I'm the only one."

Her eyes tracked over each of them, brows raised expectantly. *Secrets shared*, Huxley concluded, seeing how Plath and Pynchon shifted in discomfort. *It's not just me.*

"I'm on a beach," he said. "There's a woman there. I don't know who she is, but I'm pretty sure I used to."

Pynchon let out a slow breath before speaking, face tensed and guarded. "Some dusty village somewhere. Air smells like shit and smoke. Lot of bodies on the ground. I think I killed them."

"A boy I think I knew," Plath said. Her closed expression made it clear no more information would be forthcoming.

Rhys's eyes clouded and she hugged herself before unfolding her arms. "An emergency room. Frantic, chaotic. I try to help, but it's not enough. People keep dying. I think I'm the only doctor there."

No one spoke for at least a minute, digesting the implications until Pynchon gave them voice: "Dreams are memories, aren't they? We're remembering when we sleep."

"Fact is," Rhys replied, "neurological science is pretty vague when it comes to dreams. No one's ever been able to come up with a convincing evolutionary rationale for why we do it. Most credible theories centre on the notion that they're simply a by-product of random electronic impulses produced by the brain during sleep. Memories are a major part of the dream state, that's true, but dreams alter them. When processing random input the brain defaults to its hard-wired need to craft a narrative. What we're seeing may be memories or just something cooked up by the millions of synapses in our heads."

"Like infinite monkeys with infinite typewriters producing Shakespeare," Huxley said.

"Exactly. However, although we can't trust anything we see in a dream, they seem a little too specific to not have a memory component." She looked again at the microscope screen. "I'd need to run more tests to confirm it, but I'd be very surprised if our count of these little fuckers didn't increase when we sleep."

"'It starts with the dreams.'" Plath's mouth gave a sardonic quirk as she spoke Abigail's words from the laptop. "She tried to warn us."

"Wouldn't have made any difference," Pynchon said. "Turning back was never an option."

"For you, maybe."

"For any of us. We're all infected, remember? As whoever sent us here knew we would be. Even if, by some miracle, we made it out of this city on foot, the only reception we'd get would be a bullet." He turned back to Rhys. "How long do we have?"

"There's no way to know for sure. Clearly, the treatments we've received have bought us some time, but, for all I know, this thing could accelerate at any second."

"Why send us here just to get sick and die?" Huxley asked.

"Could be we're supposed to find a cure," Plath suggested.

"If that was true—" Rhys patted the microscope "—we wouldn't have had to scavenge this. They gave us no means of analysing our environment. And none of us really has the expertise for it anyway."

"Except you," Huxley said.

"And I'm pretty much groping in the dark here. I suspect my role is to just keep us alive. And think about it, isn't that the only thing we're doing as we proceed along this river? Our collective skills are geared towards survival." She gestured to Pynchon. "Combat skills." Her finger moved to Huxley. "Investigative skills. Useful if one of your group might turn into a monster at any moment. Dickinson was a mountaineer, an explorer, accustomed to survival scenarios."

"Golding didn't strike me as a born survivor," Pynchon commented.

"He had a considerable reservoir of knowledge, some of it actually useful. And, for all his fear and whinging, he never panicked once. It's clear to me we were all selected for this, and selection must've been pretty rigorous. Resistance to panic is a key survival trait."

"And me?" Plath enquired, eyebrow raised.

Rhys met her gaze squarely, speaking in flat and unambiguous tones. "Your scientific acumen is useful, but your pathological focus on your own needs gives you an increased chance of survival."

Plath's mouth quirked and she shrugged. "And I thought we were getting close."

"Whatever we're here for," Rhys went on, "it's not research or data collection or reconnaissance. We're here for something else. Something that requires us to stay alive, at least for now."

The engines started up then, the boat accelerating briefly before settling into its typical, unimpressive speed. Huxley looked at the sat-phone in expectation but it failed to chirp.

"Small mercies," Pynchon muttered, taking a seat at the chain gun controls. "Don't really feel like following orders just now."

They passed under more bridges and through the ruined remnants of others. The fog obscured much of the banks save for glimpses of vegetation that grew thicker and taller with each passing mile. The bridges also became increasingly festooned with root-like growths spiralling around supports and railings. "Too much," Huxley heard Rhys murmur as she tracked her carbine sight over one particularly overgrown bridge.

"What?"

"Too much growth. Looks like a jungle reclaiming abandoned infrastructure. The city's fallen, sure, but nature doesn't move this fast."

He raised his own carbine and peered through the sight at the north bank, making out what appeared to be the base of a huge tree. He initially marked it as an oak or a yew, its mass of roots half hidden by the water. But as he looked closer he recognised a chaotic but still discernible pattern in the overlap of the roots, one he had seen the night before.

"Not nature," he said. "Some of the bodies we found last night had sprouted. Like plant pots, Plath said. This—" he tracked his sight along the misted bank, finding a jumble of twisting vegetation "—this was all people. This is what happens when it's done turning you into a monster."

"Not just a disease," Plath mused. "A multi-stage organism. A new form of life."

"From outer space?" Huxley lowered his carbine and grinned at her scowl. "C'mon, the thought must've occurred before now."

"Abigail didn't say anything about . . . spaceships or meteorite impacts or strange lights in the sky. If it is an invasion they must've been pretty quiet about it."

"Makes a certain kind of sense though. When you think about it?"

"Sense?"

"Let's say you're an alien civilisation and you find a nice shiny, blue-green planet to colonise. Problem is, it's got several billion sentient apes living on it. Or infesting it, depending on your point of view. Not only are they likely to take exception to your arrival, they're also busy poisoning the place with all manner of polluting chemicals. Maybe for them this was no more significant than us spraying a houseplant with bug killer."

Rhys gave a faint laugh, shaking her head. "Not buying it. Any race capable of interstellar travel wouldn't need to resort to something so elaborate. Their technology would be so far in advance of ours they'd be like gods. Besides, if you can zip around the entire galaxy at light speed, why bother coming here?"

"I'm fully open to alternative theories, Doctor."

"Diseases, pandemics, they happen. All through history there has been at least one major outbreak of serious infectious illness every century. This one is just the most . . . unusual to date."

"That's your theory? Shit happens?"

"I'll admit it's not exactly Darwin or Einstein. But I'm sticking with it until more data makes itself available."

A sound came drifting through the fog then, a voice, but very different from the discordant screaming of a Diseased pack. It was more rhythmic, a series of sharp grunts echoing for several seconds before fading. A little later they heard a near identical sound, but this time dimmed by distance.

"What is that?" Huxley said, straining to hear more.

"Language." Plath moved to his side, resting her arms on the rail. "They're communicating."

"Like birds," Rhys said with a note of agreement. "Or apes. Chimps warn other troops away from their territory by taking to the trees and grunting."

"Why not just talk?" Huxley asked.

"Could be they don't know how any more," Plath said. "As the doc says, this thing is multi-stage. The further along the infection tree you get the less human you become, if you don't die and turn into a tree first."

The calls fell silent for the space of about a minute then started up again, louder this time. It sounded to Huxley as if the unseen Diseased that produced them were parallel with the boat.

"Are they following us?" Rhys wondered.

Plath's eyes narrowed, features tightening. "I think

so. Territorial behaviour implies an intolerance of intruders." Huxley took an involuntary backward step when she drew a breath and screamed into the fog: "FUCK OFF YOU MUTANT BASTARDS!"

A short interval of silence then the grunts resumed. Huxley felt they had grown in volume, something Plath also noticed, to her considerable annoyance. Retrieving her carbine, she began to prowl the aft deck, raising and lowering it repeatedly, peering through the sight with predatory keenness before hissing in disappointed frustration.

The calls continued for the rest of the day, providing a constant and increasingly irritating soundtrack to their journey. Lacking anything else to do, Rhys set about analysing the sample of growth matter they had retrieved during their foray. Pynchon retired to the crew cabin and embarked on a mission to disassemble, clean and reassemble their weapons. Huxley settled himself into the seat in front of the map display, eyes flicking between the slow track of the dot along a wide blue line and the inert plastic block of the sat-phone. It occurred to him that its silence might be a ploy, a means of feeding their fears, although the purpose of it eluded him. Alternatively, he speculated that the powers controlling the device simply had nothing to say at this juncture. *Or*, he reflected, *they want to avoid any more questions.*

As the day wore on Plath maintained her predatory

vigil on the aft deck, her agitation increasing in concert with the rising cacophony from the riverbanks. The sound had taken on a decidedly aggrieved pitch, overlapping voices indicating multiple Diseased were now tracking their progress.

"Just one," Huxley heard Plath mutter. "I just want one. This fucking fog . . ."

Having momentarily abandoned his scrutiny of the map display, Huxley loitered in the wheelhouse entrance, reaching up to rest his hands on the lintel. He saw how Plath's nostrils flared as she spoke, as if trying to catch a scent. "Can you smell them?" he asked her.

Her face twitched, head moving in a marginal shake. "Smells of rot, something else it has in common with the Everglades."

A sudden upsurge of calls from the north bank caused her to spin about, moving to the starboard rail to aim her carbine into the shrouded depths. "Both sides now. There's more of them too. I can tell." Apparently glimpsing movement in the swirling red haze, her finger moved to the carbine's trigger. Huxley watched it tremble before relaxing as she fought down the urge to fire.

"Take it easy," he said, which earned him only a dismissive glare before she resumed her fruitless hunt.

"Just one," he heard her whisper as he turned back to the wheelhouse.

"Anything?" he asked Rhys. The way she crouched

at the microscope reminded him of Plath in its singular focus.

"If I was a real biologist," she said, not looking up from the eyepieces, "I think I'd be using the word 'fascinating' a lot just now."

"Unusual, huh?"

"If you call protein matter assuming a cellulose structure 'unusual', then yeah."

"And in English, please?"

She sighed and moved back from the microscope, punching a button to activate the screen. The image resembled an irregular series of narrow ovals on a reddish brown background. "It looks like a plant," Rhys explained, "but it's made of meat, and a number of additional compounds not usually found in human tissue. Cell division is remarkably rapid, too. It's literally growing before our eyes."

"So, the plant pot thing wasn't too wide of the mark."

Rhys inclined her head, brows arching in agreement. "A grow bag would be a more accurate analogy. My guess is death is a signal for the infection to shift into another mode. It uses the organic matter of the body to fuel . . . this." She tapped the screen. "Self-replicating cells that form branching structures."

"To what purpose?"

"Unknown, but it must somehow relate to the disease's life cycle. Else, what's the point?"

"Does there have to be one?"

The glance she gave him was only marginally less scathing than Plath's dismissal. "Life always has a point."

"And what's that?"

"Something it has in common with us: survival. Continuance of its species."

Huxley gave a rueful grin and began to rise, intending to return to the map display, stopping when he noticed the mark on Rhys's neck. It was small, the size and shape of an average mole, but he was certain it hadn't been there in the morning. "What?" she asked, but the sudden chirp of the sat-phone forestalled his answer.

Moving forward, Huxley paused to shout down the ladder at Pynchon – "Mom and Dad are calling!" – before moving to the front of the wheelhouse. He watched the phone vibrate until the others crowded round then hit the green button.

"Do you have casualties?"

"No."

"Do any . . ."

"Enough of that shit! Of course we're displaying aggression and irrational behaviour. Why the fuck wouldn't we? Just get on with it."

Clicks and silence then the boat's engines died. "Rest period," the phone voice said. "Communications will be resumed in seven hours. Maintain a rotating guard in pairs until dawn. The Diseased in this region are extremely hostile."

"You ever going to tell us what we're doing here?"

"Final phase instructions will be provided shortly. Continue to monitor each other for signs of sudden mental or physical change."

Clicks. Silence.

"If that is a real person," Pynchon said in a flat monotone, "I intend to survive this just so I can hunt them down and kill them. Slowly."

Huxley and Rhys took the first watch. He kept to the foredeck, debating over whether to tell her about the mark on her neck. *Could be nothing.* He knew it wasn't. *Just because her infection might be getting worse doesn't mean the rest of us are too.* He knew this to be pathetic optimism. *She would want to know.* Probably true. *She'll resent you for telling her.* Also true.

This continual babble of question and answer was underscored with a competing background hum of other thoughts. Plath's new-found animation. Pynchon's new-found morose fatalism. The fact that they were alone in the middle of a city of monsters and all infected and he was going to die soon and he couldn't even remember his life more than three fucking days ago . . .

You're missing something. The statement cut through his rising panic with hard, insistent clarity. If cop instinct had a voice he knew this was it. *Something important. Something that'll get everyone killed if it's not addressed. But what is it?*

He turned his gaze outward, hoping the dark swirl of the fog would provide distraction, but the ongoing chorus from the Diseased denied him any peace. It occurred to him that, in any way that mattered, he was only a few days old, an infant sent forth into a world of terrors. *Without memory, what are we?* Golding had asked. *No one. Nothing.* He was a child pretending to adulthood only because of the skills they left him. The cop instinct that made him useful. So why wasn't it working now?

Too much to think about, he decided. *Too many clues. Clear the decks. Make room.*

He found Rhys at the microscope once again, but she wasn't engaged in any analysis. The device's in-built computer featured a clock that, as far as they could tell, provided an accurate readout on the display screen.

"Ten minutes left on our shift," she said when he entered the wheelhouse.

He tried not to let his gaze linger on her neck, but found it impossible. The mark had grown to the size of a penny now, dark red in colour. "I noticed something earlier . . ."

"This, you mean?" She pointed at the mark. "Yeah, me too."

"I'm sorry . . ."

"Don't be." She hesitated, wincing. "You've got one as well. Behind the left ear."

His hand immediately went to the spot, probing, exploring. If she hadn't pointed it out he wouldn't have noticed it, a small patch of raised skin that failed to produce any pain when he poked a trembling finger to it. "So . . ." He swallowed, forcing moisture down a dry throat. "It's started."

"I'm not so sure. Are you remembering anything? More than before, I mean."

He shook his head. "Just the dream, and I still have no idea who she is."

"Same with me. Memory is the trigger, we know that."

"Then what is it . . . ?" He trailed off when the answer came, shaming in its obviousness. "The vaccine. It wasn't a vaccine."

"Not sure about that either. These marks could be a side effect. A by-product of the inoculant fighting it out with the infection."

He poked his mark again, perversely annoyed by the fact that it didn't hurt. "Can you test these?"

"They're a bit too small for a viable biopsy using the instruments I have. Given the current rate of growth, though . . ." She raised her eyebrows, grimacing as she patted a hand to the microscope. "I'll draw some fluid in the morning, see what she can tell us."

She'll tell us we're dying. The realisation, uncoloured by even the smallest crumb of doubt, failed to produce the upsurge of terror he expected. It appeared he had, without articulating it in word or thought, already accepted the inevitability of his own demise. *This was always a suicide mission. Why would you ever think otherwise?*

"OK," he said, letting his hand fall to his side. "Pynchon and Plath?"

"Haven't noticed any marks, but it stands to reason they'll have them too."

"Do we tell them?"

"They may have already noticed. Besides, it's not like we can do anything about it." She flicked the microscope's power button to off and turned to the ladder. "Best to wait for morning."

Chapter Eleven

Unsurprisingly, sleep eluded him. Plath and Pynchon roused themselves from their half-slumber and assumed watch duties without a word. As a dull-eyed Pynchon climbed the ladder, Huxley made out the small red mark on the underside of his wrist. *No way he missed it.* The utter absurdity of their security now depending on the alertness of two amnesiacs, one a melancholic soldier, the other a high-functioning psychopath, brought a chuckle bubbling to Huxley's lips. He quelled the urge with memory pain, knowing surrendering to humour right now would invite hysteria.

Where did you go to high school? he asked himself, the question sending a sharp bolt of discomfort through the front of his skull.

How old were you when you had your first wet dream? More pain, sharper now. An ugly memory perhaps? *A complicated sexual awakening? Or had he been abused like Dickinson?*

He summoned the woman from the dream, watched her twirl in the sun. *What was her name? Where did you meet her? What did her laugh sound like? How did she smell . . . ?*

He shuddered now, agony raging in his head, but it stopped at this particular question. Not because he had an answer. It was the question itself. *Smell.* Cop instinct welled, setting his heart beating faster and making him sit up. *What does anything smell like?*

Hot dogs? Nothing. He could see a hot dog in his head, dripping with onions, red ketchup contrasting with yellow mustard, steam rising from the concoction of reconstituted meat and white bread lacking any nutritional value. He had a vague notion of how it all tasted, much as he knew how the bourbon they found on Abigail's barge would taste. But no inkling at all of how it smelled.

"Onions," he said aloud and the memory of that sweet but savoury tang came to mind. "Ketchup." Same thing. "Now hot dogs." Once again, nothing.

The woman on the beach. He closed his eyes, watching her move across the sand, long hair trailing. He knew there should have been salt on the wind, perhaps carrying a trace of her perfume. But once again he found himself reaching into the same empty box.

Rhys had apparently managed to sleep, something that stirred as much annoyance as it did admiration. "In the morning, I said," she groaned, pushing his hand away as he nudged her shoulder.

"Your dream," he said, voice low but urgent. "What did it smell like?"

She blinked, frowning at him, her tongue working around her mouth. "I dunno, it's a dream . . ."

"What does it *smell* like?"

A crease appeared in her forehead, the blinking of her eyes slowing to a stare.

"A busy ER has to stink, right?" he said. "Blood, shit, vomit. But you can't remember that stink, can you?"

She continued to stare, shaking her head.

"But you can remember what blood smells like?"

Her frown deepened and she nodded.

"Context," he said, dipping his head closer to hers. "Individual smells we remember. Combine them with a context and it goes away."

"Smell is a very strong memory trigger," she said, matching his whispered tone. "In some ways more powerful than vision. An interesting effect of what was done to us, but . . ."

"Plath can remember the smell of the Everglades. Like rot, she said. And she's mentioned them twice now."

She blinked at him again then reached for her carbine. "No hesitating. We just kill the bitch."

He nodded and retrieved his pistol before moving to the ladder. He had almost reached the top when they heard it, a loud splash of something heavy meeting the water followed by a short series of grunts and a shout of pain, one that came from a male throat. *Pynchon.*

Huxley heaved himself into the wheelhouse, crouching instantly, pistol extended in a two-handed grip, scanning for targets. The wheelhouse was empty and, he noted as he scanned the rear of the compartment, the microscope was gone. A grunt and scrape from the left snapped his gaze to the aft deck. Pynchon stood there, staring at him with wide eyes, his teeth gritted in pain. *Not standing*, Huxley realised, looking at the soldier's feet: only the toes of his boots touched the deck, the rubberised surface spattered with an ongoing trickle of blood. Huxley's eyes tracked the falling blood to a wound in Pynchon's shoulder, pierced from back to front by something long, dark and sharp.

"Sorry," a voice said, the sound coming from behind Pynchon. "Did I wake you?"

It was simultaneously Plath's voice and yet not: her usual even cadence overlaid with a more sibilant note. Her words were partially mangled, as if coming from distorted lips.

"Or did you finally make an intelligent deduction, Detective?" Plath enquired.

Something moved behind Pynchon, his body swaying, puppet-like with the motion. Huxley inched forward, making room for Rhys as she ascended the ladder. He could discern a shape in the gloom to Pynchon's rear, something larger than it should be but he couldn't see enough of it to shoot at.

"How long?" he called back, shuffling forward another few inches. "Since you started to remember. How long?"

"Hard to say really." Plath's tone was jarring in its marriage of convivial normality with rasping malice. "Some things haven't come back. My name for instance, but I never had much attachment to it anyway. Other things . . . well, they've become very clear indeed."

Pynchon's suspended form jerked in response to Rhys moving across the middle of the wheelhouse, carbine at her shoulder. As she shifted her shield, Huxley caught a slightly better look at Plath's deformed person, glimpsing her face and seeing something that mirrored her voice. It was still recognisably her, but narrower, the chin elongated to a point, cheekbones expanded, long teeth extending over her lower lip. He tried to centre his pistol sight on her forehead but she shifted again, placing Pynchon in the path of the bullet.

"Careful now," Plath warned. "Don't you want to hear my story? I promise you'll find it interesting."

Rhys edged forward, Huxley glancing across to see her features harden when she noted the absence of the microscope. "Where is it?" she demanded.

"You didn't need your little toy, dear," Plath replied, taunting delight in her voice. "They were right about not providing any diagnostic equipment. It would only have distracted you."

"From what?" Huxley asked. He stood straighter, seeking a different angle but still a clear shot eluded him.

"From what they sent us to do, of course." Plath laughed, the ugliest sound she had yet produced. "I should know. It was my fucking idea, I just don't remember volunteering for it . . ."

The boat's engines came to life with a roar, the craft swaying from port to starboard with enough energy to send Plath staggering. Pynchon screamed as he swung, somehow finding the strength to jerk his body. Kicking his legs, he jack-knifed, the motion succeeding in freeing him from the object skewering his shoulder.

Huxley fired the instant Pynchon collapsed to the deck, two shots aimed at the dark shifting mass now disappearing over the stern. "Fuck fuck fu—!" Rhys yelled, the sound swallowed by the bark of her carbine as she strode forward, firing round after round into the foggy darkness. Huxley hurried to Pynchon, clamping his hands over the gushing hole in his back.

"Help him!" Huxley called to Rhys. She continued to cast bullets into the void, each shot accompanied by an enraged yell. "Doctor!" His shout succeeded in drawing her attention. Glancing down at Pynchon with both anger and annoyance, she shouldered her carbine and crouched to inspect the wound.

"Get the med-kit," Rhys instructed, shoving his hands aside and replacing them with her own. As he rose, Huxley heard a gasp from Pynchon, accompanied by a plume of blood as he forced the words out. "Lies . . . she said it's all just . . . lies . . ."

★   ★   ★

Come dawn, the boat continued to chug its ponderous course along a waterway that might as well have been a sea. They could discern so little of the world beyond the fog now that the map display provided the only guide to their location.

"Somewhere between Richmond and Kingston . . . is my guess," Pynchon said. He spoke with slow deliberation, each word emerging in a tightly controlled cluster of syllables formed by features that twitched constantly in pain. Rhys had judged his wounds too severe to be stitched. She packed them with bandages and swiftly rejected the soldier's suggestion that they cauterise it.

"The igniter from the other flame-thrower . . ."

"Forget it. The shock'll kill you. And drop the tough-guy posturing. It's getting tedious."

They strapped him to the seat in front of the map display, Huxley berating himself for failing to make a more thorough search for painkillers in their foray ashore. Pynchon experienced bouts of suffering, his body taking on a violent spasm before subsiding into a torpor, although the tension in his face never faded. Despite this, he insisted on providing an account of Plath's transformation.

"Happened so fast. I was on the foredeck, checking over the chain gun, not that there's much to check. Just something to do. Wiping down the targeting optics, stuff like that." He paused to endure a shudder, swallowed water from the canteen Rhys held to his lips then continued. "She was aft, where I wanted her to be. Haven't felt too comfortable around her for a while now. Guess none of us have, eh? I heard something . . . like a ripping sound, then a yell. Like she was in pain. When I got there . . ." He trailed off, features forming a baffled frown. "She was heaving the microscope overboard. But her face, her arms. They were changed. I didn't get that good a look. Soon as I brought my weapon to bear she chucked the microscope in the river and came at me, way too fast for anything human. It all got blurry after that. Felt like fighting a giant scorpion." A small, bitter laugh escaped his lips. "Didn't win, did I?"

"She say anything?" Huxley asked.

"Not much. Just the stuff about lies, but it was pretty garbled until you two turned up. Thanks for that, by the way."

Huxley turned to Rhys. "D'you think it was true? What she said about this being her idea?"

"Who knows? Psychopaths often delight in dishonesty. It's all part of their manipulation schtick. Obviously the disease has changed her physically. Personality-wise, not so much."

"You sure you hit her?" Pynchon asked Huxley.

"Pretty sure. But it was quick, and we've seen other Diseased soak up a lot of punishment."

"She's still out there." Rhys spoke with conviction as she peered through the wheelhouse windows. "Tracking us. I mean, it's pretty obvious we're here to put an end to the Diseased – and she is one. Why wouldn't she try to stop us? She'd probably just do it for shits and giggles."

"From now on," Huxley said, eyeing the denser-than-ever fog beyond the windscreen, "we keep the night-vision goggles handy at all times. They're the only means we have of seeing through this shit."

"Battery life . . ." Pynchon began, raising a limp hand in warning.

"I remember." Huxley took his hand, easing it down. Before releasing his grip, Huxley felt the roughness of the mark he noticed earlier. It had grown, forming a long crimson stripe from Pynchon's wrist to his elbow.

"I hate it," Pynchon said, Huxley looking up to find a weak grin on the soldier's lips. "Spoils the look of my tats." His eyes shifted to Huxley's neck, narrowing in sympathy. "Not just me, then."

The mark felt identical in texture and size to Pynchon's, a frond-like shape tracing over the skin from Huxley's ear to his collarbone. Once again, he found it strange that it didn't hurt. "Wouldn't want you to feel left out," he said, a poor joke spoken in a thin, reedy voice that shamed him.

"I think it's the inoculant reacting with the disease," Rhys told Pynchon. "It's safe to assume the compound we were given was experimental, something rushed through without the required trials and tests. Severe side effects are to be expected."

He gazed at her in dull-eyed silence before grunting, "Guess you must've skipped the bedside manner bit of med school, huh, doc?"

"Whatever we took didn't work on Plath," Huxley said to Rhys. "How do we know it's working on us?"

"For a start, we haven't turned into monsters yet. Secondly, I didn't notice any marks on her. It's possible she had innate resistance to the inoculant."

"She said . . . she started remembering a while ago," Pynchon pointed out, gritting his teeth as another bout of suffering coursed through him. "Maybe it doesn't work if you've already recovered your memories, or some of them, anyway."

"Memory is a wound," Huxley said, echoing his conclusion when Rhys had analysed the sample of Diseased tissue. "Once infected, you're done."

They should have been accustomed to the sat-phone's signature chirp by now but still managed to flinch when it started up.

"At the risk of facing a court martial for mutiny," Pynchon said, "I raise no objection to chucking that fucking thing over the side."

Reaching for the device, Huxley felt a strong compulsion to do just that. But they had come so far and still knew so little. The phone-voice, for all its infuriatingly bland obliqueness, at least offered the prospect of enlightenment.

"How honest are we going to be?" he asked, finger hovering over the green button.

Rhys crossed and uncrossed her arms. "At this stage, we might as well just tell them everything."

Huxley looked at Pynchon who grimaced as he replied with a shrug.

"Honesty it is," Huxley said, hitting the button.

As usual there was no delay before the phone-voice asked its inevitable question: "Do you have casualties?"

"Plath transformed into . . . something unpleasant. She attacked Pynchon. We injured her but she escaped."

"Is Pynchon dead?"

"No. But his condition is . . ." Huxley watched Pynchon raise an eyebrow, pain-filled eyes blinking slowly ". . . serious."

Short pause, one click. "You will find another container has opened in the hold. Take the phone and examine the contents."

Rhys followed Huxley down the ladder to the crew cabin where the lid of the previously sealed storage locker was now raised at a slight angle. Inside, they found a computer tablet sitting atop a suitcase-sized box of heavy duty plastic. The box had an LED panel and eleven-digit keypad on its upper side, the screen a blank pale blue. The tablet activated the instant Rhys picked it up and a map appeared on the screen: a simple representation of northern Europe. A red dot pulsed in the south-east of the British Isles and the phone-voice began speaking:

"What has been named the M-Strain Bacillus was first identified in London approximately eighteen months ago. You have seen the results of mass infection at first hand." More dots appeared, forming a sprawling track from west to east. "Dieppe. The Hague. Oslo. Copenhagen. All cities where infection has taken hold. Infected subjects have also been identified in various locations throughout Poland, Belorussia and the Russian Federation. All borders have been closed for over a year, all civilian flights grounded and maritime trade suspended."

"It's carried on the wind," Rhys said, taking advantage of a slight pause in the voice's monologue. "The prevailing winds in the northern hemisphere blow east."

"Correct." The screen changed again, showing what appeared to Huxley's eyes as a mass of white fibres sprouting from a central core. "The primary infection vector. An airborne spore produced after the expiry of an infected host. This vector rendered standard pandemic response plans ineffectual. Quarantine produces only a temporary delay in contagion as it does not require human contact to proliferate. Infection occurs both through inhalation or dermal absorption. Bio-hazard clothing offers a measure of protection but only in areas where the spores have already been detected. Once a sufficient number of victims has been amassed the spread is unstoppable."

"Except in amnesiacs," Huxley said.

"In the early stages of the outbreak numerous hospitals reported limited rates of infection among patients with Alzheimer's, neurological injury or other illnesses involving symptomatic memory loss. Trials confirmed that, while such patients were not immune from the bacillus, they were highly resistant to it."

"Meaning," Rhys cut in, "you rounded up a load of people with Alzheimer's, exposed them to the spore and timed how long it took them to die. Right?"

No pause. "Correct. For obvious reasons, subjects suffering from dementia could not undertake effective field research. Volunteers were sought for trials. Your mission is the outcome of those trials."

"But this mission isn't field research," Huxley said. "Is it?"

The screen switched back to the map and zoomed in on London. The picture acquired more resolution as the city filled the screen, the simple graphic changing to a satellite image. At first it showed only a smear of fog covering the city from end to end, pink at the fringes and deep crimson at the western edge of the city. It reminded Huxley of one of the cells from the microscope display, that crimson blot the nucleus to something vast and malignant.

"Fog that isn't fog," Rhys said. "It's the disease, isn't it? The fog is made of those spores and we've been moving through it, breathing it, absorbing it for days."

"Yes," the phone-voice confirmed, as uninflected as ever. "The inoculant you administered has proven the most effective formulation yet."

"You've gone to a lot of trouble just to get us to this point." Rhys tapped the crimson nucleus. "Why?"

The picture changed once more, still showing the same region of London but with the fog vanished to reveal a monochrome image of the city below. At first Huxley thought it had been blurred or corrupted. Streets were formed of fuzzy-edged lines, often disappearing completely into a discordant, irregular mess that bore a vague resemblance to a forest viewed from above.

"This is the most recent imaging radar scan of what is termed the Prime Infection Zone. In the early days of the outbreak a large number of infected gathered in this region to die. The reason for this was unknown for some time although it was assumed that its proximity to a sustainable water source was a primary factor. An estimated ten thousand people expired here within twenty-four hours, with the number increasing exponentially over the next seventy-two hours. The growths that emerged from the dead quickly combined to form the structure you see here. It has created a canopy of sorts that blocks sunlight and prevents surveillance of what may be occurring beneath. However—" the image altered, shifting from black and grey to pink and red "—thermal imaging indicates considerable biochemical activity. Also the spore count in this area is far higher than elsewhere."

"It's a nursery," Rhys concluded. "Where the spores are born."

"We believe this to be correct."

"Then bomb it," Huxley said. "Few thousand tonnes worth of incendiaries would do it."

"Four months ago a thermobaric explosive device was dropped onto the central mass of the PIZ. It created a scorched area half a kilometre square. Within forty-eight hours the damage had disappeared from our scans. This mass is capable of repairing itself."

"Drop a nuke. Nothing's going to repair that."

A pause and a click from the phone, then: "Please turn your attention to the case in the locker."

He looked at the hard, rough plastic of the box with its as yet unchanged display screen. Then he looked at Rhys, knowing his face undoubtedly showed the same absurd mix of shock and understanding he saw on hers.

"You have to be kidding me," he said.

"Any airdropped munition capable of damaging the PIZ creates more problems than it solves," the phone-voice told them. "The blast would scatter spores over the northern hemisphere. It would also create a radiation cloud damaging to agriculture and long-term health. The device in the case is a low yield thorium bomb. Satellite X-ray scans of the PIZ indicate there are numerous deep hollows beneath the canopy. The blast from this device will incinerate the inner workings of the mass and create a localised but contained radiation plume that will destroy organic matter over the following months, including the spores."

Rhys let out a laugh, shrill and short. She rose from a crouch, wandering the crew cabin, hand rubbing continually at her stubbled scalp. "Strictly a one-way trip, I guess," she said in a breathless sigh she managed to keep from turning into a sob.

"You all volunteered for this mission," the phone-voice said. "As did the members of the previous research missions. All mathematical modelling predictions came up with the same result and no margin of error: if the M-Strain Bacillus is not stopped, all human life on this planet will become extinct in nine to twelve months."

As Huxley's eyes lingered on the case, the memory pain surged to previously unknown levels, as did the cop instinct. *Lies*, Plath had said. *Is this what she meant?* "What happened to the other missions?" he asked the phone.

"The memory suppression surgery used in the prior attempts proved insufficient to ensure success. The pathogen is capable of repairing memory synapses as well as altering them. For this attempt, surgical interventions were augmented by gene therapy and use of an adjuvant to boost immune response and combat the pathogen's ability to restore memory loss."

"So," Rhys said after a few calming breaths, "the red marks *are* a side effect of the inoculant?"

"Yes. You will have noticed they're growing in size and lividity as the amount of bacillus in your system increases."

"How long until it stops working?"

"Outcomes vary considerably depending on the subject, as you've seen."

Huxley exchanged a long look with Rhys. *Might as*

well tell them everything. "Plath said something," he told the phone. "When she . . . changed. She said this was all her idea. What did she mean?"

"That is irrelevant . . ."

"No. No! NO!" He thumped a hand to the floor alongside the phone. "No more of that. You want us to carry your big firework into the heart of that thing you answer my question, or we're not fucking going anywhere. Understand?"

Twenty seconds of silence, three slow clicks. "The volunteer you knew as Plath was a research physicist with an additional expertise in the biomedical applications of radiography. She was seconded to the team that oversaw initial subject trials as part of a joint international effort to combat the M-Strain Bacillus. She later contributed to the development of the thorium device. While this mission did not originate with her, she did form part of the planning staff and oversaw selection."

"She's a fucking psychopath," Rhys grated, pausing her pacing to stare at the phone. "You must've known that."

"Her personality profile raised concerns that were accommodated due to her expertise. The more troubling aspects of her character became apparent during the human trials stage."

"The Alzheimer's patients," Huxley said. "She got a real kick watching them die, I bet. Playing God, she'd have loved that."

"Her methods generated considerable discussion, however her results were inarguable."

Rhys rested her back against the wall, sliding down to sit on the floor. She looked at Huxley as she spoke, the clear and obvious question shining in moist, unblinking eyes. "So, the idea is we just stroll on in there, flip the switch and get atomised. I don't know who I used to be, but I'm pretty sure I wasn't a hero."

"You have a ten-year-old son," the phone-voice replied. The screen displayed a photograph of a boy, frozen in mid-run, casting a smile over his shoulder at the camera. Huxley thought he might have glimpsed some echo of Rhys's face in the boy's features but couldn't be sure. He held the tablet up for her to see. She stared at it with welling tears but no glimmer of recognition.

"Pynchon has a husband, parents and two brothers," the phone-voice went on, the tablet display running through a series of photographs. This time the familial resemblance was unmistakable and Huxley felt a pang of gratitude that Pynchon had been spared the sight of the family he didn't remember. It was a favour the voice couldn't reach him.

"Huxley, you have a wife." He felt no surprise at recognising the woman on the screen from his dream, she even wore the same hat. Her smile was a bright, wonderful thing he couldn't look at for long. He shuddered as the memory pain jolted through his head, unable to restrain himself from seeking knowledge, asking himself her name.

"Any reason you didn't tell us this before?" he asked, closing his eyes when the pain became unbearable.

"Prior studies indicate the memory-blocking procedures can be eroded by repeated exposure to personal details. Efforts were made to ensure the mission featured no reminders of who you were. All of you were kept isolated from each other during training so there would be no risk of familiarity."

"That's why you're a machine voice. No chance you might stir any memories."

"Correct."

"And now it doesn't matter?"

"Now the risk is considered tolerable due to your evident resistance to the bacillus and the need for motivated reasoning."

"Motivated reasoning?" He managed to smile. "You're asking us to die for people who might as well not exist to us."

"The entire human race is facing an extinction-level event. Norms of ethics and morality are no longer relevant." A pause then a single click. "However, the studies did indicate the human capacity for hope in survival situations to be an important factor. Turn your attention to the display on the device."

Leaning forward, Huxley saw that the LED screen now featured a number in black characters: 120.

"The readout is a timer," the voice went on. "Time to detonation can be manually adjusted using the keypad. Once the device is activated you will have a maximum of one hundred and twenty minutes to return to the boat and attempt escape. The blast radius will be contained by the mass of the PIZ."

"But we're still infected."

"You have demonstrated that the inoculant is an effective treatment. Further treatment will be required but our analysis indicates your chances of long-term survival can be estimated at ten per cent."

"Ten per cent?" Rhys lunged for the phone, putting it to her mouth and shouting into the receiver. "Fuck you!" She tossed it to Huxley and made for the ladder. "Turn it off."

"It doesn't have an off switch."

"Then just leave it here." She started climbing. "We need to talk about this. All three of us."

Chapter Twelve

"Handsome fella, don't you think?" Pynchon had insisted on looking at the photographs on the tablet, flicking through them with no sign of the discomfort that had assailed Huxley. He lingered longest at the first image, the man the phone-voice claimed to be his husband.

"Too tall for my tastes," Rhys said. She spoke with forced humour, eyes red from the tears she wiped away with angry determination. "Prefer men I don't have to stand on a box to kiss. At least, I think so."

"It didn't . . ." Pynchon winced, head bowing under the pressure of another agonised spasm. The bandage covering his wound was dark with matted blood, the seat he was strapped to streaked with it. He straightened and swallowed, breathing deep then trying again. "Didn't give you . . . a name, I suppose?"

"Sorry." Huxley shook his head.

"Wonder how long we were together." Pynchon

traced a trembling finger over the tablet. "Wonder why I didn't . . . dream about him."

"We, uh." Rhys coughed. "We have a decision to make. I think it should be unanimous."

"To nuke or not to nuke." Pynchon tossed the tablet onto the dashboard. "That's the shitty question." He reclined, quelling a shudder as his eyes flicked between them. "Not sure I should get a vote. After all . . . it's not like I'm going anywhere."

"Even so," Rhys said. "Unanimous. Or I'm not doing it."

"My vote may be biased." Pynchon gave a weak smile. "What with my imminent death and everything . . . but I vote yes. It's what we came to do. Remembering it doesn't matter. I *know* I chose to do this. Also, gotta nagging suspicion . . . so did you two."

"Two-hour timer," Huxley reminded him. "It's possible we can make it in there, get back to the boat, get you out of here . . ."

Pynchon flailed a hand in dismissal. "Enough . . . I voted. Your turn, Mister Policeman."

Huxley glanced back at the ladder, knowing the sat-phone lay below awaiting their word. The phone-voice was a machine but he also knew there were people behind it, a whole room full of white-coated or uniformed figures staring at a speaker in tense trepidation. He found he hated them. Hated them for the test subjects they had killed to make this all happen. Hated their remoteness from the horror they had sent others into. Where were they? Deep underground in some bunker? Safe from it all. Perhaps they even had food supplies and water to last a lifetime in the event their grand scheme went to shit. He was aware they felt they had no choice, that they were the guardians of a species driven to extremes. But still he hated them, because he was here and they weren't.

"They could be lying," he said. "We could carry that thing in there and it'll go boom the instant we switch on the timer. We go ahead with this, we have to assume we're not coming back."

"Agreed," Rhys said. "Your vote."

The promptness of his reply surprised him, even though he hadn't known how he would vote until the word slipped from his lips. "Yes."

Rhys's face remained impassive as she spoke, her tone as flat as anything said by the phone-voice: "Yes."

The receiver on the sat-phone must have been far more sensitive than they suspected, or a hidden listening device had eavesdropped on their discussion, because at that moment the boat's engines roared to life. A chorus of electronic whirring drew Huxley's attention to the dashboard. Panels slid aside to reveal hidden controls, each of the previously inert display screens flaring to life.

"Looks like I finally get to be . . . captain of the boat," Pynchon muttered. He reached out a tremulous hand to the newly revealed throttles but it quickly fell back into his lap, revealing the mark on his wrist. It had more than doubled in size and its texture was different, a glistening, angry red, swollen into a series of blisters. Huxley's hand instinctively went to his own mark, finding it marginally larger but the rough feel of it unchanged.

"I'll get the phone," he said.

"Steer twenty-three degrees to starboard of current heading," the phone-voice instructed. "Maintain speed. Hostile infected are known to proliferate in this area so keep an armed watch."

Huxley took over the controls while Pynchon advised on how to steer and interpret the various dials and readouts. Rhys retired to the aft deck with their remaining weapons, night-vision goggles in place. "Plenty of movement," she called to them above the growl of the engines. She had her carbine raised, continually tracking for targets as the boat ploughed through the water at walking pace. "Hard to tell one from another."

"Low level drone reconnaissance indicates the outer wall of the PIZ is dense and possibly inaccessible," the phone-voice said. "You will need to create an access point."

"How do we do that?" Huxley asked.

"Improvise."

"That's really useful. Thanks."

"Relax," Pynchon groaned, extending a finger to the chain gun controls. "This beauty can cut a hole in just about anything. Even if she can't, we've still got plenty of C-4 left."

"If we're left alone long enough to use it."

As if to underline his statement, Rhys opened fire, three rapid shots. Huxley looked over his shoulder to see tall spouts cascading in their wake. "Something below the surface," Rhys shouted by way of explanation. "Something big."

"Plath, maybe?" Pynchon wondered.

"Who knows?" Huxley adjusted the joystick controlling the tiller to bring the heading back in line with the readout on the display screen. "Got a feeling she isn't far away, though."

"Whatever happens . . ." Pynchon paused to cough, wiping the red smear from his lips. "Before this is over . . . you *get* her. For me. Yeah?"

Seeing a broad swathe of darkness loom in the fog beyond the spider-webbed windscreen, Huxley reached for the throttles and powered down to dead slow. "Yeah," he said. "I'll get her." He turned towards the aft deck, shouting to Rhys: "Looks like this is it."

"Lotta disturbed water out there," she called back, tracking her weapon in a broad arc. "Pretty sure they're chasing us!"

"Gun display," Pynchon said and Huxley moved to the chain gun controls. At Pynchon's direction, he adjusted the camera settings to reveal what lay ahead. The growths were taller and denser than they had seen before, a wall of overlapping, bulbous organics arcing away into the fog. In accordance with the phone-voice's prediction, Huxley could see no obvious entry point.

"OK." He moved his hands to the gun controls. "Where's best to aim?"

"Try . . ." Pynchon coughed, shuddering through the pain. "Try just above the waterline. Short bursts . . . Ammo stocks, remember."

"Right."

Huxley depressed the trigger for a half-second, fighting the urge to shrink from the screaming, accelerated rattle of the chain gun. A blaze of muzzle flash and tracer beyond the windscreen then a thin drift of vapour as he released the trigger. At first the damage appeared considerable, a ragged, dark lateral tear in the fabric of the wall. However, closer inspection of the gun camera screen revealed only marginal penetration and still nothing that resembled a way in.

"Try again," Pynchon told him. "Aim for the centre of the damaged region. Two second burst."

More flashing tracer, producing a chaotic, arcing torrent of shredded matter. When he stopped firing, Huxley saw a deeper rent in the wall, but no hole. His rising annoyance turned to surging anxiety at the sound of Rhys's carbine now repeatedly loosing off three-round bursts.

"Getting closer!" she shouted. Huxley glanced back to see her slotting a fresh magazine into her carbine. Beyond her, the water rippled and splashed in several places, a spiny, elongated limb rising up here and there to flail in predatory hostility.

"Looks like they don't appreciate our company," he observed to Pynchon.

"Fuck 'em . . . for being antisocial." Pynchon gestured at the gun controls. "Keep at it."

Huxley proceeded to blast the barrier with four long bursts before the chain gun ammunition ran out, creating a deep horizontal gash in the wall that refused to turn into an entry point. All the while, the bark of Rhys's carbine grew ever more frequent.

"All right," Pynchon groaned as they both stared at the damaged but unyielding wall. He coughed again but this time didn't bother to wipe the blood from his lips. "Reverse engines. And bring me the C-4."

Huxley could read Pynchon's intention in the resignation and resolve evident in his sagging features. "We could try priming a block and throwing it . . ."

"Just do it, Mister Policeman!" The soldier jerked as he grated out the order, clenched teeth red with blood. "We're all out of time."

Huxley bit down on further argument and took hold of the throttles, shouting a warning to Rhys: "We're scooting back! Look alive!"

Water rose in a white froth as he reversed the boat, closing the throttles when Pynchon began to nod. "Now get . . . the stuff. And pack enough ammo . . . for you and her. Hurry!"

Huxley scrambled down the ladder to the crew cabin,

filling two packs with all the pistol and carbine magazines he could find. He also added canteens of water
and some protein bars. *What the hell. Might get hungry.*
He tossed the packs to the upper deck then turned to
gather up the C-4, pausing at the sight of their remaining
flame-thrower. *Most things that live are scared of fire.* He
pulled the flame-thrower's strap over his head and hefted
the pack with the C-4. The climb up the ladder took
less than a minute but felt interminable, his ears thrumming with the sound of more gunfire from Rhys and
Pynchon's rasping demands he get a move on.

"Prime one block," Pynchon said when Huxley
opened the C-4 pack on the seat next to him. "Don't
worry about the timer."

Huxley jammed a detonator into a C-4 block then
raised a questioning gaze. "The controls . . ."

"I'll manage." Blood plumed from Pynchon's lips as
he shifted forward, clamping one hand to the steering
column and latching the other to the throttles. "Get
the bomb in the inflatable then . . . cast off. I'll go as
soon as you're clear."

Huxley wanted to say something but all he could
do was meet Pynchon's fevered but steady gaze. They
stared at each other for maybe two more seconds until
a thin, reflective smile played over the soldier's lips. "I
think his name . . . was Michael," he said, voice just a
thin croak now. "He looked . . . like a Michael."
Pynchon gave a minuscule jerk of his head and Huxley
tore his gaze free.

The bomb was less heavy than he expected, weighing about four kilos and easily lifted thanks to the handles its designers had placed on both sides. Even so, he had to shout for Rhys to help him get it to the top of the ladder and together they hauled it into the inflatable.

"Is he . . . ?" she began, turning towards the wheel-house.

"Staying. Yeah."

The surrounding water continued to ripple and splash as things beneath shifted, though a few judicious shots from Rhys succeeded in keeping them at bay. "I think they're confused," she said after casting another bullet at a flailing appendage a dozen yards off the stern. "Don't know how to react to all this."

"Hope they stay that way." Huxley dumped the flame-thrower into the inflatable and gave it the final shove it needed to slip into the water. "Get in."

He held the small craft in place as she climbed aboard, taking station at the outboard. Before jumping clear, he allowed himself one last glance at the wheel-house. Pynchon was just a dim, slumped silhouette against the displays. Huxley saw no movement but something told him the soldier still clung to life. *Surrender isn't in him.*

"We're clear!" he shouted, the instant the inflatable swung away from the boat's stern, the engines drowning his voice with a roar. The upsurge of churned water threatened to swamp them until Rhys activated the outboard and steered them clear. Huxley perched himself at the inflatable's prow, carbine at his shoulder. He should have been scanning the water for signs of Diseased but couldn't look away as the boat sped towards the barrier.

Pynchon steered the prow directly at the ragged tear left by the chain gun, building speed all the way. The boat shuddered and swayed upon colliding with the wall, water fountaining from the stern while the engines continued to try and drive it forward. Huxley's view of the prow was obscured but he guessed Pynchon had managed to bury the boat in the barrier up to the windscreen. He hoped it would be enough.

He turned to Rhys, gestured for her to get lower. "Best hunker do—"

The explosion came sooner than he expected. He knew there must have been multiple detonations as the single primed block of C-4 shared its energy with the others, but it felt like just one huge blast. Before protective instinct clamped his eyes shut, Huxley saw the boat evaporate in a flare of white-yellow light, the subsequent destruction swallowed by the blossom of flame. The surrounding water seethed with falling debris, most of it mercifully small. It also had the beneficial effect of dissuading the submerged Diseased from resurfacing, at least for the moment.

Huxley blinked and peered through the pall of grey-black smoke, finding the boat completely gone, the only sign of its existence a dark smear surrounding the rent in the wall. Pieces of matter fell from the edges of the damaged region, the smoke preventing Huxley from making out details.

"We're in," Rhys said, Huxley turning to find her peering at the rent with her night-vision goggles. "Can't see much of what's inside, but there's definitely a hole."

Something churned the water a few yards ahead of the prow, Huxley reflexively bringing his carbine to bear and blasting it with two quick shots. "Then let's go."

Rhys took them directly towards the rent, the inflatable infuriatingly slow as it traversed a surface scummed with bobbing debris and slicked by a rainbow-sheen of oil from the boat's disintegrated fuel tank. Twice more something raised bubbles in the surface in front of the prow and twice more Huxley shot at it. The wisdom of Pynchon's instruction to aim the chain gun just above the waterline became clear when Rhys was able to steer the inflatable straight into it. The blast had created a ramp of sorts from the destroyed growths, enabling her to push the prow clear of the water before killing the outboard. Huxley found the surface surprisingly firm as he leaped from the inflatable, holding the bow rope while Rhys went about unloading the remaining gear.

"Didn't skimp, did you?" she grunted, dragging the flame-thrower and one of the packs onto the ramp.

"Thought it best to be prepared."

The shape that sprang from the water behind her

bore a vague resemblance to a crab with its elongated limbs, each one ending in a hand deformed to resemble a pincer. However, the head that leered at them from atop shoulders thickened by impossibly honed muscle was all human. Huxley half expected to find Plath's stretched visage but this was a man, the face swollen into a grotesque parody of something from a superhero comic. As he trained his carbine on it, Huxley experienced a spark of amazement at the fact that it wore glasses. Round, John Lennon-style shades, concealing the eyes, the stems embedded in the enlarged flesh that had expanded the wearer's temples. He screamed as he lunged for Rhys, pincers aimed for her back, garbled words smothered by the crack of Huxley's carbine. Although he raised and fired the his sights one handed, his aim surprised him, one round through the Diseased's gaping, leering mouth to explode the rear of his skull. The bespectacled face went slack, trailing blood as the crab-like form collapsed back into the water and slipped from view.

The death appeared to act as a signal for the Diseased's aquatic brethren, water roiling as a forest of flailing, elongated arms broke the surface. "The bomb!" Huxley shouted to Rhys. He lowered his sights and fired a volley at the emerging Diseased, keeping hold of the bow rope as she dragged the bomb clear of the inflatable. She pushed it up the ramp then turned to retrieve the second pack. Another Diseased surged into view at the inflatable's stern, this one with arms tipped by daggers of revealed white bone. Rhys reeled away as the daggers descended, shredded rubber rising as it ripped into the inflatable's hull.

"Leave it!" Huxley shouted, seeing Rhys dart a hand towards the remaining pack. "Let's go!"

He released the bow rope, raising his carbine to his shoulder, thumbing the selector to fully automatic and unleashing the rest of his magazine into the Diseased's face. As it slumped in lifeless ruin, another, smaller creature scrabbled onto its back. It splayed webbed hands at Huxley while its child's face chattered a set of elongated teeth. Huxley slung his carbine and dived for the flame-thrower, activating the igniter and pressing the trigger, releasing a fiery torrent that caught the chattering Diseased in mid-air as it leaped at him.

The thing landed close to his boot, wreathed in flame but still moving, making a sound that was far too much like a human child in extreme pain. He kicked it into the water and backed away, triggering the weapon again when he saw more Diseased claw their way clear of the water. The fire-stream swept over them, setting each alight and producing a chorus of shrieks, then licked over the oil-covered water beyond. The blast of heat and displaced air sent him onto his back, making him grateful for the fact that he had no hair, though he was obliged to expend a few seconds pawing at his eyebrows to banish a cascade of embers.

Regaining his feet, he found the water dotted by islands of flame. Ripples disturbed the surface in a few places but apparently the surviving Diseased still harboured some survival instincts and none revealed themselves.

"Huxley!" Rhys hissed urgently and he turned to join her at the crest of the ramp. She crouched in the ragged hole created by Pynchon's sacrifice, night-vision goggles in place, scanning an interior that appeared solid dark to Huxley.

"Movement?" he asked, settling his own goggles over his eyes.

"Nothing." He saw her mouth form a bemused grimace. "Lot more spacious than I expected."

Activating his goggles, he saw what she meant. The green and black scene before him resembled a cathedral more than anything else. Tall growths formed dense spiralling columns ascending to an undulating ceiling twenty feet high. Lowering his gaze, he found the floor a sprawl of pooled water interspersed with ridges that resembled the ribs of some fallen titan.

They both started as the sat-phone clicked then spoke: "Proceed inside. Further delay will endanger the mission."

"Oh, shut up!" Rhys snapped back. Taking a breath, she glanced over her shoulder at the flame-speckled water and sighed. "Though, she's probably got a point."

"You want to carry it?" Huxley asked, nodding to the bomb case she had dragged to her side.

"Wouldn't want to undermine your masculine pride." She gestured at the flame-thrower. "Swapsies?"

Chapter Thirteen

Huxley found the air within the structure unpleasantly humid. This, coupled with the weight of his pack, weapon, and the nuclear explosive device he carried, produced constant sweat and mounting fatigue. His discomfort was exacerbated by the stench of mingled corruption, oil and sewage that arose whenever they were forced to wade through a stretch of pooled water. He knew that he trod on not just the remains of those who had died here, but the collected effluent of a dead city. Evidence of its demise was all around. Mangled cars and vans protruded from arcing walls of what Rhys had taken to calling 'veg-meat' along with twisted lampposts and traffic signs.

A few hundred paces in, they found a double-decker bus, its passengers providing the seeds for the huge growth sprouting from its roof. Of course, there were bones and bodies too. Curiously, the bones were mostly human but the bodies were not. Dogs, cats and rats snarled in frozen fear or anger from their veg-meat prisons, crushed, mangled and part-rotted, but other-wise unchanged. The bones were a different story. Denuded of flesh in most cases but all showing signs of deformity. One in particular was so grossly altered that Huxley came to an involuntary halt, transfixed by its sheer ugliness.

The cranium had been narrowed and stretched. The eyes, teeth and cheekbones were a distorted convex mask that could only be described as demonic. It lay amid the remains of a car, a small electric hatchback, its structure shredded, presumably by the scythe-like claws this Diseased skeleton bore at the end of its six-feet-long arms. He had a vague sense of what it had looked like when still clad in skin and muscle but no firm mental image, except to say that it would truly have been a living nightmare.

"Hey, phone-voice lady," he said, continuing to linger in scrutiny of the skeleton. The phone had been guiding their steps, clicking every now and then before uttering an instruction to "bear left in twenty metres" or "keep straight". Sometimes, the route it dictated turned out to be an impassable wall of growths, confirming its claim that this grotesque cavern system was impene-trable to the varied imaging tech at the disposal of those Huxley had begun to think of as their "Overseers". Apart from directions, the phone hadn't consented to offer any more enlightening details on this new en-vironment, something he was no longer willing to tolerate.

"Bear right in fifty metres," the phone-voice said, updating a prior instruction with typical blandness.

"Forget that for now," he said. "It occurs to me you haven't told us where the M-Strain came from. Origin story. Patient zero, all that shit. There must have been one, right?"

He expected another statement regarding the irrelevance of his question. Instead the phone clicked twice before providing a prompt response. "The origin has never been determined. Informed speculation produced conjecture but no testable or substantive theories."

"But not aliens, right?" Rhys asked. She had come to a halt a few yards on, flame-thrower held at waist height, sparing the phone a sour glance as she turned in a slow circle, scanning for threats.

"No evidence of extraterrestrial origin has ever been found," it stated.

"There must be something," Huxley insisted. "It can't just have sprung out of nowhere."

"The first identifiable case was a forty-three-year-old male warehouse worker located in the Enfield borough of London. Witnesses reported a rapid transformation into something they insisted looked a great deal like a werewolf. There were several deaths before the subject was subdued. Some have suggested that a box containing spores was delivered to the warehouse at some point. It handled international deliveries so, if the hypothesis is correct, the consignment could have originated anywhere. However, it is likely there were numerous prior cases missed due to the absence of a violent outcome."

"Werewolf," Huxley repeated, gaze still captured by the grotesquely deformed face. He discerned something reptilian in it now, the curve of the jaw and the pointed teeth adding to the sense that he was looking at a dinosaur. *Something that might scare you as a kid watching* Jurassic Park, *or an old stop-motion Harryhausen flick.*

"Nightmares," he said, realisation adding a soft gasp to his voice. "That's what it does. Turns you into your nightmares."

"The M-Strain Bacillus multiplies at a greatly increased rate in the centres of the brain most connected with memory," the phone-voice said. "Also emotion. Fear and memory combined could be said to equal a nightmare. Via a mechanism yet to be identified, the M-Strain is capable of forcing rapid mutation of human cells, guiding the process to produce deformities that are sometimes vaguely recognisable as characters from popular culture."

"A plague of nightmares," Rhys said. "I'm finding it increasingly hard to believe this thing had a natural origin."

The laughter started then, a faint but unmistakable echo that seemed to come from multiple directions. Rhys tensed, flame-thrower raised, while Huxley set down the bomb and unslung his carbine. The laughter persisted for some time, clear in its mockery and, once

Huxley detected the female tones that inflected it, recognisable in origin.

"Plath," he said.

"Got here ahead of us." Rhys's lips drew back from her teeth as she brandished the flame-thrower, answering the laughter with a loud snarl: "Got something here for ya! Come and get it, bitch!"

The laughter continued with unconcerned hilarity for another minute or two, dwindling into a chuckle then fading away.

"How'd she get in here without blasting a hole like we did?" Huxley asked the phone.

"Unknown."

"Seems she found our conversation amusing. Why's that?"

"Also unknown."

Liar. He sighed and shouldered his carbine, hefting the bomb. "How long until we can set the timer on this thing?"

"Keep following my directions. The location of the Primary Detonation Site will become evident soon."

"The PDS, huh?" Rhys said, straightening and resuming her slosh through the stinking water. "You folks really love naming things, don't you?"

Another hour of navigating befouled pools and heaving their burdens over growth mounds brought them to the largest space they had encountered yet. Emerging from a narrow confluence of growth columns, Huxley drew up short as his night-vision goggles were swamped by a blaze of light. Removing them, he found a single street lamp casting a mostly steady glow over a portion of road abutting a park. Roots snaked over tarmac and pavement before enmeshing themselves in the park railings. Beyond this a small patch of green lawn ended abruptly in a wall of dense matter. Opposite the park lay a parade of shops not yet swallowed by the encroaching veg-meat.

They paused to survey it all, Huxley using his carbine sight to peer into every shadowed corner. Since assaulting them with laughter, Plath had remained silent and unseen yet Huxley harboured no doubts she surveilled every step of this journey. *Waiting for us to rest*, he concluded. *Sleep, even. Like we could in here.*

"No prizes for guessing what he was afraid of," Rhys said, using the flame-thrower to gesture at the park railings. Seeing a figure splayed across the wrought-iron barrier, Huxley moved closer. He guessed it was a man from the breadth of the torso but the level of deformity and covering of roots made it hard to tell. The body was pierced by railings through the legs and arms. These were outstretched, the head thrown back, mouth gaping, bone sprouting from the skull in a spiny circle.

Not just a circle, Huxley thought, stepping closer. "A crown," he muttered aloud, gaze shifting to the hands, where more bone had sprouted to form the semblance of nails hammered into the palms.

"Think this happened more than three days ago?" Rhys quipped with an arched eyebrow.

"Whoever you were," he said, turning away, "I'm guessing you weren't Catholic."

"*Au contraire.* I can remember the words to the Hail Mary, Our Father, the Act of Contrition and a load of other shit, in English, Spanish and Latin, no less. On the boat I'd recite it to myself, expecting to feel . . . something. I didn't. Maybe faith just doesn't survive surgically induced amnesia."

Huxley inclined his head at the cruciform corpse. "Looks like it survives the disease."

"For all the good it did." The sardonic curve of her lips faded abruptly, gaze narrowing as it scanned the parade of shops. "Upper window. Above the mini-market. See it?"

He saw it: a dim, flickering yellow glow behind besmirched and cracked window glass. "Something on fire?"

Rhys shook her head. "No smoke. I think it's a candle." She took a firmer grip on the flame-thrower. "Could be *her.* Trying to lure us into something."

"She'd never be that obvious."

"Check it out or move on?"

"Move on," the phone-voice said. "This is not the mission."

"Really?" Rhys leaned closer to Huxley, hissing into the phone's receiver. "And who says you get a vote? Just for that, I think we will take a look."

"Rhys," Huxley said as she turned and strode towards the mini-market. She didn't turn, kicking in the part-destroyed door and disappearing inside.

"Signs of aggression," the phone-voice said. "Irrational thinking . . ."

"Shut the fuck up," Huxley snapped, taking a firmer grip on the bomb and following Rhys at an awkward trot.

The interior of the mini-market featured bare shelves and a floor strewn with ravaged food packaging. A light bulb flickered in one of the refrigerated cabinets, the smell it exuded indicating it had stopped functioning weeks ago. A desiccated body lay in front of a self-checkout terminal. Unlike all the others encountered since stepping into this place, it showed no signs of deformity.

"Skull bashed in," Rhys said after a cursory glance at the dried matter leaking from the corpse's sundered head. "Looter, maybe?"

"Or someone who tried to stop a looter. Must've happened pretty early on, just when things started falling apart."

Rhys shone her flashlight at the rear of the market. "Door back there."

She shifted the flame-thrower onto her back and switched to her carbine, carefully easing the door open to reveal the stairs beyond. A dim, inconstant glow from above played over the carpeted steps. She started up without hesitation, Huxley briefly debating the wisdom of leaving the bomb behind before dismissing it and following. He dragged his burden up the stairs one handed, his pistol in the other, the hard plastic emitting a soft but audible thump with every step.

"So much for stealth," Rhys murmured, crouching at the top of the stairs. She tracked her carbine around the landing, finding nothing to shoot at, the weapon halting at the door leading to the room overlooking the street. It was outlined in soft, wavering light, a repeating, dull click sounding within.

"Could just torch the place and move on," Huxley pointed out, seeing the sweat beading Rhys's upper lip.

"Curiosity," she said, forcing a smile and a shrug. "Can't help it. Some things amnesia doesn't erase, I guess."

She straightened to a half-crouch, approaching the door slowly, then darting out a hand to shove it open. She stepped back a little, carbine ready to counter any threat with a burst of fully auto. But, instead of firing, Rhys became very still. Huxley moved forward to peer over her shoulder.

The man sat on a two-seater leather couch flanked by tall stacks of neatly arranged food cans, most of them empty as far as Huxley could tell. He wore a striped shirt and grey slacks, the fabric stiff from lack of washing. His lowered head was mostly bald with tufts of unkempt grey fringing his ears and nape. His scalp shone in the meagre light of a candle stub burning on a small dish on the coffee table before him. The man didn't look up to regard their intrusion, hands moving over the surface of a large jigsaw puzzle covering most of the table. It was nearly complete, with only a small gap in the centre, rapidly diminishing as the man's deft hands took pieces from the carefully arranged row alongside the puzzle, slotting them into place with unconscious precision.

"Erm," Rhys said. "Hello."

The man didn't pause in his task, but did consent to raise his head. Huxley tensed in readiness, expecting to find the leering, gnashing maw of some creature plucked from modern media's ample supply of horrors. But the face he saw was just that of a tired old man. Curiously, he saw no fear in the old man's eyes. Instead, they creased as he offered a thin, weary smile of welcome.

"Hello to you, young lady," he said with the precise, slightly lilting inflection of someone who had learned English as a second language. "Please do come in. Your friend too." His hands didn't stop as he spoke, each piece clicking into the near-finished image on the table. "I regret I have no refreshment to offer."

He smiled again and returned his focus to the puzzle. Rhys shot Huxley a wary, baffled glance and stepped into the room. She kept her weapon trained on the old man, maintaining a wide gap as she edged around the table to the right. Huxley went left, sliding his pistol into its holster. Something – cop instinct probably – told him this aged puzzler presented no threat at all.

"May I?" Huxley asked, resting a hand on the armchair positioned next to the couch.

The old man inclined his head, eyes still on his puzzle. "Please do."

The sheer pleasure of sitting brought a surprised groan from Huxley, one that drew a chuckle from their host. "You have been travelling a while, then?"

"Yes, sir. A long while, at least it feels like it."

"So you are soldiers from America."

Huxley looked at Rhys, finding her engaged in a careful inspection of the room, a suspicious scowl on her face.

"It might surprise you to hear that we have no idea what we are," Huxley told the old man. "I'm probably some kind of detective and my friend is some kind of doctor. But we can't even tell you our real names."

"Why is that?"

Seeing absolutely no purpose in a lie, Huxley said, "They took our memories. It was this whole surgery, implant deal. Not sure how it worked, exactly. But it protected us, from the disease, y'know."

"Ah." The old man clicked another piece into place. "Very clever."

Huxley angled his head to gain a better look at the puzzle. Instead of a landscape or classical painting, it was a photograph, a family photograph in fact. Six people, two women, four men, arms about each other's shoulders, laughing. The man at the centre of the group stood a little stiffer than the others, attempting a more dignified pose that had apparently amused those around him. The picture had been taken at the moment when their contained laughter burst. The stiff man was younger with far fewer lines to his forehead than this old man on his two-seater couch surrounded by a dwindling food supply, but Huxley still recognised him.

"Your family?" Huxley asked.

"Yes indeed. The last time we were all together. My neighbour took this photograph. My wife sent it to a company that makes jigsaw puzzles from any picture. It was my sixty-fifth birthday present."

He fell silent as the final piece slotted into place. Huxley watched his finger tremble as it tapped the last piece, a tremble that spread to his hand, then his arm until soon his entire body shook.

"Forgive my rudeness," the old man said as he immediately went about disassembling the puzzle, hands splaying over the finished image, breaking it apart. "But I must do this, you see."

"Why?" Rhys asked him.

"It holds me. I must do this."

"Holds you? To what?"

The old man began to separate pieces from larger segments, turning them face down on the table. "To here. To me. To them. That way I continue."

Huxley looked around the room, struck by the sense of careful organisation gradually gone awry. Ornaments gathered dust on shelves but not as much as they should have. Sparse cobwebs glittered in the candlelight. "You've been here from the start," he said. "Haven't you?"

The old man bobbed his head, hands still busy on the disassembled puzzle. "After . . ." He paused, Huxley seeing his throat constrict, a distance showing in his gaze although his hands never stopped moving. "At the start . . . The first day when it all began to happen. There was a great deal of noise in the street outside, screaming and shouting. They went to look. I was in the storeroom . . ." He swallowed. "After that, I saw no reason to leave. My wife . . ." He made a sound that Huxley thought might be an attempt at a rueful laugh, but it instantly transformed into a shrill screech of pain. The sound might have been unbearable if the old man hadn't contained it, raising a hand to jam the knuckle of his thumb between his teeth. Blood welled and trickled over scabbed and scarred skin. Huxley fought the instinct to reach out to him, feeling more impotent and angry than at any point since waking on the boat.

The old man lowered his hand after a few seconds, showing no concern at the blood he dripped over his puzzle pieces. When he spoke again his voice was as pleasant and even as when he greeted them. "My wife said we should have left when the first soldiers came. One of many times she was right when I was wrong." This time he succeeded in voicing his laugh.

"The first soldiers?" Huxley leaned forward in the armchair, cop instinct piquing. "Soldiers came here before your . . . before it started to happen?"

"Oh yes. About a week before, in fact. They did not dress as soldiers and came in vans that had no insignia. But I was a soldier once and I know how they look, uniforms or not. They had armoured vests under their jackets and weapons too. They parked their vans around the warehouses opposite the stadium. Police came too, cordoned off streets, arrested people who started to film with their phones. Of course, they couldn't stop everyone but my daughter told me nothing appeared on the Twitter or the other places. There was nothing on the news either."

The phone clicked then but the voice didn't speak. Huxley unhooked it from his fatigues and stared into the receiver, head filled with the image of the Overseers in their uniforms and white coats all exchanging tense glances.

"Did you ever find out what they were doing?" he asked the old man.

"No, no. They stayed for an hour. My daughter captured video of them taking many boxes and computers out of the building, escorting people into the vans too. She said she saw one man struggling but the soldiers got him out of sight very quickly. When they left the building was shut up, police stationed around it. People didn't like it, of course. Rumours flew all around. My wife said we should leave, just in case. I said we were a month behind on the business loan . . ." He paused again, turning over the final piece so that they all lay face down. A brief moment of hesitation, palsy once again causing his arm then his body to tremble before he began turning the pieces over.

"Any idea what was in the warehouses opposite the stadium?" Huxley asked.

"All manner of things, there are several there." With all the pieces now turned, the old man set about sorting them into piles: edges, corners, the others grouped according to colour. "You have a purpose here, I assume?"

"Yes." Huxley slapped a hand to the bomb's case, forcing a jovial note into his voice. "When this thing goes bang it's all over, so we're told."

"Will it kill everything here?"

"That's the plan. You've still got time to try and make it out . . ."

Another shrill, pained exclamation bubbled from the old man's lips, though mercifully this time he managed to quell it without biting his hand. "No. There is nowhere to go for me. This is where I belong. This is my reward and my punishment." He blinked wet eyes and began to slot pieces together, forming a corner with swift dexterity. "At first I could maintain a routine. Eating, cleaning, toilet. I closed my ears to all the terrible things I heard outside and mostly I sat and I completed this puzzle. I maintained the routine for a long time, but not now. Now there is only this."

He stopped, the tremble returning as he straightened, turning to face Huxley. "When I was a child I would run around my grandmother's garden in Mumbai, until one day a snake bit me. It hurt a great deal. So much I thought I would die." His hands moved to the buttons of his shirt, carefully undoing them to reveal the skin beneath. Huxley couldn't suppress the revolted shudder that ran through him, unable to look away from the sight. Small marks covered the old man's flesh from chest to belly, and they seemed to ripple. Huxley's disgusted but fascinated gaze saw that each one was opening and closing, gaping like the mouths of goldfish. *No*, he corrected himself, seeing the minuscule fangs protruding from each mouth, leaking venom as they gnashed. *Snakes.*

"They bite less when I do the puzzle," the old man said, shaking from head to foot now. "I think it slows it, remembering the good things, I mean to say. If you can keep the bad thoughts at bay, you live. But no one can do that for ever." He blinked, tears trickling down his twitching face. "I request that you kill me before you leave."

Huxley found he couldn't meet the old man's gaze, keeping his eyes on the puzzle pieces as he rasped out a soft response. "I don't think I can do that, sir."

"You must." Desperation trilled in the old man's voice. "I deserve it. You see, I killed someone. A young man. My customer. He tried to steal from me so I killed him. His name was Frederico. He would come in every few days and buy a six-pack of the cheapest lager in stock and a copy of the *Racing Post*. He would give me tips, for bets you see. They never won."

The body downstairs with the smashed skull. One of countless murders in a city claimed by nightmares.

"It changes things, you know." The old man's tone softened, hands returning to the puzzle. "Memories. It twists them, makes lies of them. I loved my family more than anything in this world, and they deserved my love. But, whenever I allow myself to pause, I remember things. Things that make my wife into a liar and cheat, my sons into thieves. Things that I know never happened. I think it feeds on ugliness. I think it needs us to hate, that is how it spreads. If you do not kill me, I know I will surrender to that ugliness, and then—" his fingers splayed on the pieces "—they truly will be dead and I will no longer be . . . me."

His last word was a barely legible explosion of spit and desperation and he immediately returned to his task. His hands moved so fast they seemed to blur, turning and fitting pieces together with a speed and accuracy far beyond merely human skill.

"Huxley," Rhys said. He looked up to find her inclining her head at the door, finger moving to the fire selector on her carbine. Huxley shook his head and stood up, releasing his hold on the bomb and drawing his pistol. He expected his arm to shake as he trained the muzzle on the old man's temple, expected a bout of last-minute cowardice, but it didn't happen.

★ ★ ★

"First soldiers." Huxley held the phone close to his mouth as they exited the mini-market, his words clipped and very precise. "Soldiers who showed up at the warehouses opposite the stadium. Soldiers in plain clothes who arrived weeks before the army. You heard all that, right?"

No clicks or hesitation, but the very promptness of the response made him suspicious. "M-Strain infection is known to produce hallucinations and false memories. The situation described by the Diseased you encountered simply did not occur."

"Bullshit. You selected me for this because I'm a detective. Years of experience getting to the truth makes me a living lie detector, whether I remember how or not. He wasn't delusional and he wasn't lying." He and Rhys paused beside the overgrown ruin of a police car while he continued to harangue the phone. "Get it straight, whoever the fuck you people are, we are not taking one more step until you tell us exactly what—"

The shot was poorly aimed, missing him by a clear foot to smash through what remained of the shop window behind. His response was instinctive and immediate, crouching behind the remains of the police car, dropping the phone, one hand still clutching the bomb case while he raised the carbine with the other. Rhys had already begun returning fire, two aimed shots fired into the sprawl of growth dominating the park. He couldn't see what she was shooting at until he caught the answering flare of a muzzle flash, a flickering strobe accompanied by a rhythmic growl that told of automatic fire. He ducked, shredded metal and shattered glass lacerating the street.

"She got herself a gun," he observed to Rhys.

She crouched behind the police car's rear wheel hub, shaking her head and shrinking from another burst of fire. "It's not her." The firing ceased before Huxley could ask what she meant. "He's out," Rhys grunted, bobbing up, carbine at her shoulder, snapping off two more shots. Huxley saw something shift behind the park railings, a grey-green, vaguely human figure staggering as Rhys's rounds struck home.

Huxley put his eye to his carbine sight, the figure leaping into stark clarity. It was a man, or had been. Growths snaked over his form from ankles to head, obscuring identifying details. However, the bullpup assault rifle he held in his enlarged hands marked him as a soldier. Another salvo from Rhys tore gobbets of veg-meat from the figure's chest, making him stagger but causing no appreciable delay as he went about reloading his rifle.

"Covering's too thick," Huxley said, centring the sight's reticule on the soldier's forehead. The shot tore away the growths covering his face, producing a plume of blood. Still he didn't fall. "Shit." Huxley aimed for the same spot, firing again. It took three attempts before he succeeded in putting a bullet in the Diseased's brain. Once again, he failed to fall, reeling about and firing wildly, bullets striking sparks from the railing and tearing holes in exposed tarmac.

Huxley and Rhys crouched low as the bullets zipped around them, cautiously raising their heads when the soldier's rifle fell silent. "Seriously?" Rhys said. Apparently robbed of the motor skills required to reload his rifle, the Diseased soldier had dropped it. He charged towards them, arms outstretched and a guttural cry of wordless fury emerging from his mouth along with a spray of blood. He continued to rage after colliding with the park railings, casting out a torrent of dark-red fluid, arms flailing through the gaps in the iron barrier.

"Fuck," Rhys swore in a soft, elongated sigh, Huxley turning to find her staring at something on the pavement. The sat-phone lay shattered in several pieces, plastic and wiring scattered. Stooping to pick it up, Huxley knew pressing the green button to be a pointless act but he did it anyway.

"Now where do we go?" Rhys asked, voice laden with weary despair.

Huxley spared a glance at the mini-market's upstairs window where the candle still flickered. "The stadium sounds like a good bet."

"Great. I'll ask for directions, shall I?" Rhys hefted her flame-thrower and strode towards the still gibbering and flailing Diseased pressing himself into the railings. "Excuse me, sir. Is there a stadium nearby, perchance? No? Oh well, fuck you then."

The flame-thrower's roar smothered the soldier's enraged cries and the short-lived scream of pain that followed. He took an absurdly long time to die, arms waving and hands clawing at Rhys with fingers reduced to blackened stubs. She blasted him twice more, stepping back with a disgusted grimace at the stench as he finally subsided into ashen stillness.

She stared at the smoking mess for a short while then sniffed. "Guess the old man might've had a map somewhere. *A–Z*, maybe."

"No need." Huxley pointed over her shoulder at a part-obscured junction twenty yards on. The sign had been twisted and morphed by the growths to resemble an arch, but some words remained legible, the most salient being the four positioned next to an upwards pointing arrow: Twickenham Stadium 1 Mile.

Chapter Fourteen

Deciding they needed to move faster, they divested themselves of any excess weight. Rhys surrendered her carbine for the combination of pistol and flame-thrower. Huxley kept his carbine and pistol but dumped everything else save the bomb. They both retained their night-vision goggles, electing to spare the batteries until needed. Before setting off, they gulped down protein bars and drank the remaining water in their canteens. With only a mile to go there seemed little point in saving it. Huxley hadn't realised the scale of his hunger until his first bite, wolfing down the whole bar and quickly unwrapping another. He wondered if his hunger arose from the imminence of his own demise, some innate, desperate desire to accrue sensation before the chance to do so disappeared for ever. Or he was just tired and really hungry.

Beyond the street sign arching over the junction the growth columns became denser and more numerous, forming a forest of sorts which soon narrowed into something resembling catacombs. Street lights continued to flicker among it all, meaning they didn't need to resort to the goggles. Still, it was an unnervingly quiet place of plentiful shadows and yet more floodwater, so the stink was as bad as ever.

"Raised some interesting questions, didn't he?" Rhys asked, leading the way once more while Huxley followed with the bomb. The density of the growths obscured much of the urban landscape but the edges of roadways and pavements were easily discerned, enabling them to follow a reasonably straight line.

"Who?" Huxley asked.

"The jigsaw man. What he said about the disease. Doesn't just feed off memories, it changes them. Like it needs us to hate, needs our rage. My guess is hormones act as a stimulus, adrenaline, cortisone, all the chemical soup that churns when you're stressed. That's its fuel."

"Makes sense." Huxley spoke in a cautious mutter, concerned by the rapid animation of Rhys's speech. *Aggressive. Irrational, maybe?* Words the phone-voice would have said. Words he thought now.

"And to do that it has to play with our thoughts, change our memories," Rhys went on. "Makes me wonder. About Dickinson, I mean. Had she really been abused or was it just something the M-Strain cooked up to make her crazy?"

"Also raises the possibility that Plath might not be the psycho we think she is."

"Oh, she's every bit the psycho we think she is. I doubt the M-Strain needed any help with her. She had a whole headful of bad shit to draw on already. Wouldn't surprise me to learn that the people who survived longest in this place without showing signs of mutation were the psychopaths, the sociopaths, the selfish, deluded fucks who do so well in this shitty world . . ."

"Rhys . . ."

". . . and why not? Why wouldn't they? We already made a fucked-up world for them to flourish in, a world where all the greedy, thieving liars get to rule the rest of us. Why wouldn't they flourish in this one too?" She had come to halt now, shoulders slumping in fatigue although her invective flowed thick and fast. "The first soldiers. Who were they? Not a coincidence. Can't be . . ."

"Rhys."

She started at the hardness of his voice, falling silent with a gasp. She didn't turn and he saw her tremble.

"Have you remembered anything?" he asked her.

She didn't speak for long enough to make him acutely aware that he had both hands full with a nuclear explosive device. Should she choose to immolate him he would have great difficulty drawing his pistol in time. However, when she did finally turn, his fear dissipated at the sight of her face. Instead of a picture of delusion he saw only grief. No deformity and no unreasoning hate. Just a profound sorrow that was, in its own way, just as hard to look upon.

"That's just the point," she said in a hoarse whisper. "I looked at my son and I felt nothing. There should have been something, shouldn't there? If he was real. If I was really a mother. There should be something. But I didn't know him. I don't even dream about him. I just dream about that fucking ER shift. Whatever they did to us, it's permanent. Even if we make it out of here, the people we were died before this whole journey ever began."

"He's real." Huxley removed a hand from the bomb case to grip her shoulder, drawing her closer. "As real as me and you and the woman I'm married to. We have to hold on to that. It's all we have."

She rested her forehead against his chest, allowing herself a few gasping sobs before drawing back. "I just wish they'd told me his name."

They found the first flower a short while later. The catacombs narrowed for a time then opened out to create cavernous tunnels. For the first time since leaving the river Huxley saw fog again. It lay in a thick bank towards the end of the largest tunnel, perhaps indicating a larger space, one that might even be open to the air.

"Pretty," Rhys commented, pausing next to a mound of growths. Moving closer Huxley perceived a vague resemblance to an embracing couple. Had they been lovers? Friends? Strangers even, seeking some comfort from another human body in the face of oblivion. The object of Rhys's interest sprouted from what he thought might have been the head of the larger figure: a short stem crowned by a closed cup of dark-red petals.

"Haven't noticed much plant life," Rhys added. "Every tree or bush we've seen has been dead or close to it."

"I don't think it's a plant," Huxley said. He nodded to the fog-shrouded tunnel ahead. More dark-red flowers covered its floor and curving walls. Moving closer, he saw these were open, the petals drawn back to reveal a mouth-like opening. Glancing ahead, he found the flowers became thicker in number as he began to emerge from the tunnel, petals spread even wider to form a carpet of red blossoms stretching away into the most impenetrable crimson haze he had seen yet. Cars, trucks, and buses rose from the field, blanketed into vague outlines by the flowers.

"They're responsive to light," Rhys said, coming to his side. She activated the flame-thrower's igniter and stooped, bringing it close to one of the half-opened blossoms. The petals twitched and spread, a small but visible pink cloud of particulate matter emerging from the mouth in a gentle puff. Rhys straightened, surveying the swathe of flowers before them. "The nursery of the M-Strain Bacillus," she said, turning to Huxley, brows arched in an obvious question.

"We're not quite at the heart yet." He took a firmer hold on the bomb case and resumed wading his way through the flowers. The ground felt uneven beneath his boots, rough growth mounds interspersed with infrequent patches of bare tarmac and pavement. "We haven't reached the stadium."

"Twickenham Stadium." She fell in alongside. "Sounds very quaint, don't you think? Almost Hobbit-esque. Wonder what they played there."

"Soccer," he said. "It's always soccer here, even though they call it football."

"Rugby."

They froze. The voice had come from the fog, echoing in a way that sounded far from natural. Front, behind, right, left. Huxley couldn't tell. They had drawn close to one of the overgrown buses, Rhys training the flame-thrower on it as the most obvious hiding place. Huxley crouched, setting down the bomb case to unsling his carbine.

"They played rugby," the voice said. Despite the echo Huxley had no trouble recognising it. His carbine sight tracked over a field of red blossoms that merged with the haze about twenty feet away. He saw no movement and when Plath spoke again, he still couldn't discern a location.

"I have to confess, I never thought you two would make it this far," she told them, her tone lightly conversational. "Always thought it would be just Pynchon and me at the end. All the models predicted it."

"That's really fascinating," Rhys replied, face set in a mask of eager animus. "Why not come on over and we'll talk about it some more?"

A faint, hollow laugh. Hearing a soft, rhythmic

ticking to his right, Huxley jerked the carbine up, the sight revealing beads of moisture detaching themselves from an overgrown car's shattered wing mirror.

"So keen to kill me, Doctor?" Plath asked. "I guess the Hippocratic oath doesn't survive amnesia."

"First do no harm." Rhys pivoted slowly, eyes bright and finger tense on the flame-thrower's trigger. "You are nothing but harm. I'd guess you were a pestilence long before all this shit came along."

Another sound, a soft rustling, Huxley seeing only a swirl of displaced mist.

"Pestilence is a silly word." Plath's words were accompanied by a weary sigh. "It suggests that sickness is somehow an aberration in the environment we evolved to live in. In fact the opposite is true. This world is designed to kill us and we are designed to live only long enough to reproduce. That is the true balance of nature. I can see it now. Disease is not an aberration, even this one, despite its unique origin. *We* are the aberration. A species so successful it eventually devours its environment and secures its own doom. What is happening now is merely a necessary corrective."

Rhys took her hand from the flame-thrower's trigger to pat Huxley's arm, nodding urgently at the bus. When he replied with a doubtful grimace, she added a hard squeeze of her hand for emphasis. He nodded, reaching down to take hold of one of the bomb case handles. Rhys started towards the flower-shrouded vehicle, moving low and slow while he followed, dragging the case.

"Don't you want to know?" Plath asked them as they skirted the bus. Huxley strained to discern some sound from within the vehicle, hearing nothing. Rhys, however, remained fixed on it, ploughing an arcing line through the flowers as she led them closer.

"Know what?" Huxley called back, hoping the answer would reveal a target.

"Why, the origin of course. The genesis of the M-Strain Bacillus."

"Sure." His eyes roved the misted flowers, carbine aimed one handed. "Tell us all about it."

A pause during which he entertained the absurd image of Diseased and deformed Plath stepping up to a podium, notes in hand, a professor about to deliver her keynote lecture. "It's both surprising and mundane," she said finally. "Predictable and incredible."

This time Huxley had a definite sense that she was closer. He reached out, patting Rhys's shoulder to bring her to a stop. She halted with a visible effort, Huxley sensing a desperate keenness to unleash her flames on the bus.

"It's all about hubris in the end, you see," Plath went on. "The arrogant conceit that has possessed humanity since an ape first struck sparks from flint. The delusion that we can transcend the natural laws that bind us. Always we are driven to understand the world, not for the pleasure of enlightenment, but for control. For power. We are a species engaged in an endless quest to bend nature to our will. Specifically, in this case, the power of mutation."

Rhys let out an annoyed grunt. Huxley divined she was torn between curiosity and her keen desire to watch Plath burn. "Tell us something we don't know," she called out. "Of course mutation is a component of the M-Strain. That's obvious."

"Mutation is the engine of evolution," Plath responded. "But it is fundamentally random, unpredictable. All major advances in natural selection take generations to appear, thousands of years of labour by what Dawkins called the Blind Watchmaker. But what if mutation could be guided, directed, controlled?"

Although her voice still possessed the frustrating echo, cop instinct drew Huxley's focus away from the bus. *Way too obvious a hiding place.* He turned, crouching back to back with Rhys, setting down the bomb case once again to take a firm hold of the carbine.

"The work of millennia could be done in decades, or less," Plath went on. "Diseases cured, intelligence enhanced – higher, faster, stronger. Human potential unlocked to the fullest. There was a man – you won't be surprised to hear that he was a man with a huge amount of money. A man as terrified of his own mortality as he was of losing his wealth and power. The kind of terror that drove him to invest his fortune in gene research, viral research, synaptic research, a grand project to connect human will with evolution.

He wanted to be all he could be, all he *wanted* to be. Instead, he gave us the ability to become our worst nightmares, and in so doing spelled the doom of the world."

"The M-Strain is artificial," Rhys said.

"Of course it is. Only humanity could have produced something so perfectly cruel. So insidious. Nature's cruelty is inherent, but also unsentimental. Sadism is a feature but also a teacher. A cat that doesn't enjoy killing will go hungry, but only humans torture for sheer pleasure. In that sense, the M-Strain is humanity distilled into its purest form. We have always been a nightmare."

"So some rich guy created this thing," Huxley said, scanning the fog for some betraying twitch or vortex. "And dumped it in a warehouse in west London."

"Not quite. Creating a pathogen of such complexity and danger in complete secrecy required a great deal of effort. Covert labs were established in various locations. The work of years at the cost of billions. The London site was merely a testing station. Despite being one of the richest cities in the world, it also boasts some of the worst poverty and homelessness statistics. Finding subjects no one would miss was not particularly difficult."

Huxley detected a cadence to her voice that spoke of both nostalgia and regret. "You were part of it," he said. "That's what made you so useful to this mission. You helped create the M-Strain."

"I'm not sure the word 'create' works in this context. I was merely one of many who facilitated its birth, a birth that was inevitable. It might surprise you to learn that we didn't know what we were making, the nature of our child was too complex, too powerful. It was never intended to be contagious, never intended to be something that could reproduce itself. Our billionaire paymaster envisioned a minion bringing him a single pill on a silver plate once a year to maintain his godhood. But you can't tap into the very essence of evolution itself and expect to control it."

"Tell me something," Rhys said, Huxley feeling her tense in readiness. "Did it get out or did you set it loose?"

The subsequent pause was long, Huxley detecting the first sign of movement in the fog: a sudden spiral in the mist accompanied by a flurry of displaced flower petals. He resisted the impulse to fire, knowing whatever Plath was now, she was moving too fast to hit, at least at this range.

"She's not in the bus," he whispered to Rhys just before Plath started speaking again. She was closer now, but still maddeningly unable to place.

"You think so poorly of me, Doctor. And yes, I'll confess to certain . . . predilections that place me outside of societal norms. But, much as I've come to embrace its necessity, all this isn't on me. This is where we arrive at the mundane aspect of the story. You see, it all came down to a combination of bureaucracy and laziness. Somewhere in the logistics train a mid-level project manager decided to save a few cents on a security protocol with only a ninety-nine per cent assurance rating. In a complex system, one per cent is a huge margin of error. A bored security guard took a little too long on his piss break and one of the test subjects escaped. It wasn't long before the authorities picked him up and he was still rational enough to tell them all about his ordeal. They tried to be circumspect about it, keep it under wraps. No scandal. No criminal charges. After all, what government wouldn't want to get its paws on something so powerful. But, of course, it was far, far too late. I'll spare you the tedious genies and bottles metaphors."

"They arrested you," Huxley said, carbine shifting left and right of where he had seen the flurry of petals, widening the arc each time. "Recruited you to work on the cure."

"Recruited is far too pleasant a word for what they did to me. The more desperate a power structure becomes the more vicious their methods. I was fully cooperative from the start, but that didn't stop them claiming I might be holding something back. I believe there was a good deal of basic vindictiveness in all their torments. Eventually, as the outbreak got worse, they set their pain-inducing nerve agents aside and made me a conscript to the International Outbreak Response Team. I think you can guess the rest."

Another flurry of petals ten yards to the right. "She's

circling," Huxley whispered to Rhys. They turned together, maintaining their back-to-back crouch.

"You said it was your idea," Rhys called out. "Get a bunch of volunteers together, wipe their memories, dose them with an inoculant and give them a thorium bomb to deliver. Guess you didn't realise they were going to send you along for the ride."

"It was a bit of a shock when I started to recover my memories, that's true. Then, when I realised the truth about the inoculant, I started to get angry. A rare emotion for me."

Huxley's mind flashed to the marks he and Rhys bore, the marks that had blossomed into raw wetness on Pynchon's body. Marks he couldn't remember seeing on Plath. "Your injector was empty," he said. "They vaccinated us but not you."

"Vaccinated?" Plath let out an ugly sound that he assumed to be a laugh but resembled more a grating screech. "You still think that's what it was? You fucking idiot. And my applicator wasn't empty, it just didn't work on me. So it goes with experiments at the edge of known science. All the brightest medical minds in the entire world tried for months to come up with a working vaccine and the best they could do was invasive brain surgery. The absence of memory is your only protection, and it won't last. And as for your bomb . . ."

Her charge was so fast Huxley barely had time to bring the carbine to bear, pivoting to train it on the explosion of petals, raised like a wake by something dark and very fast. A stunning, iron-hard impact to his side, casting him into the air with so much force he turned a full somersault. A yell escaped him as he collided with the ground, sharp, deep pain and grinding of bone leaving him in no doubt Plath had cracked most if not all of the ribs on his right side. His carbine was gone, even though his hand kept reflexively pulling an invisible trigger.

Carbine! He rolled amid the flowers, still shouting, shock robbing him of any action but ineffectual flailing. A roaring whoosh sounded from Rhys's flame-thrower, but it was short-lived, followed by a scream and a series of crunching thuds. *Get your fucking weapon!*

Spittle spouted from clenched teeth as he forced action into a stunned form, rolling onto his front and blinking tears as he cast about for the carbine. It lay at least three yards away, a distance that had suddenly acquired marathon proportions. He began to crawl towards it, grunting with each heave of his damaged body, blood colouring the spit that flew from his lips. His vision swam in concert with the waves of agony that swept him, but he didn't allow himself to stop. By the time he clamped a hand to the carbine's stock, there was a good deal more blood than saliva flowing from his mouth.

He tried to stand but collapsed instantly, instead forcing himself into a sitting position, bringing the carbine to his shoulder. As he aimed it, his vision blurred again, clearing by sheer effort of will to reveal a figure so impossibly deformed he required several precious seconds to accept it as real.

Plath's elongated face remained much the same as that parting, leering glimpse he caught before she fled the boat, apart from the blackened and scorched flesh that covered its left upper portions, the result of Rhys's final blast with the flame-thrower. Everything else that had made Plath a human being was different. Her body was stretched to a length of at least three metres, torso far narrower than her hips. Her arms featured two additional joints and had grown by several feet. Her legs were even longer, jagged arcs of muscle and sinew sprouting from her rear. The most severe change was the fact that she had acquired two more legs, both positioned at her waist. They were smaller than the others, the flesh that formed them raw and wet in places. These and the rear legs ended in a sprawled, clawed parody of human feet, while her arms narrowed to irregular spikes.

She dangled these over a stunned, possibly lifeless Rhys, arms and legs splayed, blood leaking from nose and mouth. Huxley saw no animation in her at all. For some reason, Plath was reluctant to impale her helpless prey with her spikes, though her still smoking, part-ruined face displayed naked hate as she leaned close to Rhys, hissing a single word: "Bitch!"

Huxley squeezed the carbine's trigger, too driven by pain and panic to remember to flip the safety off. His hands shuddered as he got a thumb to the lever, flicking it to full-auto by which time Plath had closed the distance between them in a few bounds of her impossible limbs. A blurring swipe of her spiked arms sent the carbine tumbling from his grasp before she brought the enlarged foot of one of her new-grown legs down on his chest.

Pain exploded in a blinding flash. He would have screamed if there had been any air left in his lungs.

"Just wait a while longer," Plath said, her blurred bulk retreating from sight. "We haven't finished our little chat."

He lay gasping, surprised by the fact that he was capable of such a thing. Although, the bloody spray that accompanied each gasp made him doubt it would last much longer.

"A thorium bomb." He heard Plath laugh again, looking up to see her crouched over the bomb case. "I'm insulted they thought I would actually fall for that. Wouldn't've worked anyway, the roots of this nursery go far too deep. A hundred megatons wouldn't be enough."

Huxley sagged as another wave of pain swept through him, his gaze slipping from Plath, becoming filled by the sight of the red-petalled flowers. It was then that he saw it.

"That wasn't my idea, by the way," Plath went on, her voice dimmed as the flowers captured his full attention. *Black.* He flailed a hand at the closest flower. Its petals were still mostly red, but were also speckled in black.

"I wanted to call it a biological dispersal unit, but they were worried Rhys would see through it. Some sort of nuke was considered more convincing. I guess they bargained on the fact that fissionable devices were way outside my specialty."

Huxley coughed, a thick wad of blood emerging from his mouth to land on the nearest flower. Instantly, its petals darkened, stem wilting until it was a pitiful blackened remnant. The other flowers nearby also withered; wherever his blood had touched them, they turned black, and it was spreading. Looking around, he saw that he lay in the centre of a widening pool of darkness, flowers dying all around.

Antibody. The word came back to him in a flash, accompanied by the image of it scribbled in blood. *Antibodies . . . That's what we are . . .*

Plath loomed above him, spiked limbs descending to pierce the ground on either side of his head. Huxley's eyes slipped towards the one next to his right ear, the one she had used to impale Pynchon. It was thinner than the other, scarred, reduced.

"That's the thing about ignorance," Plath said, lowering herself so that her face was only inches away. "It's so very dangerous. But not for me. I learned at an early age that to successfully navigate this world, I would need to learn just about everything I could, such as the fact that there's no such thing as a thorium bomb."

Her left eye was sunken beneath a mass of blackened flesh, the other gleaming clear and bright as she leaned closer. "I read your file, Special Agent," she said, voice a solicitous whisper now. "I wasn't supposed to, but I had ways of securing access. Such a brilliant career you pissed away. Did they tell you you're still married? That beautiful wife of yours." Her ruined features formed a taunting parody of a sympathetic frown. "Think she's waiting for you . . . ?"

The woman on the beach, the way she looked at him. *A goodbye? A final rejection of the drunken failure she'd married?* He didn't know why, but he didn't think so.

Huxley took a long, shuddering breath, fixing his gaze on Plath's one eye, shining with the cruelty that defined her, and spat a thick wad of blood directly into it.

Her reaction was spectacular in its immediacy and violence; massive, deformed body rearing, twisted limbs thrashing as a scream of agonised rage erupted from her throat. Huxley fought through his pain to roll to the left, avoiding Plath's withered spike as it stabbed into the ground an inch from his back. He kept rolling, shouting with the pain of his broken ribs, until the drumbeat of her multiple limbs receded, craning his neck to see her engaged in a crazed dance across the field. A constant stream of hate-filled, garbled obscenities leaked from her gaping mouth, along with a torrent of thick, dark blood. She danced a while longer then slumped, shuddering in pain, and Huxley felt a flare of hope that she would simply subside into death.

Unwilling to trust to luck, he looked for his carbine, finding nothing but more blackened flowers. *Pistol*, he remembered, hand moving to his holster, finding it empty. Probably lost when she first hit him. *Shit* . . .

"YOU FUCKER!" The screeching challenge was dispiriting in its loudness, as was the determination Plath displayed in heaving herself upright on her deformed limbs. "Pathetic, worthless, fucking loser . . ." she raged, each word accompanied by a thick gobbet of both flesh and blood as she clawed her way back to him, drawn, he assumed, by nothing more than predatory instinct. Both sides of her face were black now, one burned, the other shrivelled and sunken like the flowers that had felt the touch of his blood.

Huxley scrabbled back, heels scraping over dead, blackened growths and tarmac. From the way Plath continually stumbled in pursuit, coughing out chunks of her insides all the while, he attempted to find some comfort in knowing she would be dead shortly after she killed him. It didn't work.

The stream of flame licked over Plath's spiked arms first, bringing her to a sudden halt. A screech even more painfully loud than before pealed out as she pivoted towards the origin of the flames. The fire stream grew more intense as its source closed on its target. The blazing yellow-orange tongue stripped away much of Plath's upper mass, wreathing her in roiling black smoke and swirling embers. Rhys appeared at the edge of the heat haze, limping through the smoke, flame-thrower still casting its blazing cascade onto Plath's diminishing husk. Rhys halted and fell to her knees, keeping her finger clamped to the weapon's trigger until it expended all its remaining fuel. A few final dregs of burning chemicals arced out to join the flames consuming Plath before it guttered to silence.

Huxley watched Rhys slump, expecting to hear the slowly diminishing beat of his own heart accompanied by a dimming of vision. Instead, he convulsed in an energetic bout of pain and coughed more blood onto already dead flowers.

"You don't sound so good," Rhys croaked, turning towards him, her face a mess of mingled soot and blood. "No offence."

"It's just . . . a flesh wound." He laughed then wished he hadn't, although the resulting agony served to dispel his remaining fatigue, at least for now. What felt like at least five minutes of painful gasping enabled him to lever himself onto his knees. Another minute and, incredibly, he was on his feet. He clutched at his ruined ribs, fearing that some of what was inside would spill out if he didn't, staggering towards Rhys.

"Thought she'd killed you," he said by way of redundant commentary.

"Yeah?" She managed to raise an arm, pointing a wavering finger at Plath's smoking remains. "Well, I fucking killed her, didn't I?"

She winced and lowered her arm, Huxley seeing that the mark on her neck had grown in size, joined by several more. Like Pynchon's just before the end, the texture was different, glistening wet and blistered instead of rough. Putting a hand to his collarbone he shuddered at the touch, the pain, sharper and deeper than all the others, communicating itself to his back and thighs where he knew more marks would be appearing.

"Injury," he said. "That's what triggers the final stage."

Rhys squinted up at him. "What?"

He didn't reply, instead looking around until he found the bomb case. Stumbling towards it, he fell to his knees and dragged it closer, peering at the timer.

"Don't!" Rhys said, not quite managing to shout as he punched in the sequence and activated the count-down. "We're not there yet."

Huxley set the bomb case down and turned the timer display towards her, the readout already counting down: 00:28, 00:27, 00:26 . . .

"Stop!" Rhys groaned and forced herself upright. "Stop it!" She managed only a few feet before falling, staring at him with desperate eyes. "We can't . . . not now . . . not here . . ."

"A thorium bomb," Huxley said, watching the timer tick down: 00:15, 00:14, 00:13 . . . "There's no such thing, according to Plath."

"You . . ." Rhys clutched at the black remnants of flowers, dragging herself closer. "You can't . . . believe her . . ."

"No." Huxley inclined his head in agreement. "Not

about everything. But this—" he tapped the timer display "—this I do."

00:06, 00:05, 00:04 . . .

"Huxley!" She flailed an outstretched hand at him, fingers splayed. "Please!"

"That's not my name."

00:00.

The timer blinked the zeroes twice and went dark. Huxley stared at the case for the space of two seconds before weakly shoving it away. "And this is not a bomb."

He hissed through clenched teeth as he regained his feet, moving to slump down beside Rhys, helping her sit up. "See?" he said, tugging the collar of his fatigues to reveal the raw, expanded mark. He could feel it pulsing now, like something ready to burst. "It was never a bomb. It's us." He took her head in his hands and pressed their foreheads together. "We're the bomb. We always were. Survival, remember? This mission was all about survival. We had to survive long enough to get here."

She pressed herself against him, the violence of her shudders telling of pain that matched or exceeded his. "I guess . . ." she grunted eventually, putting both hands to his shoulders to raise herself up. "We should do . . . what we came to do."

He looked up to see her offering a hand, a deep, bitter weariness bringing a firm refusal to his lips. *The woman on the beach . . . My wife. Rhys's son. Pynchon's husband. Whoever the hell Golding and Dickinson did this for.*

Huxley took her hand, almost pulling her over as he hauled himself to his feet. They had to hold on to each other to prevent falling as they made their way onwards, although they stumbled many times. Their destination was obvious now, a bank of fog so thick it resembled a vast, formless bruise. They both bled as they walked, leaving a trail of blackened, dying flowers in their wake. Huxley could feel the inoculant working within him, a feverish, busy nausea that wracked him with pulses of the purest agony, making each step an exercise in masochism. Rhys sobbed with the effort, but every time he thought she might fall, she gripped him tighter and kept moving.

When the bruise filled his vision Huxley began to make out a form within it, broad and monolithic in scale. "The stadium," he said, the effort of speaking causing him to convulse and vomit up a chunk of something wet but solid. He would have fallen if Rhys hadn't jerked him back to a measure of sensibility. He straightened from an agonised crouch to take in the sight of the stadium. The fog remained thick but he could make out the dense mass of flowers that covered it.

"This is where . . . they came," Rhys gasped. "Thousands . . . came to die here."

Huxley hugged her closer and they walked into the fog. A few minutes of stumbling brought them in sight of a huge wall of flowers. Huxley looked up to see the stadium was completely shrouded in blooms, each one with petals spread wide to cast out what Plath had called a necessary corrective.

"Maybe she was right," he said in a low, slurred mumble.

Rhys shifted against him, unable to raise her head. "What?"

"Plath . . . Saving the world . . . For what? So they just . . ." He raised his arm, flailing at the wall of flowers. "Just do this . . . all over again."

Rhys's answer came in a soft sob accompanied by a movement he took as a shrug. "Maybe . . . they won't."

Pynchon's husband. Rhys's son. My wife. "Yeah." He started forward again, pulling her along. "Maybe."

They stopped a foot from the flower wall, Rhys's eyes leaking red tears as she blinked at the barrier. "No way in."

"I don't think . . . it matters." Huxley looked back the way they had come, their passage marked by a trail of withering blackness slowly expanding across the field. The ground beneath had a wet sheen to it, a sludge like softness that caused it to subside in places, fissures appearing as the corruption spread from flowers to roots. *The roots of this nursery go far too deep . . .*

He tottered back from Rhys, taking her hand. "Ready?"

Incredibly, she managed to smile at him and reply with a weak squeeze of her fingers. Words, however, were beyond her now. Looking into her veined, reddened eyes he knew she wasn't seeing him, she was seeing a smiling boy whose name she couldn't remember.

He smiled back and together they turned, walking into the wall. At first the flowers shrank from their mere touch, subliming into colourless threads. The barrier thickened a few feet in, the flowers still dying but their number so great they created a dense, soft mass. Huxley kept walking for as long as he could, forcing steps from his shuddering legs. When, inevitably, they gave way, Rhys fell with him, their hands still clasped. As the withering growths embraced him, the marks defacing his body opened to spill forth their final torrent of poison. There was pain, then cold, then a perverse feeling of connection. It may have been the product of a fading mind, but he felt he could feel the entirety of this monstrous nursery dying, the poison leaking from his sundered body spreading to every stem and petal. He took joy from its death.

The last few pulses of his heart stirred the shielded corners of his brain as it mistook death for sleep, and in those seconds he dreamed. A woman on a beach, hair trailing in the salted wind. She turned to him, face drawn in a terrible sadness.

"Don't go," she told him, pleaded with him. "We only just found each other again."

"I have to," he said, and she crushed herself to him. He held her as she wept, savouring the feel of her against him, the smell of her hair as the wind played it across his face. Shifting to place her lips close to his ear she whispered something.

"My name," he stuttered with the last fluttering spasm of his body, still holding Rhys's hand, but it was lifeless now. "She said . . . my name . . ."

extras

orbit

meet the author

Ellie Grace Photography

A. J. RYAN is a pseudonym for Anthony Ryan, the *New York Times* bestselling author of the Raven's Shadow, Draconis Memoria, and Covenant of Steel series. He previously worked in a variety of roles for the UK government, but now writes full-time. His interests include art, science and the unending quest for the perfect pint of real ale.

Find out more about A. J. Ryan and other Orbit authors by registering for the free monthly newsletter at orbitbooks.net.

if you enjoyed
RED RIVER SEVEN

look out for

DEAD WATER

by

C. A. Fletcher

From the author of A Boy and His Dog at the End of the
World *comes a haunting and suspenseful story of isolation
and dread within a small island community.*

There's something in the water. . . .

*On the edge of the North Atlantic lies a remote island. The islanders
are an outwardly harmonious community—but all have their own
secrets, some much darker than others. And when a strange disorder
begins to infect them all, those secrets come to light.*

*Ferry service fails and contact with the mainland is lost.
Rumors begin to swirl as a temporary inconvenience grows*

into a nightmarish ordeal. The fabric of the once tight-knit island is unnervingly torn apart—and whatever the cause, the question soon stops being how or why it happened, but who, if anyone, will survive.

Chapter 1

Islander

A pair of ravens ride the brightness on the thin morning breeze above the islands, wheeling high on the updraught as the wind makes first landfall since sweeping off the barren rocks of Labrador more than two thousand cold sea-miles to the west.

From this height, the main island makes a shape like a hog-tied bullock lying on its side, neck stretched for the knife as its mouth gapes wide in a final bellow of protest. The rocky tangle of the skerries to the south looks like a flying gargoyle snapping at the rearmost hoof of the doomed animal.

The island is not big and lacks the mountainous majesty of its wilder Hebridean siblings to the north. The two low humps of land don't quite amount to eight miles nose to tail and barely two miles at the widest point, and the tallest hill only squeaks above four hundred feet if measured to the top of the deep heather covering it. It is, however, both first and last land, a barrier island standing guard with its face set to the North Atlantic and its back to the Highlands of Argyll thirty-five ferry-linked miles away.

The birds spot movement in the water and arc across the

ridge of higher ground towards it in case it means food. As scavengers and klepto-parasites, the carrion birds aren't fussy about where the next meal comes from.

Something red and white and splashy is disturbing the gunmetal deckle of the inshore waves in a westward bay to the head of the main island, where a long curve of shell-sand makes the back of the bullock's neck. The beach is deserted.

The ravens dip a wing and swoop lower still.

The red is a buoy, one of two at either side of the bay, and the splash is a swimmer, a lone figure in a wetsuit who jackknifes into a slow and very controlled duck-dive. The ravens see the long black swim-fins break water and wave a brief farewell in the air, just like a whale sounding, and then the swimmer is gone.

Sig is unaware of the ravens above her as she kicks slowly but determinedly away from the light, head down as she matches the angle of the line tethering the buoy to the unseen lobster pot far below. The pot is beyond her reach on the one lungful of air that is all the life she carries with her, but that's not why she does this.

She's not swimming towards something. Freediving without oxygen tanks is a thing she does for its own sake. It's the closest she gets to a small escape, one she can live with, a way she can find a place where the constant pain in her broken body goes away for a while. More than that, in freediving like this Sig finds – for a minute or two – not just the purity of the practice itself but the end of magical thinking, the death of extraneous thought and a place where the past is finally, mercifully silent. And of course the small escape carries with it the possibility of the larger one if she should lose focus. That's what gives it the hard straight edge, like the bone-chilling cold in the water around her: in the freedive, nothing matters but the present and the exercise of the rigorous self-discipline needed not to drown in it.

She fins calmly downwards with slow, stiff-legged kicks for the first ten metres as the buoyancy of air-filled lungs pulls her body in the opposite direction, back up towards the surface. At the ten-metre mark, the all-round pressure of the water is twice what it was at the surface, and her lungs are now half the size they were. She has trained for this and can read the signals her body is sending her, which calms her enough to no longer feel the panic she once did when the physics change abruptly as she hits twelve metres, as the buoyancy that's been pulling her upwards back to safety disappears and the sea begins to pull her in the opposite direction. She has come to think of this as the invisible trapdoor to the deep: she stops finning and puts her arms at her sides like a skydiver, letting gravity pull her downwards.

For the next ten metres, she glides deeper into the gloom, feeling a great calmness as she becomes one with the liquid world all around her. And although she is alone, she does not feel lonely, not in the way she has grown used to in what she thinks of as her land-mammal life. Here she feels more and more like a sea creature the further down into the comforting squeeze of the water column she goes. A solitary sea creature, alone, but – here, at least – comfortingly and correctly alone. It's like meditation for her, this daily practice. And where some meditate to achieve an inner quiet, Sig does it to hear herself. It is here, away from the world, doing this one hidden thing with no one else to rely on, that the chatter disappears and she is able to remember the one voice she misses. Time has worn away the precise memories of other voices she's lost – her sister's, for example. Down here, alone in the dark, she's fallen into the habit of giving herself the necessary calming reminders in that other lost but not forgotten voice.

At thirty metres, there is a red tag on the line and the pressure is triple that of the surface, and the only sound in what is now the last quiet place in the world is her heart beating about once every three seconds as it slows to half her normal resting rate.

Below the red tags are four more white tags spaced a metre apart, and then another red tag. They're depth markers. Once there were more, all the way up to the ten-metre mark. She has slowly built her capacity over the months by snatching them off the rope one by one, going deeper and deeper as her resilience increased.

This is where she feels the urge to push on and see how much further she can go. To reach the next red tag, deeper than she's ever been.

NO. ENOUGH. NOT TODAY.

The moment she feels that urge, her discipline kicks in hard and she imagines the voice telling herself to turn head to tail. She begins finning again, this time steadily heading upwards towards the light, fighting the impulse to kick frantically as she moderates the oxygen burn to make the most of what's still usable in her lungs. She has to get back through that trap-door. The screaming ache in her lungs at this stage used to scare her, but now it's an old friend, a way-station on her return to the surface and the waiting air. She knows that for one more day she has managed not to push it further than her own self-defined safety boundaries, and she smiles as she rises unhurriedly towards the waiting buoy overhead. This was the right decision for today. Maybe in a couple of days she'll push it deeper. Today she has a promise to keep. Today isn't the day to flirt with checking out.

SMILE.

Smiling is also something she has disciplined herself to do. It no longer comes as naturally as it once did. She believes the positive feedback of the physical act of smiling calms both the mind and the body and goes some way to muting the pulmonary alarm bells that are now jangling with an ever-growing insistence.

The ravens look down on Sig as she breaks water and clips herself on to the red ball bobbing in the light chop, regaining her breath: she's too big for prey, too small to be a fishing boat with the chance of scraps tossed over the side that might drift in and land where the ravens might hop from rock to rock and pluck them from the salt water.

They're about to move on when they see dark shapes in the depths below her, submarine shadows that lazily swim towards Sig on a converging angle. There are three of them and even the smallest is easily four times as long as the swimmer, who hangs there steadily getting her breath back, normalising her breathing as she floats by the buoy, unaware.

The ravens wait.

Maybe there will be breakfast to be picked off the water's edge after all.

Below the birds, Sig rolls on to her back, her face a white flash in the black neoprene hood.

She sees the ravens hanging in the vault of air above her, a pair of ragged black crosses beneath a lead-lined sky, black feathers whiffling untidily in the wind like battle-torn pennants.

She watches them as she waits. Only when she is sure she is safely re-oxygenated and her pulse is respectable again does she trust herself to unclip and start to swim the home-stretch of her daily routine. She keeps her eyes fixed on them as she arches her spine and stretches out into a regular backstroke, arms reaching far into the wavelets ahead and then pulling deep scallops of water as her legs churn like a machine, powering her towards the other buoy at the north end of the bay.

Her heart's pumping normally again, and the water is no colder than it was yesterday. That's not why she shivers.

The familiar ravens look ominous and unchancy today. And because it's early and she's alone and over deep water, even Sig – who has spent a lifetime honing her mind to be as perfectly rational a tool as humanly possible – has to remind herself she isn't superstitious, that she can't afford to be, and concentrates on something she can control, like counting strokes and not getting cramp and above all not wondering what she looks like from the birds' viewpoint or – worse – to anything watching her from the unknown depths below.

She doesn't see the change in the water surface thirty yards to her right, the upward bulge in the sea travelling towards her. She doesn't see anything until she finishes her set of one hundred backstrokes and rolls into position for the front-crawl.

Then she sees them.

The shock hits her with a sledgehammer of adrenaline, spiking her heart rate and stopping her breathing in the same moment.

She abruptly stops swimming and hangs there, unmoving.

Dead in the water.

orbit

Follow us:

f /orbitbooksUS

/orbitbooks

/orbitbooks

Join our mailing list
to receive alerts on our
latest releases and deals.

orbitbooks.net

Enter our monthly
giveaway for the chance
to win some epic prizes.

orbitloot.com